Cougar Tales

By

Sandra Kitt

Evelyn Palfry

Laura Castoro

Noire Passion is an imprint of Parker Publishing LLC.

Copyright © 2008 by Sandra Kitt, Evelyn Palfrey, Laura Parker Castoro
Published by Parker Publishing LLC
12523 Limonite Avenue, Suite #440-438
Mira Loma, California 91752
www.parker-publishing.com

ISBN: 978-1-60043-048-0
First Edition

Manufactured in the United States of America
Printed by Bang Printing, Brainard MN
Distributed by BookMasters, Inc. 1-800-537-6727
Cover Design by Jaxadora

Parker Publishing, llc
www.Parker-Publishing.com

How To Handle A Woman

By

Sandra Kitt

DEDICATION and ACKNOWLEDGEMENTS:

To all the men I have loved…who were ALL younger than me!

Chapter One

When she finally spotted the one lone space, between two mammoth SUVs, Geneva Springer sent up a silent prayer of thanks. After circling the school parking lot for the third time she was about to give up and resort to the nearby residential streets for a place. She deftly maneuvered her Honda Civic into the spot, an ironic smile playing around her lips. It was not lost on her that, once again, size mattered.

She turned off the engine, grabbed her bag, and climbed out. Flipping open her cell phone Geneva speed dialed a number from her directory. It was answered on the first ring.

"Aunt Eva?"

"Hi Trey. I'm here."

"Oh, man. I thought maybe you forgot about the auction. It's almost gonna start," the young male voice rushed anxiously. "I saved a seat for you. Hurry up."

"Where will I find you?" she asked, crossing the lot as she maneuvered between cars.

"We're in the stands in the fourth row. Right next to the doors going to the girl's locker room."

"I'll find you. Bye."

"Wait! I got something to tell you."

"Can't it wait 'til I get there?" Geneva asked.

"I guess, but..."

"Okay, then. See you in a minute."

Heading toward the entrance of the three storied brick building, Geneva was well aware that she was late, but it couldn't be helped. She squinted at her watch. 40 minutes. Not too bad. It was annoying that she had to go overtime late on a Friday afternoon, but paying clients and deadlines came way ahead of high school events for favorite nephews. Nevertheless guilt sped up her steps. As she reached the door it was suddenly pulled open from the inside and a burly middle-aged security guard blocked the entrance. Geneva nearly plowed right into him.

"Hey! Slow down! You kids know you're not supposed to...Oh. Sorry, Ma'am," he grinned, seeing his mistake. "Thought you were one of the students. The gym is down the hall to your left."

The guard politely stood aside as Geneva, moving more sedately... and like a grownup, followed his directions.

"Thank you," she said over her shoulder as she passed by.

"You haven't missed anything. They haven't started, yet," he called after her.

Just ahead she could hear the rumble of voices coming from open doors at the end of the corridor. At a table just outside was a folding table behind which was seated two women. One, her blond hair pulled back into a youthful ponytail, smiled as Geneva approached, already holding out a clipboard with papers and a pen.

"Hi, thanks for coming tonight. The kids appreciate your support. It's all for a good cause. Here's your bid number. If you'll just fill out this form for me."

"We can't hold anything you buy tonight. It's cash and carry. Or credit card and carry," the other woman joked, her long dreads pulled back from her brown face into a single crossover knot at the back of her head. She held out a yellow photocopied page. "Here's a list of what's up for sale. Now, that little star next to some items means there's a minimum bid. There's some nice stuff in there," she added.

Coming from inside the gym a garbled voice made an announcement from a microphone. Geneva frowned as she bent over to fill out the form.

"What's he saying?" she asked.

"He said there's ten more minutes to look over the auction lots, and then they're going to start. Better go on in. There's a lot to see."

Geneva shook her head. "I wasn't planning on buying anything."

"But it's for charity," the blond reminded her.

"I know, my nephew told me. He's been begging me for weeks to come tonight. So, here I am. But I'll probably just write a check, if that's okay," Geneva asked, looking from one to the other.

"We'll definitely take your money," the woman in dreads said.

"And you never know. Maybe you'll see something you can't live without," the blond added. "Pick up early holiday gifts."

"Yeah," her companion said. "Me, I never have trouble spending money. Ask my husband."

Geneva chuckled as she continued on into the gym.

It was noisy and crowded, people pressed together, moving slowly like a rolling wave, as they passed the displayed merchandise. The spectator seats and bleachers, normally packed with cheering fans for school basketball games, was slowly filling up.

She was surprised by the number of people, and the number of tables neatly laid out with every manner of no longer wanted things to be auctioned. The students and teachers themselves, all identified by the orange t-shirts they wore with the school name stenciled across the back, stood at the ready to bring things to the auctioneer as they were to be bided on. To Geneva it was like a large contained flea market, or outsized garage sale.

Despite her decision not to buy anything she began walking along the first aisle of tables, putting off trying to find her sister and brother-in-law.

She stopped at a table with old costume jewelry, drawn to a black display case with sterling silver earrings, pins, and bracelets. There was one piece in particular that she studied closely. The interlocking motifs on a bracelet were inlaid with Mother-of-pearl. She reached to pick up the bracelet for a closer look, when another hand appeared at exactly the same moment. Large, white skin, male. A man she wasn't even aware of standing next to her had reached it first.

"Ooops. Sorry. Ladies first," he said. He lifted the bracelet from its niche and held it out to her.

Geneva turned her gaze up at him and found a pair of very dark, almost black, eyes looking at her apologetically. His hair, thick and a bit longish with a slight wave, was also very dark. She shook her head.

"That's okay. You go ahead. I don't really need another bracelet."

He raised his brows as he continued to study her, steady and thoroughly. "Did I just hear right? A woman turning down a piece of jewelry? Of course you don't need it, but do you like it?"

"Well, yes. It's unusual. Beautiful. That's why it caught my eye, but..."

"Then, go ahead; take it. It won't look good on me, anyway."

Geneva gave him her attention, seeing the comic wistfulness in his eyes, and the hint of humor around his mouth. She slowly grinned.

"Glad you realize that. Doesn't mean you shouldn't buy it. Maybe your...er...wife, or girlfriend...sister," she fumbled. "It would make a nice gift."

Rather than blink under his continued scrutiny, Geneva found herself staring back. His face was starkly masculine, and his voice a pleasing baritone. Not the kind that rumbled and sounded threatening, but a voice that was smooth and kind of silky. Definitely a bedroom voice, she considered. The thought made her momentarily avert her gaze...just in case he could read her thoughts.

"The gift idea is really what I had in mind," he said. He held the bracelet out to her once more. "Last chance."

Geneva took a last look at the bracelet. It was such a great looking piece. "No thanks. It's all yours. Good luck." And stepped around him.

A school bell trilled through the gym and a voice came over the microphone again.

"Okay folks. We're going to get started. Please take a seat. Will all the student helpers get to your assigned stations."

Geneva walked faster along the aisle sorry there wasn't enough time to see everything. Her head swiveled back and forth from table to table, her gaze trying to take in what she could as she made her way to the seats.

She again stopped abruptly when, this time, she spotted a small handmade crib quilt hung from a jeri-rigged clothesline. It was beautiful. Geneva wondered if it had actually been used to dress a crib, or a baby carriage. But she could imagine it hung, like a tapestry, on a wall somewhere. She reached to lift a corner to examine the stitching.

"We really have to stop meeting like this."

That voice.

She turned around.

The stranger was standing behind her. Now, Geneva really paid attention to him. The first time was a mere encounter. But a second time felt like something different. Especially looking into his eyes that seemed to pull her into their mysterious depths and hold her attention. He made her feel as if he was invading her space, and getting too close. But, rather than feel threatened by him she felt challenged. Like they were playing cat and mouse with just their eyes. She boldly faced him.

"Are you following me?" she asked dryly.

"As a matter of fact...no."

Taken aback by his blunt denial, Geneva was stumped for a quick come-back.

"But it seems like we're drawn to the same kind of beautiful workmanship." He pointed to the quilt. "Reminds me of one I had as a kid. My grandmother made it for me. I dragged it around everywhere. Talk about security blanket," he said disarmingly.

"Do you still have it?"

He shook his head. "Don't know what happened to it. I grew up. I moved. I went away, and came back again. Things change. Things get lost." He shrugged.

Geneva nodded at his short-handed life story. "So, you're telling me you're interested in bidding for this as well?"

"Maybe. You?"

She looked at the quilt again. "I like it. Unlike you I've never had one."

He took a step closer and grinned down at her. "Want to arm wrestle me for it?"

The absurdity of his challenge made her chuckle, even as it caught her off guard. Having him stand this close also had an affect. She casually took a step back.

"I don't want to embarrass you. Enjoy the auction. May the best person win," She said, walking away. Behind her she heard a short barking laugh.

"I plan to!"

She grimaced at his arrogance.

Thirty-five, she calculated his age. She was aware that, irritating even to herself, she had a tendency to do that with men. As if trying to judge their suitability. Thirty five wasn't too bad.

Reaching the parameter of the gym Geneva heard her name being called. Scanning the seated crowd she finally spotted her brother-in-law, Bradley, waving his arms. She waved back and began climbing into the stands toward him.

Bradley, a pleasant looking man in glasses carrying about thirty extra pounds around his middle, gave her a brief kiss on the cheek and made room for her to squeeze past him to get to her sister.

"Aunt Eva, I gotta talk to you," her young nephew said, talking over his mother's head.

"Give me a minute, Trey. Hey, Gee. How's it going?" she asked her sister. She looked her up and down. "You look like you lost weight."

Several inches taller and three years older than herself, Geneva knew her sister was battling bulge from almost twenty years of solid, comfortable married life.

Grace struck a pose with her hands on her round hips, showing off a woman who was attractive, with coiffed hair a la Oprah.

"Ten pounds as of this morning. Twenty more to go."

"Good for you," Geneva said. They hugged and air kissed.

"Aunt Eva..."

"I'm never going to be tiny like you..." Grace interrupted her son.

"And I'm never going to have what you have," Geneva said.

"You can't do that. Compare my life to yours. I can't do what you do, Eva. Too much work. Too stressful. And believe me, you would not want to put up with what I have to deal with sometimes."

"I have no sympathy for you. Bradley is a saint, and you know how I feel about Trey," Geneva said.

"You're right. But nyway, that's all beside the point. There's someone I want you to meet. He's eligible, straight, and a professional. A good Black man."

"Will you stop? I don't need your help planning my life," Geneva said in annoyance.

"You need all the help you can get," Grace shot back. "I know I don't need to remind you you have a birthday coming up that puts you right on the edge of extinction! You don't want to start the new year at a disadvantage."

"I have no problem with turning thirty nine."

"It means you're closer to forty. And it means if you ever expect to have a baby you better hurry up!"

Geneva shrugged off her sister's comment and stepped around her to take the empty seat next to fifteen years old Trey. She gave him a warm hug, frowning at his troubled expression.

"What's wrong with you?"

"I got something to tell you," Trey said, now looking shamefaced. "I know I should have told you before, but..."

Geneva frowned at her nephew as they sat down. "What are you talking about? Did you change your mind about the mountain bike for your sixteenth birthday? I told you I didn't think your parents..."

"No, no. That's not it."

"Then what?"

"I put your name into the auction," Trey finally blurted out.

Geneva stared at him as if he'd spoken in a foreign tongue. Then, her gaze narrowed on him. "You did what?"

Trey lifted his shoulders up to his ears, and raised his hands as if in surrender. "I put your name in. I mean, the name of your business. I put it on the auction list."

Dumfounded, she stared at him. "Why on earth would you do that?"

"I told you to ask her first," Grace said, leaning forward to speak to her son.

"I didn't think she'd mind. Aunt Eva's really good at fixing up places and stuff."

"Don't think a compliment is going to let you off the hook," Geneva said sternly.

"It's for a good cause," Trey reminded her.

"And I have yet to hear what this good cause is," Geneva argued.

"We told you Trey took this advance computer class over the summer with this Silicon Valley guy," Bradley explained. "He said he'd be willing to set up a computer lab for the school, with recording and taping equipment and everything, if the school can raise the money for the hardware."

"Yeah. And Mr. Fairway said he'd give us the software for free," Trey added.

"That's great, guys. But I don't have the kind of something to sell that people want to buy at an auction. It's not like they're getting a table, or a carpet."

"Why not? At my church fundraiser last year somebody was offering six months of hair styling. Women went after that like crazy, and it sold."

"Shhhhh," Bradley suddenly hissed at them.

The lights began to dim, and the female Principal of the high school came to the mike to welcome the audience. Everyone settled down. She went on to talk about the purpose of the auction and thanked everyone for their support, particularly Fairway Future-Tech and Games for the generous offer to develop a computer lab for the school.

Geneva was still trying to process what her nephew had done without her knowledge. In principle she didn't mind that Trey had volunteered her services. But she knew he didn't understand that, while the school might get money if someone made a successful bit, she would actually be doing a lot of work for free. It was too late to explain that to him. It was too late to say no.

She missed most of what was said next, including the introduction of the person who influenced the organizing of the auction. A man stood and waved briefly, sitting down again before she could see him clearly. Nonetheless Geneva was sure it was the same man she'd encountered as she browsed the sales items. She squinted and craned her neck trying to find him again. It should have been easy. The majority of the attendees were African American. He was white.

"After the summer program ended Trey was offered an Internship with the company this year," Grace informed her sister.

There was no time for Geneva to put it all together in her head. Another man came forward who was introduced as the auctioneer. While he told how the bidding was going to work Geneva turned to Trey and spoke in a low voice.

"I hope you won't be too disappointed if no one bids on my company. Interior design is very expensive."

"I know someone who wants it," Trey said, excited. "He needs it bad. Daddy said there's a high opening bid. I'm not sure what that means," Trey admitted.

"Shhhhh." Bradley said again.

"We'll talk later," Geneva told Trey and gave her attention to the action on the gym floor.

The volunteer students and teachers paraded each item around the arena, so that everyone would have a chance to see the objects.

The auctioneer was professional and fast, moving the lots of merchandise in an orderly manner. Bradley got in on the action and successfully won a set of golf clubs. Grace bought a box of old cookbooks. Geneva saw a number of things that caught her interest, but she didn't really perk up until an assortment of old sterling silver jewelry was offered. As described by the auctioneer the lot included the bracelet with inlaid Mother-of-pearl that she'd looked at. She immediately thought of the man she'd sparred with over it, and wondered if he would try to buy it.

The bidding started low and, surprising herself, Geneva joined in, suddenly excited by the prospect of winning. But she didn't.

"That's too bad," Grace murmured. "We could have shared what was in the box."

"And you would have paid for half," Geneva said tartly. Her sister laughed.

When the quilt came up for sale she again tried her luck, her family cheering her on. Suddenly, she really wanted the crib quilt. And this time, Geneva won. She was thrilled. Even so, she couldn't help feeling a little guilty that she had bested that intriguing stranger, especially after hearing of the one he'd had as a child.

Probably was making it up, she shrugged.

The last things to go on sale were the unusual stuff, like dinner for two at a top rated restaurant, a vineyard tour and tasting in the Sonoma Valley, and Geneva's design services Comfort Zones. The first two went easily. When it was time for her offerings, she was nervous. Not for herself but for Trey. This meant so much to him.

She crossed her fingers.

As soon as the auctioneer began several offers immediately came in. Trey put his arm around her, shaking her.

"See? I told you."

Geneva listened in utter disbelief as the price rose higher and higher, drewing gasps and cheers from the audience. As far as she could tell it was only between two people. Three, at most. The figure kept rising. Finally, it stopped.

"Going once, twice...sold to number..."

Geneva never heard the rest. The audience rose to its feet and cheered and whistled and clapped. A lot of money, thousands of dollars, had just been given to the school. In exchange, the successful bidder got her expertise.

Bradley whistled through his fingers. Grace was jumping up and down, her amble bosom bouncing comically under her sweater. Trey, in his own exuberance, lifted Geneva clear off her feet.

"Trey, put me down!"

The auction shortly after. Those who'd made purchases hurried to the three tables of cashiers to pay. Those who hadn't began to stream out the exits. Others milled around chatting. Geneva, Grace and Bradley made their way down from the bleacher seats to center court and joined the cashier line to pay for their things. Geneva accepted the small brown paper wrapped package that contained her quilt. Accepting it Geneva broke into a broad grin, feeling as if she had just been given a wonderful gift...even if she had paid for it herself.

"Come on," Trey urged, pulling on Geneva's arm when they were done. "We gotta see who won."

It was still crowded, as people were now trying to get out carrying their just purchased treasures. Trey took the lead, making way for them to get through."There he is," Grace suddenly said behind Geneva, poking her in the back. "Remember I said I had someone you needed to meet?"

"Here?" Geneva asked, skeptical.

"Hurry, before he leaves," Grace said, gently pushing her sister forward.

"Over here," Trey interrupted, pointing to a small cluster of people nearby. He rushed ahead but then seemed to disappear in the gathering.

Geneva began to hang back.

There were parents and students surrounding a tall Black man. Geneva could only see part of his profile. His face was long and rectangular; chiseled and clean-shaven."That's him. Clifford Dailey,"

Grace hissed behind her sister. "He's the new Assistant Principal," she added with significant emphasis.

"Aunt Eva!" Trey tried again to get her attention.

Geneva, annoyed by her sister's determination to introduce her to the Assistant Principal tried to squelch her efforts.

She failed.

"Hi, Mr. Dailey. Remember me? I'm Trey Savages' mother, Grace..."

"That's it. I'm outta here," Bradley said to Geneva, juggling his new golf clubs and his wife's box of cookbooks. "Tell Grace I'm waiting in the car."

Geneva turned to her brother-in-law reaching to grab his arm. "Bradley, don't you dare leave me..." He was already gone.

She watched speechless, as her sister boldly insinuated herself into the center of the gathering and captured the Assistant Principal's attention. Geneva was sure that he probably didn't remember Grace, but to his credit he was gracious and gave her his full attention.

"Yes, I believe we met during student orientation last month, right after school started."

He took her offered hand and Grace promptly took hold and pulled him around to face Geneva.

"I want you to meet Trey's aunt, my sister. Geneva Springer."

Geneva had only a second to direct a murderous glare at her sister. Grace blithely ignored her. Geneva had no choice. She forced a smile to her lips and looked up at the man who quite literally towered over her.

"Aunt Eva..."

Briefly distracted, Geneva turned to Trey. "I'll be right there. Sorry," she apologized to the man now studying her.

"Clifford Dailey," he introduced himself, smiling at her in a way that showed his interest.

Despite the circumstance a long dormant part of her was flattered. He was a very pleasant looking man.

"It's nice to meet you," she said automatically.

"Yes, same here. Did you buy anything tonight? You know, the money is for a good cause," Clifford Dailey said with a smile.

Geneva nodded, indicating her package. "I did. A handmade crib quilt. How about yourself?"

She tried to ignore the fact that behind Clifford Dailey's back Grace was grinning like a Cheshire cat and giving her a thumb's up.

"'Fraid not. I missed out on..."

Trey appeared, practically in her face, ready to pull her away. Then he remembered himself.

"Hi, Mr. Dailey."

"Trey," the assistant principal nodded. "I just met your Aunt."

"Look, I'm sorry, but I really need my Aunt for a minute, okay?"

"What's so urgent?" Geneva asked.

"I want you to meet the man who won your design service."

Clifford raised his brows and regarded Geneva again. "You're the interior designer? I was in the bidding, too."

"Oh. Well...thank you for trying."

"I might still be interested in contracting with you privately. I have a project in mind," Clifford said.

"Okay, but...I think I better..."

"Go on," he said in amusement, as Trey began dragging her away. "Give me a call." He smoothly reached into a pocket of his jacket and pulled out a business card, giving it to her.

Geneva didn't have a chance to do more than take it as she let Trey lead her a few more steps and she found herself facing...that man.

"Here she is," Trey said triumphantly.

Geneva stood before a tall white man, not as tall as Clifford Dailey, but close to six feet. He was wearing a white oxford shirt with the cuffs folded back beyond his wrists and a pair of black jeans. The ensemble lent a casualness to him that made him seem non-threatening and easy, as she'd already found out.

"So. You're Trey's Aunt Eva," he murmured with thoughtful smile.

His words held her attention. Geneva couldn't help feeling something significant in the way he said it. Like he already knew so much about her. Like he'd already formed an opinion.

"Mr. Fairway won you," Trey announced.

Geneva and the man raised brows at Trey's turn of phrase. He thought it was very funny, if his expression and broad grin were any indication. She didn't.

"Not me, Trey. Just my services."

Geneva sighed. Still sounded too much like the same thing.

"I know what he meant," he said kindly. "Reed Fairway."

"As in Fairway Future-Tech and Games," Trey added.

"I guess I should thank you for your contribution to..."

"Oh, my bid was real enough. I'm glad the school gets the money, but I do need your help."

"You mean...you really intend to..."

He grinned. "Get my money's worth."

The innuendo caused her stomach to flip-flop.

He pointed to the brown package. "What did you get?"

"The quilt."

"Good. I know you really wanted it."

"How about you?"

He gazed at her again, his black eyes unreadable, but his mouth forming a seductive, playful smile. "Can't complain. I got you."

She was about to correct him again, but Reed gave her no chance. He held up his hand and Geneva now saw that he was holding a small black box.

"I did get something else."

"The silver jewelry."

"Right. I'm taking your advice. These will make great gifts."

She waited to hear for who, but he wasn't specific and she didn't ask.

He turned to Trey. "He's a great kid. Did he tell you he's interning with me this semester?"

"I just found out this evening."

Someone leaned close to Reed and whispered in this ear and quickly left again.

"Do you have a business card?"

"Oh. Yes," she said, digging in her bag for her card folder. She gave one to him.

He tucked it into the front pocket of his jeans. And then he ran his fingers through his hair, which only moved the glossy strands into interesting disarray. He considered her for a moment.

"I'll call and set up a meeting. Listen, a bunch of us are going out for drinks. Come with us. Unless you have other plans."

Behind Reed, Grace was vigorously shaking her head, and nixing the plan with her waving arms. Geneva pretended she didn't see her.

But she was surprised by the sudden invitation. And she was just as surprised that she wanted to, if for no other reason than to wrest control back from Grace. Her sister had always behaved as if she knew what... and who...was best for her. Didn't seem to matter that she'd always been wrong.

"No plans, but you really don't have to..."

"I can let Mom and Dad know," Trey offered.

"Great. So, you'll join us, " Reed said. His attention suddenly shifted to someone behind her. "Cliff. I just asked Trey's Aunt..."

"Geneva," she said.

"To join us. We're leaving now."

Geneva glanced covertly from Cliff to Reed, and back again.

Forty-two. Maybe forty-four. Middle-age.

She found the thought dispiriting. That would make Clifford not much older than her self. Suddenly, Geneva wasn't sure she wanted to go after all.

Trey took the quilt out of her hands. "You can get it on Sunday when you come over."

Cliff steered Geneva toward the departing group.

"Call me when you get home!" Grace shouted after her.

Geneva pretended not to hear.

"We can talk a little bit about my project. I have a small room..."

She was only half listening. She was more aware of Reed walking ahead chatting with another man, and three other people who joined the entourage. All women. All pretty. All dressed in casual but meant-to-be-seen attire. All white. All clustered close to him.

Chapter Two

"It's probably too small for a guest room, so I figure a small office or library would work."

"Sounds good," Geneva nodded, trying to stay focused and interested on Clifford Dailey's comments.

He leaned toward her. "The thing is, I probably could make it a small guest room because of my mother. She likes to visit from..."

Geneva continued to give him her undivided attention by sheer force of will, even though the music made her shoulders twitch, and now and then her foot would tap to the rhythm. It was lively. But she wasn't about to get up and dance with Clifford Dailey again.

A short time earlier, after nearly an hour of nonstop me and I conversation from his end, Geneva had looked at him and said abruptly, "Let's dance."

It was not her habit to take the lead in social situations like this. She liked to be asked. It signaled that someone had noticed her, and liked what they saw. But she'd grown desperate. Surprised and somewhat reluctant, Cliff had agreed. Almost immediately Geneva realized she should have left well enough alone.

Cliff was a tall man, and his movements were stiff and awkward. He followed the beat, and his dancing was more than acceptable, but she would not have conceded that he had natural rhythm. Geneva also didn't realize what a comical pair they would make on the dance floor. A few people around the room were actually chuckling until finally she understood why. She must have looked like she was dancing with her father...and he, with his daughter...or a date that was way too young or too small for him.

She decided that conversation was the safest interaction between them.

But Geneva was growing envious of the laughter that kept bursting forth from the other end of the table, where Reed, and the other four members of the party were engaged in lively conversation. They certainly seemed to be having a great time.

At one point a brunette approached from another table, and it was clear that she and Reed knew each other. Geneva wasn't going to try and guess how well. There was a warm embrace between them, a light kiss, brief conversation, and then they took the dance floor. With a deep inward sigh Geneva turned her attention back to Cliff.

"Are you from the San Francisco area originally?" she asked.

He was off and running again.

The saving grace to the evening was that the small club was comfortable, and the music was great, and great for dancing. The others were nice people, out to enjoy themselves and each other. And despite what she saw as obvious attempts by the three women to capture Reed's attention, he didn't appear to single out any one of them.

However, several times she caught Reed watching her. Twice she detected something in his eyes to which she had a near physical response. Curiosity? No. It felt like something else. But only once to he come to her end of the table. To bring her a glass of red wine. A tangy merlot.

How did he know?

"...but I always knew I'd come back to the bay area. My mother is in Oakland."

"Right. Right," Geneva nodded. She finished the rest of her wine, and reached for her purse. "You know, I think I should be heading home..."

Someone touched her shoulder. Squeezed gently. She glanced up and found Reed next to her. She didn't recall him saying anything, but he reached for her hand and pulled her to her feet. Geneva let him. He took her purse away and put it on her chair. He said nothing to Cliff, certainly didn't ask permission. He led her to the dance floor.

Geneva went with him without question, mostly because she was glad to get away from Cliff. She didn't care if Reed Fairway had two clubbed feet, she was so grateful for a break.

Reed didn't have two clubbed feet. It was quickly obvious to Geneva that not only could Reed dance, he had a fluid sensual way of moving that showed he understood the connection between the musical beat, his steps, and the sway of his body. A slow smile of surprise curved her lips and she smoothly followed his lead, step for step. Even nicer, Geneva really liked that he didn't make her feel small.

There was something almost ritualistic about them dancing together. Like a mating dance. Like Reed showing her a little about himself. And she responding to him in the same way.

When the dance was over she expected them to head back to the table. But the next number began; slower so that everyone could catch their breath. A smooth, romantic, perfect-to-sway-to number. Reed took her hand and put his arm around her waist, holding her in position as he led her effortlessly into the moves. She had to adjust to having him hold her close, to the sense of strength she felt in his hands, the breadth of his chest, the firm support of his thigh.

Geneva tried to keep her breathing even. Natural.

Thirty-seven.

Not bad.

She chuckled nervously, staring at a sprinkling of dark hair through the top opening of his shirt. "Did I look like I needed to be rescued?"

"Cliff's really a great guy, but it was unfair of him to monopolize you the whole night."

"It was nice of you to notice."

Reed looked down into her eyes, turning her slowly. "I also noticed that you got paired with the one Black man at the table. Were you more comfortable?"

She raised her brows, returned his look. "I don't think I really noticed."

"Are you sure?"

She sighed, rolled her eyes. "Okay, I was aware of it. So is this your attempt to be unbiased and democratic?"

"This is my attempt to finally get next to you. I wanted to get to know you for myself, without coaching from Trey."

Geneva caught her breath. "Trey? Just what did he tell you about me?"

"Pretty much everything."

Her eyes widened in horror. He chuckled.

"Take it easy. Of course I'm kidding."

She relaxed, glancing up at him. She liked that he was so sure of himself, so unafraid of her. She liked that he had a certain kind of fearlessness. That he made her feel she would be safe with him.

His face so close that she could detect the laugh lines near his eyes, the slight furrow in his forehead, a faint scar at the corner of his mouth.

His mouth.

"I did have selfish motives."

"What?"

"Trey said you taught him how to dance. I wanted a test drive."

She laughed quietly despite herself. "And?"

"Hmmmm. Hard to tell. I don't want to make a snap judgment."

"I have my own observations."

"I know," Reed said, starting to grin. "White men can't dance."

"Except for you, apparently."

"Glad you noticed."

They both laughed.

The music ended and the dance was over.

Reed held her a moment longer and then stepped back. They grinned at each other but said nothing, as if they'd still come to some sort of understanding. Geneva finally turned back to her end of the table. She again picked up her purse and Clifford stood up.

"I'm going to say goodnight."

He offered to walk her to her car but Geneva waved him back to his seat.

"Don't forget to call. Let's get together," Cliff said.

She looked to everyone at the table. "It was nice to meet all of you. Thanks for including me."

Everyone spoke at once as they said goodnight, but she didn't try to separate the comments.

She didn't see Reed as she walked to the exit. But he was standing just outside the front door.

Geneva wasn't particularly surprised to see him and he said nothing as he silently fell into step next to her. In the parking lot she unlocked the door of her car and stood with it open, facing Reed.

"I'm glad you came along," he said.

"Yeah, me too. It was fun."

"Maybe we can do this again sometime."

"Maybe," Geneva said noncommittally.

"What do you want me to tell Trey when he asks what we did tonight?"

"Tell him to mind his own business."

She took her place behind the steering wheel and Reed closed the door. He stood aside as she backed out and turned toward the exit.

"Goodnight, Aunt Eva," Reed called out.

Laughing she blinked her headlights at him in answer.

"Hey, Reed? Can I borrow that Latitude XT laptop Dell sent last week? I want to try something on it."

Reed, in conversation from a hand free headset, pointed to the Dell box next to his desk.

"Thanks, man," the visitor said, quickly snatching up the box and leaving.

With his long legs propped on another stock of boxes and manuals, Reed worked on the seventeen-inch portable resting on his lap.

"What about the language? Are we going to have problems with conversion?" He asked, reviewing data on multiple opened windows.

"Reed? Phone call," a female voice called from outside his office.

He glanced up, finding her arm waving a cordless in the air. "Take a message...Yeah, I'm listening. What about Microsoft? I heard there might be something in the next version of Windows."

Reed looked at the clock at the top of his computer screen. He was running late again. Geneva Springer of Comfort Zones was due in half an hour.

For a moment he was totally distracted as he recalled the woman talked about incessantly by Trey Savage. At first he'd been amused by the boy's clear love and respect for his aunt. And then he'd grown intrigued by someone who could command so much adoration, and who was such a strong positive influence on Trey's life as well.

Reed pursed his lips. He knew all about that part. As a matter of fact, it had come when he was just a few years younger than Trey was right now.

All that aside, that wasn't the only thing about Trey's aunt that had gotten his attention. Even before he'd actually met her there was that whole unexpected encounter at the high school auction with a gorgeous Black woman. She had a pretty if cautious smile. Large, very inquisitive eyes. A sweet riot of short, loose curls. And she was so petite. But what had also grabbed his attention was her ability to banter with him without being the least bit coy or having an attitude. She'd looked at him, not through him. He liked that. The difference mattered.

So far, everything Trey had told him about her had been right. And there was all that other stuff he'd found out for him that night. Nice surprise.

"Reed? They said it's important."

He looked up. The young woman stood by the door, phone in hand.

"Is this about an unpaid invoice," he returned, flippant.

"It's County Medical about a Mrs..."

Reed reacted instantly.

"Something's come up, Brian. I'll get back to you."

In one breath he was out of his chair, pulling off his headset and tossing it onto the desk, along with the laptop. He grabbed the phone, already rushing out the door.

"I'm on my way," Reed said without even waiting to hear from the caller.

He flipped the phone over his shoulder as he reached the office entrance. It was deftly caught by one of the techs passing by.

"You coming back?" someone asked.

"Depends," Reed answered, and then was gone.

Anxious and concerned he screeched out of the parking lot and into traffic, thinking of all the short cuts that would get him across town in the least amount of time. He still had to contend with all the approaches on and off the Golden Gate Bridge, and the short hilly streets of San

Francisco. It was a trip that could have taken twenty five minutes. He made it to the medical center in seventeen.

Reed gave his name at the reception desk.

"Where's Mrs. Lambert?" he asked.

"She should be back from Ex-Ray. Third floor, room 327."

When he got off the elevator and approached the reception desk, the first person he saw was an elderly Black woman seated with quiet regality in a wheelchair. She was fully dressed in her own clothing, and not in a hospital gown. That's a good sign, he thought.

Her handbag rested on her knees, and she clutched the straps. She was dictating information to a nurse who sat nearby with a clipboard.

"Cora..."

The woman saw Reed and the look of relief and pleasure that crossed her face sent relief rushing through him.

She reached out a hand and he grasped it, holding it as he sat in the chair nearest her. The young Asian nurse smiled at him, a bit puzzled.

"Are you her...er...next of kin?"

"Pretty much," Reed responded. "Health care proxy, Surrogate son. Good friend. Guardian. All of the above. How is she?"

"Stop talking like I can't hear you," the elder woman complained.

Reed merely nodded for the nurse to continue.

"Mrs. Lambert is fine. Nothing serious."

Reed looked to Cora for confirmation, his eyes searching for signs that he might not be getting the whole story.

"I told them not to call you," the older woman said in a strong, clear voice.

"What happened?" Reed asked her.

"I just got a little dizzy. It's those pills the doctor put me on."

"Actually, Mrs. Lambert fainted. And we're pretty sure it wasn't the medication. It seems she may not have eaten since sometime yesterday. She got lightheaded."

"How'd she get here?" Reed asked.

"That busy-body Mrs. Templeton next door came over to borrow my new iron. Had the nerve to walk right into my house just because I didn't answer the bell. She called the police."

Reed looked at Cora Lambert with a mixture of affectionate tolerance, and steely disapprove.

"I'll have to thank Mrs. Templeton anyway."

"Oh, don't fuss at me, Reed," Cora said contritely. "Last night I fell asleep reading in the living room. When I woke up it was after eleven. I just went right to bed. I still think it's those pills."

Reed squeezed her hand and allowed himself a quiet sigh. "Anything else?"

"No, nothing. Mrs. Lambert is in pretty good health."

"Of course I am. I know how to take care of myself."

Reed and the nurse exchanged silent looks. He stood up. "Then you're not keeping her?"

"I'm not staying. I want to go home," Cora declared imperially.

"There's no reason to," the nurse said. "She's really okay, but she needs to remember to eat more frequently. Sign here."

She gave the clipboard to Reed who signed off on the release form. Reed walked next to the wheelchair as they made their way back to the main floor. Soon, with Cora Lambert's arm hooked through his own, they were headed to his car.

Her posture was as erect as he'd always known, but she seemed to walk carefully, deliberately, as if to show him that she was very much in control. Reed glanced down at her Cora's face, with her still smooth, even if not as firm, sienna toned skin. At sixty-nine she was still an attractive woman, but he was beginning to see other signs of aging.

"Am I going to have to carry through on my threat to get a home care attendant in for you, Cora?" Reed asked kindly as he assisted her into the front passenger seat of his car and fastened her seatbelt. She didn't respond until he was also seated, and had swiveled to face her. His gaze on the older woman was not annoyed or impatient, but deeply concerned.

"If you do I'll never speak to you again," she threatened.

Reed patiently waited Cora out until she had calmed down.

"You know how I feel about that, Reed."

"You're one of the most important people in my life. You know I'm going to worry about you. You know I'll do anything for you, Cora."

"I know," she smiled softly, patting his knee. "Bless your heart. I'm still sorry. I hope this doesn't mess up your day."

Reed sat forward, smiling ruefully as he turned over the engine of his car. Geneva Springer would have arrived about an hour ago.

"Nothing you need to worry about."

There was no way he wouldn't have responded to a call for Cora. Geneva didn't need to know that...but he still didn't feel right about standing her up.

"You can drop me off at the house and go on back to work."

"First I'm taking you to lunch."

She glanced at him. Reed could literally feel Cora's quiet delight.

"Are you sure you have time?"

"Absolutely."

When she arrived at the offices of Fairway Future-Tech and Games, Geneva thought that maybe she'd arrived at their warehouse. Possibly a testing lab, or workshop. She realized that the space was fairly large, but seemed significantly smaller because of all the clutter, the chatter, the absurd levels of activity. It all gave the impression of being a college dorm lounge, and a video arcade. She was appalled by the lack of professional standards.

Geneva stood at the entrance, the metal door propped open with a five gallon water dispenser bottle. She checked the suite number to make sure she had the right place. She did. Now she understood why Reed seriously wanted her to take on the job of renovating his company offices.

Gaping at the circus-like atmosphere she reviewed her conversation with Reed just that morning, trying to recall if there was something she'd missed...

"It's good to hear from you," he'd said cheerfully.

"Thank you." Geneva had a strong feeling that they were both probably thinking about the previously Friday evening. "But before we go any further I just want to say..."

"You're not interested in taking me on?"

Geneva frowned. She wished he wasn't so loose and easy with his phrasing. Or maybe she was reading too much into his words.

"That's not it, exactly. I know you're trying to help the school, and I realize you paid a lot for me...I mean, for my design services. But you don't have to if you don't want to. Really."

He was chuckling.

"I'm not letting you off the hook," Reed said. "Listen, let me tell you what I have in mind. Maybe that will help," he said, getting serious. "I run a pretty good size operation. It's software development for business use. I got into video and virtual games a few years back. I'm even thinking about feature productions strictly for on-line viewing, bypassing DVD.

"I work with a bunch of incredibly smart people. But, to be frank, they're a lot like a bunch of geeky overgrown kids. They were not the popular ones in school, but they're brilliant. These are the folks who are developing our technological future. In other words..."

"In other words, you indulge their quirks because of what they offer the company."

"What they offer the world. That's it in a nutshell. And they're good, honest people."

"Hmmmm," Geneva murmured, starting to feel the challenge involved with working with such a group. "And what about you? Are you a weirdo, too?"

Reed had laughed out loud, the sound spontaneous, rich, and genuine.

"Probably. But I am house trained, I don't drool, and there are lots of people who are very fond of me."

"I'll bet," she'd responded dryly, grinning despite herself.

"Including your nephew, Trey. The kid is smart. He's already talking his own business. He loves computers, and I think he can learn a lot here. In fact, he thinks I'm a pretty cool dude. Ask him. Does that help?"

"Sort of," Geneva confessed honestly.

"Good. Can you come by around noon? You'll get to meet the inmates..."

Inmates is right, she now considered.

She stepped into the room. To her left, a man on the telephone was using his free hand to expertly and repeatedly take basketball shots into a hoop nailed between two windows! Several people appeared to actually be working, but lounged in their spring action chairs with feet propped on the edge of their desks. Someone else was clearly playing some sort of game on his computer, watched by several co-workers at nearby desks who cheered him on. Geneva nearly jumped out of her skin when a cat...a cat...sauntered past her into the office and jumped onto a vacant chair to sleep.

"This is ridiculous," she muttered, already feeling that, her beloved nephew's future potential aside, this was going to be a huge mistake.

"Who're looking for?"

Geneva turned to the young woman addressing her. "Reed Fairway. I have an appointment to see him."

"He's not here," the woman said.

"I'd already figured that out. Do you know when he'll be back? He was expecting me," Geneva said patiently.

"Don't have a clue. But, if he knows you were coming, have a seat. He might be back soon."

"Might?" Geneva asked, controlling her rising annoyance.

"Yeah, that's right. I think he got a call a while ago. Would you like some popcorn? The machine is over there."

Astonished, Geneva followed the woman's nod and, in disbelief, saw a fully operational popcorn maker, just like the ones they have at fairs... and arcades.

She dropped into the nearest chair to consider what she was going to do. She wasn't used to this. Suddenly taking on Clifford Dailey's project was starting to have appeal. After more than an hour Geneva gave up; fuming, more than a little disappointed, she marched over to the desk of the woman.

"I can't wait any longer."

"He could be back any minute."

"Are we talking today or tomorrow or next week?" Geneva asked through clenched teeth. "I want to leave him a voice mail message."

She was immediately ashamed that she was taking out her angst on the woman.

"Sure." She picked up her phone, dialed a number, and passed it to Geneva.

Geneva waited out the voice that made her momentarily waiver. That sent a peculiar sliver of tension through her as she considered the man she'd met behind the voice. As she remembered the way Reed had articulated the good, the bad and the comical about his company and its employees.

Beeep.

Too late.

"This is Geneva Springer. It seems you forgot about our appointment, or chose to ignore it. I'm disappointed in you, Mr. Fairway. And I am seriously anger that you didn't even have the decency to call. Your time is not more valuable than mine! And..." she took a very deep breath at what she was about to say. "And I'll be happy to reimburse you for the money you contributed at the auction, since you won't be getting what you paid for."

With that she slammed down the phone and marched out of the office, unaware that she left the entire staff staring silently after her.

Chapter Three

"Aunt Eva, you got to chill. Reed's not like that. You made a mistake."

Geneva stared indignant at her nephew, trying to remember that what happened wasn't his fault.

"I know you like the man Trey, but he had no right to do that to me. I had to turn down a meeting with your assistant principal to get together with Reed."

Trey frowned. "Mr. Dailey? Why you wanna meet with him?"

Geneva ignored the question.

"What he did was rude. He's arrogant, conceited, and..."

"Wow. He really ticked you off," Trey observed, as he sat opposite his aunt at a favorite seafood stall on Fisherman's Wharf. "How could that happen? Reed is such a great guy."

"So you've said. So he said you'd say." Geneva sighed, shaking her head. "I felt so foolish sitting there in that insane asylum he calls his company."

Trey guffawed, stomping his foot on the floor. Finally he stopped laughing as he stuffed French fries into his mouth.

"Oh man. That's cold. Okay, I get it. But you're wrong about him. I know you're wrong."

"He didn't say anything to you about what happened?" she casually asked her nephew.

"We sort of had a talk," Trey muttered, shifting in his seat.

"Maybe I should have given him a chance to explain," she murmured, feeling terrible about her own behavior.

"You think?" Trey asked smartly.

Geneva swatted him with her napkin. "Don't get fresh. After all I've done for you you're supposed to be on my side."

"Yeah, yeah. I know. Saving my life, taking me all over San Francisco when I was a kid, running interference with Mom and Dad."

She smiled, also protective of the tight bond between them. She loved her roll as favorite aunt. She loved thinking of Trey almost as a son.

She sighed and became reflective. Very much like a son...

"Don't worry about Reed, Aunt Eva. He never holds a grudge. Unlike other people I know."

She tried to swat him again, and he leaned out of reach.

"For a grown up, he's cool."

"I was going to ask you before but, could you do me a favor?" Trey said when they left the restaurant and walked to her car.

"Yes, of course I'm driving you home," Geneva said, unlocking the doors.

"I mean tomorrow. I left my math lab book at Reed's. I need it to study for a test. Do you think you could drive me by to pick it up? You don't have to come in if you don't want to."

"Trey," Geneva whined.

"Please? It'll only take a minute. I'll be in and back before you count to sixty."

"It's a good think I love you."

"Sure is," he cackled.

Reed answered his cell phone and waved everyone in the room behind him into silence.

"You're here...yeah, everything's ready...are you sure she'll come up? You lied to her...not a good idea, Trey. You aunt already wants to rip my heart out and feed it to the cat...okay, right...show time."

Reed hung up, surprised and even a bit annoyed that he felt butterflies in his stomach. There was no time to wonder about why it mattered so much, or why he was going to extraordinary measures to make things right with Trey's aunt. Actually, he considered, it wasn't so much that she was Trey's aunt. Maybe it was something he'd sensed when they'd first met, and then was reinforced after the auction, at the club.

He turned to the motley gathering of his employees, all fidgeting and not at all happy about what was expected of them. He raised his hand to get their attention.

"Okay, listen up. Your jobs depend on how this goes down."

Everyone moaned and griped.

"I'm serious. Now, I know that what happened wasn't really your fault. Tough."

Then, all heads turned to the door as it opened and first Trey walked through, smiling and with long, confident strides. Behind him, Reed stared as Geneva slowly appeared. She really was pretty cute. It was still hard for him to believe that she'd left that incendiary voice mail for him. There was certainly nothing small about her ability to get mad.

He watched as she appeared uncertain, her gaze puzzled at finding everyone standing in a group at the side of the room. Her gaze finding his and freezing there. Reed was relieved not to detect any lingering anger in her eyes. Just an almost wounded, cautious look he'd seen on her face that first time. It made him feel even worse about what had happened.

"Ready?" he asked softly to his gathered crew. But he didn't wait for an answer. He put a tuning whistle to his lips and softly blew.

On that cue everyone began singing, rather off key, as Reed enthusiastically conducted them through a song he'd hastily written to the music of "There Is Nothin' Like A Dame" from the musical, South Pacific.

Peering occasionally over his shoulder he could see that, at first, Geneva stared blank and wide eyed at the offering. Then she slowly began to grin with each stanza. His employees were game and forceful but it was painful to listen to. Finally, Geneva discreetly covered her mouth to hide her smile at the absurd lyrics.

"'We're so sorry we were jerks
(and for gumming up the works),
Giving you a bad impression
With our crude and rude transgression...

And we hope that you'll forgive us
We are not pigs in a pen.
What do we need?
We need you, Gen...Ev-A!"

Her shoulders were shaking with laughter. Good, Reed thought to himself, as the group went into a hearty final chorus, ending the song.

The room went silent, and Reed looked at his group as they all stood, sheepish, waiting for approval.

Geneva began to clap. Trey soon joined in with a shrieking whistle through his tongue and fingers. The group started to laugh and relax, glad that the ordeal was over. They applauded themselves as well.

"That was...incredible," Geneva said, her voice shaking. "Bravo."

Reed remembered the coup d'etat. A last peace offering. From the back pocket of his jeans he pulled out a makeshift flag. It was a sheet of paper towel attached to a ruler with Scotch tape. He waved it.

He was sure no one else saw what he saw them. The rapid fire change of emotions across Geneva's face. What would have been a blush, except for her brown skin, the rueful smile on her lips. And the silently mouthed words, "thank you", for his eyes only.

"Hi. I'm here."

Geneva stood in the open doorway of Reed's office and waited for him to see her. He had his back to her, searching through a book case behind his desk.

He jerked his head toward her, and the motion dislodged books and manuals from the shelf. Several fall to the floor.

"Hey," Reed said, before dropping to one knee to gather up the pile.

Geneva put her purse and portfolio on a chair and hurried around his worktable.

"Didn't mean to startle you," she apologized.

She crouched down, shoulder to shoulder with Reed, to help gather up the papers. Their hands and arms touched and crossed and got in each other's way. She realized that he was taking quick, covert glances at her, and each time he did it was like being touched with heat. Geneva didn't dare meet his gaze. She was already suddenly aware of Reed in an entirely different way. It was like a warning signal that sent strange sensations down her arms, up her legs, and changed the pattern of her breathing.

What is wrong with you? Geneva asked herself, as she stood up with a handful of books and papers.

"Where should I put this stuff?" she asked.

"Anywhere," he said, putting what he held on his desk chair.

Reed stood regarding her, absently trying to tuck in the tail of his white shirt into the waist of his black jeans. "It looks worse than it is. I know where everything is. I'm glad to see you." He swept his fingers through his hair.

He was nervous. Good.

She'd been busy watching the motion, and the way the shirt stretched taut over his chest. She liked what happened with his hair when he combed it with his hand.

She blinked. "What?"

"I said, I'm glad you're here. Especially after last week."

He picked up a small rectangular sign and headed to the office door. Geneva caught a glimpse of the front where a single word was printed in bold caps: CLOSED. He hung it on a nail on the outside of the doorframe. She realized for the first time that there wasn't a door.

To hide her reaction to Reed's confession, she looked around for her things and retrieved them from the chair.

"I've over it."

"I just want you to know I'm not a jerk, or a pig."

She couldn't help grinning at him. That was in that ridiculous but very sweet song his employees had song for her. "I know that."

"But I guess sometimes I can be arrogant, conceited..."

Geneva moaned and closed her eyes. "I'm going to kill my nephew..."

"And rude."

"I over reacted. I don't usually get that bent out of shape."

Reed's lips formed into a warm smile. "I know."

"How could you know that?"

"Trey. According to him you practically walk on water. He's devoted to you, and he made it clear that he would kick my ass if I dis you again."

Geneva gasped in surprise, and then started to chuckle at the thought of her skinny fifteen years old nephew taking on Reed.

Reed was grinning broadly at her, and any lingering annoyance or hesitation she might have been feeling when she arrived, quickly turned not only to total forgiveness, but a sudden rush of admiration.

He was just so different from the kind of men she was used to.

Reed's amusement slowly faded and he began clearing a space on his table and beckoned her closer.

"I have one more thing to say about what happened and then we'll close the book on it. Agreed?"

"Agreed."

"I had a really good reason for not being here on Monday. Something came up unexpectedly that I had to see to. My problem, not yours, but I should have called you when I had a chance."

Geneva again felt impressed by the lengths he was going to for damage control. He'd already succeeded. And he certainly didn't have a fragile ego. This final statement sealed it for her, combined with her nephew's obvious hero worship.

Reed Fairway was genuine. And possibly a very good man.

She also admitted to herself that his appeal just took an instant fifty percent leap in her opinion of him.

"Sounds very important."

"It was," Reed said solemnly.

"I hope it turned out alright."

"It did."

There was an unusually long pause and they stared at each other silently.

"Well..." she broke the spell, approaching his desk with her portfolio. "I have some drawings to show you. I should warn you, the changes are going to be expensive."

"No problem. I'll authorize your use of a company credit card."

"Naturally I'll get your approval before I buy anything."

Reed suddenly reached out and took her hand, an amused light making his black eyes even darker. "You already have it. You're the expert. Let's see what you have."

The sudden unexpected contact had an affect. But he quickly

37

released her hand, and Geneva fumbled to open the portfolio. She laid out half a dozen sketches of different sides and angles of the large open space of Reed's company offices. She pointed to her plans, explaining her thoughts and outlining ideas for reorganization and design.

Reed was silent for the most part, but a quick glance at his profile now and then, as he leaned partially over her shoulder to see the details, showed serious focus. Sometimes he made a noncommittal murmur, or nodded his head slightly, but otherwise it was her show, and she was on.

They were interrupted once with a call on one of two cell phones clipped to his waistband. Reed answered immediately. "Hello?... everything okay?...Good...I'm in a meeting right...don't worry about it. Why don't I stop by after work?...Can I bring something in?...Sounds good to me. I'll see you later."

He urged her to continue without reference to the call, but Geneva couldn't help but draw her own conclusion. After work. Cozy get together. Date. She tried to keep her imagination under control and forged ahead.

Almost an hour later Reed straightened and silently reviewed the drawings while Geneva stood by watching. She became a little anxious the longer he went without saying anything. Had she been too strong in her approach? Did he not see that her use of the space was more efficient? Did he resent her attempts to rein in the chaos?

"Okay," Reed finally sighed. "Feedback."

He perched a hip on the edge of the table, slid his left hand into the front pocket of his jean, and with his right hand pointed to all the areas he wanted to discuss.

"This is a great start, Gen..."

Gen?

She started to voice her disapproval, but Reed plowed right on.

"You certainly get it that the office is out of control, so to speak. My fault. I haven't been a very strict parent," he drawled, his tone self-deprecating and rueful.

Geneva hid her smile. Trey is right. Reed was very cool.

"Let's think about this..."

For almost another hour Reed and Geneva went over the drawings one more time. She made margin notes, did strike through, drew arrows to indicate relocations. Reed did the same, and Geneva had to admit that what he contributed was insightful, functional, and important to the efficient running of his business. They argued over only one salient point; the cat.

"It's probably a health department violation, Reed. This is supposed to be a place of business, remember?"

"Yeah, I know. It sounds crazy but Mac is part of the team, in her own way. She was found in the garbage one night by one of the guys. She'd been dropped into a shipping carton with three other newborns kittens. One didn't make it. We found a home for the second one. Mac became the office mascot."

"Mac? Let me guess," Geneva said dryly. "She was inside an Apple computer box."

"That's right. I'd hate to have to tell the office we have to get rid of her at this stage. She has a calming affect on my group when they're under deadline pressure and stressed to the max. Can't you do something?"

Geneva gnawed her lip, but she was moved by the quiet plea in Reed's voice. It was absurd that grown men and women needed to have a cat in the office in order to get the job done. But in an odd way, it was rather touching. "Let me think about it, okay? But I'm not making any promises."

"Good enough." He looked at his watch. "One more thing. Do you have time to give a little presentation to the gang?"

"Right now?"

"Why not? I think they should know what we have in mind. Will fifteen minutes do it?"

It was a less than subtle hint, but Geneva nodded. She liked that he was decisive. His charm and sense of humor didn't get in the way of business.

"I guess so. If you want."

While Reed went into the outer office, got everyone's attention and made an announcement, Geneva quickly formulated in her head what she was going to say. She was a little nervous. What if they didn't like the idea of changing things? What if they really didn't like her?

By the time Geneva joined Reed, there were some twenty-five people cluster at, around or on top of desks just outside his office. They were looking at her, it seemed, with frank open skepticism.

"This will only take a minute or two," Reed said, addressing them. "Gen is going to tell you about the new design plans for the office. I want the place to look more professional and less like a frat house. I want to clean up the clutter. What I don't want to do is make the place sterile, uninteresting..."

"And no fun," someone said from the back of the crowd.

There was general muttering agreement.

"You're not going to get rid of Mac, are you?" someone else asked.

"That's under discussion," Reed said, signaling to Geneva.

There was a rumble through the group as she stood before them. She cleared her throat. "Hi. I promise no yelling this time." Everyone laughed. "I'll only be a few minutes I want to show you..."

"Wait a minute," Reed interrupted.

He retrieved a clear lucite step stool placed it next to her. Immediately one of the guys rushed forward to take hold of her arm, while Reed took the other. Before Geneva could say a word she found herself lifted in the air and her feet set on top of the stool.

"Thanks," she said awkwardly, as several onlookers chuckled.

She was only vaguely aware that Reed then shifted his position and now stood facing her, but a little apart from his employees. He crossed his arms over his chest and watched closely as she made her presentation. A wave of nervous heat washed over Geneva, making her throat and hands dry. She felt on display, but raised her chin defiantly and spoke in a strong clear voice.

She kept her comments brief and to the point, reiterating exactly what she and Reed had already agreed was needed to make the office function better. Essentially, the space would be divided in a more logical manner so that worker would have space for their desk.

She stole a glancing look at Reed and found him regarding her. It was impossible to know what he might be thinking.

Genera told them she also planned for a meeting center with a conference table, and a quiet lounge partitioned off from the work place. And to keep the place from closing in and becoming smaller, she wanted to use plate glass for the partitioning walls, so that everyone could see everyone else. There was a smattering of pleased applause. She told them they would be kept abreast of plans and, at some point, for at least a week the office might shut down while all the changes were put in place.

"That's it. Not so bad, I hope. But the most important thing, and I believe Reed will agree, is that your office should be comfortable and a place you want to be everyday. I'll leave copies of the drawing so you can all see them. Now it's your turn. I'd like you to tell me what you want."

For a moment there was silence. Geneva scanned the room but they all stared blankly back at her. Reed remained calm and observant, but did nothing to help her out.

"Anyone?"

"Miss Gen."

Her eyes searched out the lone voice while a hand was tentatively raised. The instant nickname now had a familiar and comfortable sound to it that she decided she liked after all. Geneva smiled in gratitude at her savior. "Yes."

"Will we be able to eat in the lounge area?? And can we get a beverage machine?"

"I was thinking the lounge area as a quiet zone. I have included a break room with tables and chairs, a frig and microwave, etc."

"How about more closets. Or individual lockers."

"I think we can do that. Reed?"

"Fine with me," he readily agreed. "You're in charge. Make it happen."

There was genuine applause when Geneva finished. Two young men rushed over to help her down from the stool, but Reed got there first.

"I got it," he said, spanning his large hands on her waist. He gently swung her from the stool to the floor.

She felt like she was flying.

Reed didn't immediately let her go. Once again she felt as if a private message had passed between them. The look in his eyes caused that funny tingling to her arms again, and a catch in her throat. And there was suddenly that whole thing going on in her stomach.

"You had us worried, Miss Gen," a round face middle aged man, one of Reed's oldest employees, said to her.

Reed's hand slid away, but he stayed close to her side.

"Why?" she asked, dragging her gaze away and focusing on the man.

"We thought you were going to put us all in little ticky tacky cubicles, just like real offices."

"Bor-ring," Geneva intoned. "You deserve better than that, right?"

The man gave her a nod of approval. "Awesome!"

She looked at Reed again, curious to see if that look would still be there in his eyes. It sure was.

"How did I do?"

Now his gaze did change, filled with something that was hidden in the depths of his eyes, but that nevertheless signaled the disappearance of a barrier, the shortening of distance and space, a change in perception.

"Awesome," Reed said quietly.

Chapter Four

"Trey, I just know you're doing homework and not playing some fool game up there. Don't make me have to get after you!" Grace shouted up the stairwell. "It could get ugly."

There was no response and she didn't wait for one. But Geneva was chuckling when her sister returned to her kitchen. Geneva was at the sink rinsing the dinner plates and loading the dishwasher.

"There should be a law or something that says no teenager can get and play computer games without parental consent," she continued to fuss.

"Oh, leave him along, Gee. Trey is an A student. He could be doing something worse, you know."

Grace moaned. "Lord, don't I know it. He loves this internship he's doing 'cause that Fairway guy gives him all this free stuff for his computer. You should see Trey's room."

"He really likes Reed a lot. Reed says Trey has a great natural instinct for computer language and software capabilities..."

"Whatever that means," Grace muttered.

"And Reed says he could have a fabulous future in technology. The future will be computerized and digital. That's where the big money will be."

"I'm glad to hear that. Then he can support me and his father in our old age."

"I think his relationship with Reed Fairway is good. Don't do anything to discourage Trey."

Grace looked at her impatiently.

"What is it with this Reed Fairway? It's Reed this, and Reed that. Even you are starting to sound like a disciple. I don't hear any mention of Clifford Dailey."

Geneva didn't realize that's how she was coming across. Was her enthusiasm over the top? Was her admiration getting in the way of objectivity?

Was she lusting after Reed Fairway?

"Well, I'm working for him. I've had a chance to see Reed in action, up close and..." She decided against finishing the cliché, afraid that it might be too revealing. "...And I can see for myself why Trey is a fan."

"You didn't answer me. What ever happened with Clifford Dailey, the Assistant Principal?" Grace pursued.

"Nothing," Geneva said, wrapping the leftovers from Sunday dinner at the Savages.

"What do you mean, nothing? You told me you were out with him a few weeks ago," Grace badgered.

"Yes, I was. We met at his house. Don't give me that look. It wasn't a date. He hired me to redo a room."

"But, haven't you seen him since then? As in a date?" Grace asked.

"What is this? I don't owe you a blow by blow of my personal life, Gee. To be honest, he did ask me out and I said no."

"You said no? Are you out of your mind? He is a great catch. Girl, what am I going to do with you?"

"Leave me alone?" Geneva gently suggested.

The subtle hint went right over her sister's head.

"I go out of my way to find you a good Black man who's not full of you-know-what, and you act that they're a dime a dozen on the open market. Not!"

Geneva couldn't help but laugh at Grace's histrionics.

"You should know, so you can get over it, that I'm really not interested in Clifford Dailey."

"But why? He's good-looking, he dresses nicely..."

"And, I'm sorry to say, he's not very interesting. And, I might also add, I'm just not that into him."

Grace gaped at her, standing indignantly with a fist on her hip. "You could grow to love him, if you work at it."

"I don't think so. There's no point in pretending, wasting my time and his, or trying to get his feet to fit into the magic glass slipper. It ain't gonna happen," Geneva said with attitude.

Grace made an impatient sound. "You haven't been involved with a man since your divorce and that was three years ago."

"Four," Geneva corrected smoothly.

"You are running out of possibilities."

Geneva pursed her lips into a wicked smile. "Actually there is one. Reed Fairway."

Grace's mouth dropped open. "Excuse me? What did you say? That...that Reed person?"

"That's right."

"Trey's mentor?"

"Right again."

"You do know he's white."

"From the first moment I met him. Not an issue. He's been flirting with me. I think I've been flirting with him," she said in a wry tone. "He's cute, interesting and very different from any man I've met since my divorce. He's fun. I like him."

"But...but he's so young."

In the process of pouring herself a glass of wine Geneva's hand shook spilling some on the counter. Merlot. Reed knew she liked Merlot.

"Ho...how old is he?"

"Well, I don't know but, he spends all his time on computers. He plays games. He goes to work in jeans and loafers. He needs a haircut."

"I like his hair," Geneva said irrelevantly.

"I bet he's not a day over thirty five."

Geneva let out a sigh of relief. Still within the ballpark.

"You need a grown man. Someone who's mature, can take care of you financially. Who's responsible...and has a pension!"

Geneva blanched, blinking at her sister. "He's not that young," she said, but sounded uncertain. "He's been in business for at least ten years. He's got a few dozen men and women working for him, some older than he is. Reed could be thirty-six. Thirty-seven."

"And you are still on the wrong side of both numbers."

"Grace, give it a rest. It's not like I expect him to propose. There is this thing between us. But it's not going anywhere.

"You're the one that keeps reminding me I'm going to end up unmarried and a lonely old maid. If that's the future I have to look forward to then I'm having all my fun now. It's harmless. Nothing's going to happen."

Geneva grew serious, approaching her sister and giving her a loving hug. Despite her helplessness at Geneva's flippant and irreverent attitude, Grace returned the embrace.

"But I worry about you. I want you to be happy."

"You're not responsible for my happiness. I did everything the manual tells us you should. I followed all the rules, found the man that was, by any standards, perfect. I took my time to be sure he was the one, and he played his part to the letter. I thought I'd be happy. And almost the moment the words 'I do' were spoken and the ink dry on the wedding certificate, I found myself living with someone I'd never seen before."

Grace looked stricken. She hugged Geneva again.

"And you left after only five months. The bastard."

"It hurt a lot, Grace. I certainly learned there are no guarantees, so I'm not looking for any. Thanks for caring about your little sister. Life is too short. I'm having dessert first."

Grace laughed, if somewhat sadly. "Just watch out for empty calories.

Geneva sat at the nearest empty desk and, reading from her written notes, entered the latest measurements into one of the many files she'd created for Reed's renovation project. She was alone in the big room, the last employee having left just twenty minutes earlier. Even Mac, the office mascot, had been taken home by someone for the duration of the work.

But she was not completely alone. She let her gaze drift to Reed's office. He still sat at his desk, lounging back in his chair as he concentrated on no less than three laptops, typing on one and then another. He'd told her he'd stayed to make sure she'd be okay.

"I don't want you freaking out 'cause you're by yourself," he'd said. "It gets spooky late at night. And the neighborhood gets deserted in this part of town."

She wasn't afraid to be alone, but she didn't argue the point. It was sweet and gallant knowing that he was concerned, and nearby.

Geneva sighed, saved the most recent entries, and got up with her retractable twenty-five feet tape measure in hand. Reed had already given her the official floor plans, so she knew the exact square footage of the office. But she was now working on dividing the interior into workable space for his employees. Geneva stole yet another glance at Reed, sitting alone in his office, seemingly riveted to his screens and his work.

Maybe it was just as well that his powers of concentration were so great. But there was a part of Geneva that also couldn't help wondering, did he remember what she remembered of what had happened between them two nights earlier, after hours...

The employees had been told the week before that they had to pack all their belongs into moving boxes, while still being able to access anything they needed for work during the day. Given their overall penchant for being slobs, it was a tall order.

When Geneva arrived at the office, she was surprised by how much had actually been done, but it became clear that Reed had played a very proactive part in the preliminary work. As a matter of fact, it was he who was alone still packing boxes.

"Sorry it's not done yet," he'd apologized to her, looking up only briefly to give her a quick ironic smile before tackling another pile of software boxes.

"You could have hired a service to do this, Reed. Or, at least, someone should have stayed to help you," she'd complained.

"A lot of our work is highly sensitive information. I feel better having control of it," he explained. "The staff actually did quite a lot, and I don't mind. I need the distraction," he murmured.

"I'll help," Geneva had volunteered at once. "Between the two of us I think we can finish this side of the room quickly."

She'd come prepared to work, dressed in jeans, sneakers, and a black T-shirt because it wouldn't show dirt so much. She'd also brought along a cotton square to tie around her hair.

Reed had taken a momentary break to stare at her, like he was seeing her for the first time.

"You look cute. Way too small to be doing this kind of work."

She hid her reaction in the simple chore of putting aside her purse, and looking for a digital camera in its depths. "Well, no point in wishing I was taller."

Geneva felt a peculiar sense of exposure as he considered her. His face was sweaty. Sweat marks stained the entire front of his Henley shirt, and under the arms. His hair was damp and also tied back with a scarf. He looked like a very handsome modern day pirate. Or a wild Italian.

He looked very sexy.

Immediately Geneva wished that hadn't entered her mind. Because now, it was going to be impossible not to be aware of his physical appeal. Of his intense masculinity. Of the magic powers of his eyes.

"Why don't you finish that desk," Reed said, pulling them both back to reality. "I'm almost done here."

They'd worked in near silence for the next half hour. Every now and then Geneva stopped to take photographs of a particular angle or corner of the room. That's what she was doing when it happened.

She was moving backward, stepping left and right to get the shot she wanted when Reed called out, startling her.

"Geneva, watch it! Get out of the..."

Then there was a rumbling crash, making her jump.

When she jerked around it was to find Reed trying to hold back a falling cascade of boxes that had been stacked too high on top of each other. Most missed him and landed on the floor, only one spilling it's contents. Another barely missed her. The top one glanced off the side of his head, knocking Reed backwards to the floor, the box on top of his chest.

"Reed! Oh my God, Reed. Are you okay?"

She put the camera down and stumbled over the debris to reach him. He was flat on his back but he wasn't unconscious. He muttered an oath and touched his face. His fingers had blood on them. He shoved the box on his chest aside.

Geneva dropped to her knees leaning over him. Her hands gently turned his head to the side so she could see the damage. Not as bad as it might have been, but there was a pretty good abrasion high on his cheek. The box had missed his left eye by an inch. She manipulated the area with her finger-tips. There was only superficial bleeding.

"Ouch! That hurt," he complained.

"Oh, stop being such a baby," Geneva accused him, even as her racing heart slowly went back to a normal beat, seeing that he was not seriously injured. He lay still and let her examine the cut.

The water cooler had already been moved, so she went into the ladies room pulling off her bandana. She quickly came running back with it folded and wet. By now Reed was sitting up, gingerly touching his face. Geneva put the scarf on the cut and held it. Worried, she gazed into his eyes, causing him to gaze back as if she were demented.

"What? You think I'm going to faint?" He struggled to get up.

Geneva held his arm and helped him. He sat on top of one of the boxes, the lid squashing under his weight.

She held up her hand and waved it in front of his face. "How many fingers?"

Reed grunted and pulled her hand away. She giggled.

"I appreciate all your sympathy."

"That was a nervous laugh," Geneva said quietly. "I was scared."

Reed stared at her. The tension from being hit was fading from his face. It was replaced by an odd softening in his eyes...like relief.

"Thanks. I'll live."

She dabbed gingerly at his cheek, but was very aware of his scrutiny. Geneva began to feel air, light, the room closing in on them.

"Let me wet this again..." She tried to get up.

He grabbed her arm, pulled her back to his side. "No, stay here. I don't need it."

"What then? Some water and an aspirin?"

He shook his head, regarding her with a sultriness that caused a churning in her stomach.

"Oh," she whispered, with sudden understanding.

She came slowly to her knees and put her hands gently to either side of his face. Bending forward Geneva placed her lips just barely on the cut. Still holding his face she felt Reed's hand circle her wrist as she withdrew. It looked like he was expecting something more. But she came to her senses and put her hand on his chest to stay him.

"I don't think this is a good idea," she said softly.

"What?"

"You know what I mean. I don't get involved with my clients."

Reed took one of hands and planted a soft, rather sensual kiss on her palm.

She drew in her breath. Her heart began a fast trot.

"What if we weren't working together?

His voice had dropped a few decibels, the sound rasping along her nerve ends. "I don't know," she answered honestly.

"Then, consider this another test run," Reed growled, again leaning toward her, his lips parting.

"I'm serious," Geneva tried to be stern.

"Gen, so am I." Then, suddenly frowning, he took the back of one finger and gently stroked it up and down her smooth brown cheek. "It's not about this, is it?"

She knew at once what he was referring to. Geneva shook her head. "No. Not at all."

Later, she would realize hers was a feeble effort at control, decorum, false modesty. Bottom line, she didn't put up much of a protest.

The look in his eyes was so intent, as if saying, I'm going to do this. And as if daring him, she waited to see if he would follow through.

Reed laid claim to her mouth in a most determined but tender way, drawing a sigh and moan from her. There was an immediate answering tightness in her lower belly. A heaviness settled in her lower body, between her legs. A moist sensation of heat and desire. He didn't attempt to embrace her, but used one hand to glide up her back, pressing her closer to him. Then down again to curve over her butt. She instinctively arched toward him.

It was a highly erotic kiss, his tongue making an instant foray between her lips and teeth, stroking a nerve of tension that caught her off guard. She hadn't expected this reaction from herself. This instant compulsion to surrender. She didn't. But she knew she was in trouble.

And she indulged her senses, enjoying the moment and kissing Reed back, an overwhelming need taking over that she was sure would never be fulfilled again. Her objections, or rather her hesitations, went up in smoke.

To hell with the consequences.

He so knows what he's doing.

This is not a young man's kiss.

All of this flashed through her mind as she justified the moment. All of it made her feel better.

Geneva let Reed slowly end the kiss. Then, he dragged his warm lips along her cheek to her jaw, sending tingling sensations up her spine while his breath fanned over her skin.

"Well..." she uttered in a somewhat strangled voice.

"Right," he agreed.

She withdrew enough to gaze into his face, to try and see what she could read in his eyes. Reed's regard said more than she could have imagined, and it made her feel peculiarly vulnerable. She tentatively let her finger tip trace the line of the cut on his cheek.

Reluctantly, Geneva came to her feet trying to hide the fact that her knees were a little wobbly. Silently, in a state of emotional suspension, she attempted to return to the work at hand.

"Gen?"

Even though the urgency in her tone compelled her, she didn't dare turn look at him.

"No, Reed. We're not going to start anything we can't finish."

"Somehow I don't think that's going to be the problem," he teased quietly.

Finally, she turned around. "I made a commitment to your company, to you, to my nephew. You have to help me finish."

Silently, he nodded, maybe hearing the desperation in her voice. His expression filled with regret but also understanding, and purpose.

"You're right, dammit. Okay. Let's do it."

Her gaze softened. He swept back his hair and retied the bandana. The cut on his cheek was starting to discolor and swell. Reed hunched down to repack the spilt box.

For a moment she wondered if she'd made a mistake in stopping Reed. In stopping herself. Her mind was now a delirium of what might have happened. What she might have missed.

Conversation slowly and awkwardly went back to safe subjects, but Geneva was kidding herself. Her lips were never going to work properly again. She was going to remember the feel of his kiss for a long time...

The memory still had the ability to make Geneva feel lethargic. She sighed, trying to snap out of it, and saved her document. She shut down her laptop, vaguely dissatisfied that she and Reed had worked entirely separate the whole evening. Apart, their work was just about done. But wasn't that exactly what she wanted? That they both maintain their professionalism?

Stupid idea, she thought crossly.

She was essentially done. The office would shut down on Friday, and the following Monday the installation would begin of new fixtures. Electricians were coming the next day to finish rewiring and put in dedicated lines. By the middle of the next week the furniture would start to arrive and be put in place according to her design. The week after that she would be back to put the final touches in. After that... nothing.

"Gen?"

She glanced up. Her insides roiled just hearing his deep voice. Reed was standing in the doorway of his office, watching her across the empty room. She was aware of two things. That he'd removed the small band-aid she'd placed over his cut the night before, and that his hair was a little mussed, making him look a bit rakish.

"How about a break?"

"What do you have in mind?"

"I thought maybe we could get something to eat. Dinner. Together."

She tried not to show her surprise, or that the idea appealed to her. The thought of going home alone seemed so single-career-woman-without-a-life kind of thing. Single-career-woman-of-a-certain-age-without-a-life sounded even worse.

She swallowed. She knew that despite her resolve of putting clear boundaries on their office relationship, she was disappointed that he'd taken her seriously. He was being honorable for which she gave him the full ten points.

"Sounds like a nice idea. Sure."

"Let me lock up. There are a couple of places nearby. We can walk."

At the door, Reed turned off all the breaker lights and for a moment they stood in the dark.

Side by side they walked a long corridor to the building entrance, already locked for the night. They were the only ones still inside.

"You know," Reed said, as he let them out. "I should be paying you something for all your time. It's not fair that you're doing all this work for free."

"Thanks for recognizing that. You gave a lot of money to the high school. In exchange you're getting a beautiful new office. That was the deal. I'm also doing it because of Trey. His parents really appreciate all you've done for him."

"Everybody's getting something out of this project but you."

"I wouldn't say that," she demurred.

She was thinking of the night before and a devastatingly hot kiss that could have easily led to something more.

There was dancing with Reed after the auction, and the song he'd written for her and produced. There was the computer program he'd loaded on her laptop earlier in the week. It was a $4,000 CAD she couldn't afford, but that was the top drafting and design software in her field. Reed had gotten it for free as a demo and had no use for it.

But it was more than any of those things. Just with a touch of his eyes on her, a smile, the timber of his voice, he made her feel desirable, and he'd stirred her senses and brought to life an essential need that had been dormant for longer than she wanted to remember.

Little things mean a lot. Reed had already given her quite a lot, more than she knew he was aware of.

"If it makes you feel any better I'm going to make you pay through the nose for dinner. I plan on ordering the most expensive thing on the menu."

Reed grinned at her. "You're an easy woman to please."

That's what you think, she considered grimly.

Chapter Five

When they got outside Reed began to head down a street away from the building and the parking lot. Geneva didn't question where they were going. She didn't particularly care. The cool San Francisco night air felt good on her face. Calming. She was glad to be in his company, despite the increasing sexual tension between them, and their Herculean efforts not to let things get out of hand.

Reed took them to a neighborhood place. Not an upscale over populated restaurant with designer food and high prices, but an unpretentious family owned Mexican café. They sat in a quiet corner, he drinking a cold beer, she a glass of wine. They ordered dinner, but shared a dish of tortilla chips and salsa.

"How did you get into interior design work?" Reed asked Geneva.

"Totally by chance. When I went to UCLA I had a part-time job working as an assistant set designer at one the studios. I was finishing a degree in marketing, but I liked what I was doing better. I stayed with the studio for a few years.

"Then I got a job with an architectural firm in L.A. Before I knew it I was advising them and then their customers on design. Soon I was doing jobs on the side, making a name for myself. My family and friends convinced me I could start my own business."

"How long ago?"

"About seven years ago."

"You're good at it."

"You can tell me that when I finish with your office," she smiled. "Were you really a geek? Is that how you got into your business?"

"No, not really. A teacher I used to have, a really great lady, got me into computers. She thought it was a perfect outlet for...well...it required focus and quick thinking and she thought I'd be good at it."

"She was obviously right. I hope you thanked her."

"Not enough," Reed murmured thoughtfully.

"What about your family?" she asked.

"There's not much. My father was killed in a highway accident when I was about four or five. I don't actually remember him that well. My mother died when I was almost eleven. My older sister was about nineteen. She's the one who took care of me until I was sixteen."

"What happened at sixteen?" Geneva asked.

"She met a guy, they fell in love and they got married. I lived with them for a while in Sacramento, but I started to feel like I was in the way. So...I left. I moved out."

She frowned. "At sixteen?"

Reed shrugged. "It's not that unusual."

"But, how did you support yourself? Where did you live? What about school?"

Reed looked far away for a moment with his own memories of the past. But not really sad.

"It wasn't easy. To be honest I kind of bummed around, staying with relatives or friends.   could have fallen between the cracks if it hadn't been for Mrs. Lambert."

"Who was she?"

Reed's face softened, his gaze now warm and reflective. "The math teacher I had in high school. Man, she was tough. We fought like cats and dogs until...somehow it finally sunk in. She cared about what happened to me. I don't know why but she believed in me, and wouldn't let me off the hook. Where my sister left off, Mrs. Lambert and her husband picked up. They actually took me in until I got into college. It was a very lucky break for me. It could have gone the other way."

Geneva could easily guess what 'the other way' might have meant for

Reed. "And your sister was okay with that?"

"I think she was relieved. She felt guilty that I didn't want to stay with her. Cora Lambert became second mother to me." He finished his beer and signaled for another. "I think she probably saved my life."

"You sound very fond of her."

He nodded. "I am."

She was fascinated, listening as Reed opened up to her. He had a fearlessness, a confidence in himself that was breathtaking. It wasn't conceit after all, but experience and hardship and surviving beyond any limitations life had tried to set for him. He knew who he was and had gotten to that place in a very round about way, with the assistance of someone who helped him discover his strengths and talents. And who'd loved him.

Geneva liked him even more because he had achieved so much the old fashion way. He'd earned it. But, there was something wrong with the picture of a man at the top of his game. Where was the woman in his life? She knew there had to have been more than one. Reed was good-looking, successful, sexy, fun. How had he slipped under the radar? Or had he?

Their meal arrived and all through it they continued to exchange life stories, but Geneva realized they both seemed to want to avoid the subject of their past love lives, current involvements, or plans for the future. She was curious, but just as glad not to get into any of that. Whatever was going on between her and Reed wasn't going to last. This heady flirtation was going to die a natural death as soon as his office was done. But she wanted to stay in the moment and ride the wave for as long as she could. She needed it. It had been a long time.

On the way back to the company building Reed decided that there was no point in returning to the office. They'd done enough and the work was on schedule.

Their steps slowed as they reached the parking lot. The evening suddenly had a heightened anti-climatic feel to it. Geneva's anticipation antennas were up, and she could feel her own accelerated heat beat. She was reminded of all those first dates after having been brought back home and wondering, waiting, for the goodnight moment. Was this going to be one of them?

Apparently not.

Geneva realized that Reed was preparing to get into his car. She did the same.

"I'll follow you," he called out.

She saw that he was waiting for her to precede him out of the lot. They hadn't really said goodnight, or anything for that matter. Geneva accepted that, as she drove out and made her way into traffic.

She was a quarter of a mile on her journey home when she looked in her rear view mirror and realized that Reed was still behind her. Not unduly surprised Geneva gave her attention back to traffic and navigating congestion on the narrow streets of the city. By the time she reached her building there was no cars at all behind her. She pulled into the indoor lot, parked her car, and let herself into the lobby from the garage. After collecting her mail she began the walk up, three stories, to her floor. Even as she was unlocking her door Geneva could hear the buzzer inside her apartment indicating a visitor at the downstairs entrance.

"Yes? Who is it?" she asked, answering the intercom as she stood in the open door.

"Geneva, it's Reed."

She frowned, confused, even as her body went into high alert. "Reed? What are you doing here?"

"I forgot something. Can I come up?"

"You...want to come up?"

"It'll only take a minute."

Geneva stared at the intercom box on the wall through which Reed's voice had traveled. She couldn't tell anything by the sound. And she couldn't understand what he might have forgotten. But, she pushed the bottom that released the lock on the outside door.

She stayed where she was, and by the time she'd put down her mail, her tote and her purse she could see Reed bounding up the last flight of steps. Geneva stared at him but while her expression may have seemed tentative, she had only to see the intent dark fixing of his gaze on her to understand what was happening.

She never actually had a change to make a decision as to what was coming next because it happened so fast. In two easy strides Reed was in the doorway, reaching for her. In that moment she wasn't surprised at all. Most especially when she went willing, naturally, into his open arms as he embraced her.

Grace is right. I'm out of my mind.

So what.

There are worse things than this...

It was worth it just to have his mouth capturing hers again, to have Reed kiss her with a deep all consuming purpose, and desire. Her whole body felt limp. Reed held and embraced her so that she could feel his heart beating, and his arm muscles flexing, and the hard pressing of his arousal against her. Her own hands moved restlessly over his chest, reaching to circle his neck, to finger his hair, to touch his jaw and cheek, feel the thin ridge of that cut now covered with scar tissue.

Geneva forced her mouth free.

"Re...Reed. The...door..."

He blindly reached out his hand to push it firmly shut.

She got completely lost in the euphoria of being caressed and kissed. She had no idea, nor would she ever recall, how they navigated the distance from the door, through her living room, around a short corner, into her bedroom. Nor did Geneva recall how they actually got their clothing off and ended entwined on her bed. What did stay with her, to be relived and remembered over and over again, was the thrill of being made love to by a man she liked...and felt safe with. The utter delicious sensations left her breathless, panting, uttering little moans and grunts of satisfaction as Reed took his time...forever...exploring and learning her body. What she liked. What she'd never had done before.

The silky, slow, wet invasion of his fingers until she came so intensely she thought she was going to die. His tongue there as well, making her almost cry with the potent intimacy of it.

Taking her time as well to touch him, fascinated by the dark soft hair on his chest, at his groin. Their bodies together didn't feel strange at all. She was excited that she too could get Reed so hard with desire that, finally, in a quick gentle flip and reversal of their positions, she found herself on her back, arching and open, his weight forcing her legs apart. She had only a few seconds to enjoy him prostrate on top of her before she gasped as he slid into her. Reed let out such a sigh of deep content, relief, and pleasure that it was almost as if he'd somehow arrived home.

Reed shifted gears on his Audi A4 Turbo and the car surged forward with smooth rolling speed. The black baseball cap he wore keep his hair tamed, and the Blues Men styled sunglasses protected him from both the bright sunlight, and the wind. It was a California day, an on-the-open-road drive, that begged for a convertible. Even more so when Geneva admitted that she'd never ridden in one before.

He took his eyes from the road and let his gaze linger for as long as he dared while Geneva lounged in the passenger seat. As they headed out of San Francisco and north into Sonoma he was enjoying how she looked next to him, wearing a light summery dress under a denim jacket. Feminine, yet casual. The wind teased at the hem of her dress, flipping it up in places to reveal her smooth brown legs. Her loose curls were being tugged and ruffled as well, but she didn't seem to care about the havoc and disorder that it created. She, too, had a look of contentment as she tilted her face up to the sun, or looked out over the quickly changing landscape. Was she also remembering last night?

The night was just like he thought it would be. Geneva was just as he knew she would be. Warm and loving, and beautiful. He'd made sure that there was no time for Geneva to second guess or question what was happening, especially as she'd made it clear it wasn't going to happen. So much for good intentions. He wanted to show her that them together was not a figment of her imagination. Nor impossible.

He'd gotten up first that morning, Geneva curled up and still asleep next to him. He'd stroked her thigh lightly, kissed her cheek before carefully getting out of the bed to shower. By the time he'd returned to her bedroom the bed was empty. He'd found her in a robe in the kitchen puzzling over what to make to eat. Coffee dripped in the maker, filling the air with the fragrance of hazelnut. No hesitation when he took her in his arms. But, although her eyes were bright with the memories of their shared passionate night, there was also a hint of uncertainty.

Reed had cupped her face, staring earnestly into her eyes.

"I'm glad you let me stay. I'm really happy to be here, Gen."

She'd smiled tentatively, and they'd kissed. But he was still not sure if he'd convinced Geneva of his sincerity.

Reed was glad that he had arranged a consultation with a restaurant owner in the valley, someone he knew casually, who wanted him to design software specifically for tracking his inventory and stock of wine and produce based on use. He asked Geneva to go with him, finding a counter to every excuse she'd given him why she couldn't. Reed counted her assent as a victory. She wanted to be with him, too. Maybe even felt the way he did. That last night was still too fresh, too alive within them both to want to be apart.

In fact the tension had grown so great between them that they'd made love twice, in quick succession, before falling asleep. Reed reflected on how comforting and peaceful he'd felt, holding her pressed close to his body, his arms securing her in place. It would have been easy and flippant to toss it off as being satisfied. Only this morning had it come to him that his feelings were somewhat more complex.

But before morning there had been predawn nuzzling and cuddling and languid caressing, with a whispered conversation in the dark.

"Still worried about us? This?" he asked, correctly gauging her thoughts. His thumb brushed back and forth across a nipple.

She rubbed her cheek against his chest and teased her fingers over the sensitive area just below his navel.

"Yes."

"Don't be. I made a promise that I won't let this get in the way of your work. You're not regretting last night, are you?"

She sighed. "No."

"Good."

"I'm just wondering..."

"What? Why you?"

"Yes."

"Why not? You're beautiful. You're talented. You've got spunk..."

"I hate that."

"What?"

"That word. Spunk. People always say that about other people who are short."

"You're not short. Napoleon was short..." He kissed the top of her head.

She giggled.

"You're petite. Lithe. Ethereal. Adorable. Brave."

"Enough. Sorry I asked."

"You know what else?"

"What?"

He came up on his elbow and gazed down at her. "You make me feel...safe. Does that sound weird?"

"Well...yeah. Why would you say that?"

He thought about it for just a moment and decided to be truthful.

"That's what Trey said about you. He said when he's with you he knows nothing bad is going to happen."

"I didn't know that," Geneva murmured. "That is weird. I wonder why?"

"I think it has to do with the time you saved his life."

Her eyes had widened as she strained to see him in the dark of her bedroom.

"Trey told you about that? I swear that boy..."

"He said he fell into a neighbor's backyard pool during a summer party. You were the first to notice and jumped in after him. Now, that's pretty spectacular in any event, but Trey said you don't know how to swim. Is that right?"

"Don't make such a big deal out of it, Reed."

"You never even thought about yourself."

"He was a child. He was in trouble. I had to do something."

He lightly kissed her and let his lips lingered. "That's what I thought."

He shifted away and turned to lay on top of her slender body, warm and soft and pliable. His kisses grew deeper, more demanding as he easily coaxed a response.

"I don't understand...what you...aaaoooohhh...oh... Reed..."

"This is all you need to know for now," he said. against her lips.

And preceded to show her, his hands stroking and caressing her body until neither of them could hold back any longer...

Reed reached for Geneva's hand and held it. He had the feeling, one that he couldn't shake, that if he didn't hold onto her she could easily slip away. She didn't know what he knew, and if she did he was sure that she might reject him, push him away for reasons known only to herself. She could retreat so far that there might never be a way back.

He squeezed her hand and, although she kept her attention turned to the scenic unfolding of the county, seeing her answering smile made him feel hopeful. She was a woman worth fighting for, a woman of grace and strength, heart...and soul. Someone he could love.

For months Geneva had been only an anecdote, a myth as told by her fifteen years old nephew whose stories and memories had brought her to life in his own mind. And now she was real. In truth, for a long time he was merely amused by Trey's gushing about his Aunt Eva. But, in truth, he'd compared Trey's affection to that of his own, for Cora Lambert. And, in truth, it finally occurred to Reed that this Geneva Springer sounded too good to be true.

He was eternally grateful that he was wrong about that.

When the reached the vineyard and restaurant for his appointment, Reed apologized to Geneva for having to leave her own her on.

"Go ahead," she said. "I want to look around, try some wine. Visit the gift shop. All those girly things that guys hate."

He laughed. "Trying not to miss me too much?" She made a face, as if she could care less. "This shouldn't take long. About an hour. Okay?"

"I'll synchronize my watch." She waved at him. "Have fun."

Reed hesitated, feeling that little catch of apprehension again. "I miss you already."

Her expression slowly changed to one of surprise, and became shy. "You're going to be late," she said quietly.

The meeting took fifteen minutes longer than he'd expected, and by the time Reed went in search of Geneva he was anxious to be with her again. His only problem was, as he went to all of the places she'd said she wanted to visit, he couldn't find her. For a crazy moment Reed wondered if she'd had second thoughts, if she'd given up waiting, if she'd read his mind and found all her secrets stored there, and bolted back to San Francisco on one of the tour buses, leaving him behind.

"Excuse me. Are you Mr. Fairway?"

He turned to the young woman approaching. "Yes, that's right."

"If you're looking for your friend, she's in there." She pointed.

Reed followed her direction, which led him to a side entrance into the restaurant. There was a maitre'd podium, guests leaving and arriving, but no Geneva. Reed slowly approached the arched entrance into the dining area. She wasn't there, either. Now, he was convinced that she had given up and left him.

He exited the front door, bewildered that she might actually have gone back to the city without him.

"Reed! I'm here! Over here!"

Reed took a few steps onto a stone path that wound under a trellis and into an arboreal patio laid out with bistro tables and chairs for dining alfresco. Most were occupied. Geneva stood by one waiting for him. She'd removed the denim jacket, and she looked lovely and bright, smiling at him. The table had been set for two, with an opened bottle of red wine in the center.

Reed tried not to let her see how much the possibility of her not being there had affected him as he walked to her.

"How did the meeting go?" she asked, taking her seat as he held her chair.

"Great. It's an easy job, and I'm going to charge him a fortune. What's this?"

"Well, I thought it would be fun if we had lunch here. It's so pretty. I've never been to Italy, but I bet this is what Tuscany looks like," she said, pointing to the rolling hills of the vineyard, divided in a neat pattern of rows for growing grapes. "Is this okay?"

Reaching for the bottle of wine, he began to pour them both a glass, letting the action disguise his momentary attack of anxiety.

"This is very okay."

Chapter Six

"The only thing worse than trying to get out of San Francisco is trying to drive back in," Reed joked as they inched their way in rush hour traffic back to the city. They were still some distance from the Golden Gate Bridge.

"I'm in no rush," Geneva murmured, turned a little sideways in her seat toward him. "It was such a nice day."

Reed put his hand on her knee briefly. "I'm glad you had a good time."

"Have you ever walked across the bridge?" she asked.

"I've biked it a number of times. Never walked it. Have you?"

"No, but I've always wanted to."

"Then consider it done. We'll do it sometime. There's a scenic overview that's worth visiting. It gives a great angle on the bridge and the city from above it."

As he spoke Reed's cell phone chimed and he quickly attached his blue-tooth headset to his ear.

"Hi," he answered. "Is everything okay? Are you sure? Yes, I'm just getting back into the city. Drove up to the valley for a meeting. I can come by, if you want. It's no problem, you know that. I'll be there in a half hour."

Geneva only half listened to the conversation, not so much interested in what was said as in how. She could tell right away from Reed's voice and intonation that whomever he was speaking with he cared a lot about. It made her smile as much as it made her curious. And, of course, she couldn't help but question the nature of this relationship, for she had no doubt it was a woman. His sister? A friend? A significant other?

Geneva felt her vulnerability resurface, just with the recognition that she could not possibly be the only involvement in his life.

Involvement. Affair. Fling.

One night stand.

Reed ended his call.

"You can drop me off at my place..."

"No way."

"Reed, I totally understand..."

"I want you to come with me."

She stared at his profile, but grew firm. "Look, if you have something to take care of..."

"I do. But not without you." He glanced briefly at her before concentrating again on his driving. "I don't want you to leave me, yet, Gen."

She felt frustrated and nervous. "I just think..."

"Don't think. Just stay with me."

She nodded, not sure if she should have given in...but not yet ready to go home and have the day end.

In exactly the amount of time Reed had predicted they reached Oakland, and made their way through the town to a quiet residential street of modest homes. Reed pulled into a drive way of a ranch, behind an older model Cavalier sedan.

"I'll wait here," she said.

"Gen..."

"Go. I'm not moving. I'm sure I'll only get in the way."

Reed looked like he would debate it more, than gave in. He stroked her cheek. "It's not what you think," he said.

Now he's reading my mind, she thought, irritated.

He got out of the car, approached the side door and, after ringing the bell, let himself in with his own key.

Geneva sighed, sliding down in her seat to consider her tumultuous feelings about Reed. Since their night together it seemed to have grown exponentially. It was giddy and exciting. A smile played around her lips as she anticipated the evening, although she knew she shouldn't. If Reed took her home, if she insisted on it, she had the memory of him imprinted on her body and heart to get her through the night.

She looked around at the property where they'd parked.

The house was modest, but clean and orderly. The flowerbeds in the front on either side of the main door were planted with a mixture of annuals and perennials, but nothing exotic or hard to maintain.

Geneva caught movement from the corner of her eye at a window that quickly disappeared. The door opened slowly. Believing it was Reed, Geneva sat up straight. But it wasn't Reed coming out of the house. There was an older, thin, African American woman standing with the front door ajar. Geneva stared at her, curious and surprised. The woman was wearing pair of tan slacks, and coordinated V-neck sweater with broad black and cream horizontal stripes. Her straightened hair, obviously tinted to hide the gray, was styled in a neat but simple arrangement Geneva had not seen since she herself left high school. It reminded her of her late mother, and her mother's friends.

The woman beckoned her.

"Why did Reed leave you sitting out here by yourself? Come on in."

Geneva couldn't even respond at first.

"Come on in. I'm not going to hurt you!"

Geneva did as she was told, getting out of the car. She approached the thin and refined woman trying not to appear confused...or nervous. But her mind was literally spinning with conjectures about who this lady was.

"I'm Geneva Spri..."

"Yes, I know who you are."

She went back into the house, expecting Geneva to follow her.

When she entered Geneva found that she was in a small kitchen. It was immaculately clean, if dated in its décor and accessories. The woman walked quietly and gracefully through a dining alcove, and a living room, into yet another room. Following behind, Geneva realized it was a combination sitting room/library/TV room.

The woman took a seat in a Queen Anne chair with slightly worn upolstry, and immediately picked up something she was knitting, and continued to work.

"Sit over there," she instructed.

Geneva didn't even think of not doing as she was told, the woman had that kind of presence and command. She sat in an adjacent armchair. She wondered where Reed was.

"I'm Cora Lambert," the woman announced calmly. "Mrs. Cora Lambert. My husband Malcolm died three years ago."

"Oh! Reed told me about you. I'm really glad to meet you."

The woman looked sharply at her, never missing a stitch on her project, the needles clicking quietly as she worked.

"And I'm glad to meet you. Reed said you're doing over his office. I could hardly believe my ears. I've been telling him for years to do something about the mess. He's very successful but he's too old to be running his business like it was a college frat house. Disgraceful."

Geneva allowed herself a knowing grin. "I told him the same thing."

Cora Lambert gave her speculative glance, and slowly nodded. "He told me you set him back on his heels. Good for you. Mr. Lambert and I taught him better than that. Still, given what he's overcome, I think at thirty-three he's done very well, don't you think?"

Geneva stared blankly at Cora as the older woman calmly knitted.

Thirty-three.

Geneva felt a ringing in her ears. Suddenly, she couldn't hear anything Cora Lambert was saying to her. A wave of prickly heat washed right over her skin.

Thirty-three...

Inadvertently she pressed her hand to her stomach, which had begun to churn alarmingly.

"Has Reed told you about me?" Geneva finally uttered, already feeling a knot in her stomach at the thought that this self possessed and imperial woman, someone who meant so much to Reed, might judge her. A two-year difference might not have been so horrible. Three times as much seemed like a generation, as in the difference between thirty-something and...middle-age.

"Just that you're beautiful. Well, okay. I can see that. That you're talented and smart. And he likes your nephew. The young man works in Reed's office. When a son starts telling his mother about the woman in his life..."

"A son?"

The knitting stopped. Mrs. Lambert looked at her. Her eyes were bright and sparkly and Geneva held her breath as she saw the genuine love reflected in their depths.

"Reed's very much like a son. The one me and Mr. Lambert never had." She took up the knitting again, fast and precise. "I'm not going to bore you with the details. Can't be told in twenty-five words or less, anyway. We took in him, made sure he graduated. He surely did put us through a lot. We stuck with him because, just like a child of our own, we saw through the acting out, and the stubbornness. We saw his potential." She shook her head. "That boy was something else."

Geneva was speechless. She had no idea what to make of this conversation. It was too much to handle, too much to take in all at once. The only thing she could process was the cold hard fact that she was almost seven years older than Reed. The undeniable truth kept hammering at her.

Please don't ask me how old I am.

Please!

There they sat, two Black women in conversation about a white man that obviously meant a lot to them both.

Geneva blinked as that thought flashed through her mind. Was there any point in denying it? How could she have spent the night with Reed, most of it making love, without it meaning something? Without having felt something for him. Or had it been just recreational sex?

There was the sound of footsteps out in the hall, and in another moment, after the opening and closing of a door, Reed appeared in the entrance of the small room. His gaze went swiftly from Cora to Geneva and back again. He smiled ruefully.

"You've met."

"How could you leave her sitting out in the car?"

Geneva stood up. "It's not his fault. I was willing to wait outside."

"It was my fault," Reed conceded. "I know better."

"Apology accepted," Cora said briskly and stood up.

Geneva suddenly could see that Cora, despite her firm voice and elegant presence, was not as young as she first appeared. And she could see the undisguised concern in Reed's gaze, even though he lounged casually against the doorframe.

"How much is it going to cost me?" Cora asked Reed. Standing in front of him.

He took her small bony hand and held it. "Nothing. The problem seems to be a defective valve. I'm getting the company replace it at no cost. I jeri-rigged it so you'll get heat for a day or two. By then someone should be here to look at it."

"Thank you, Hon." Cora rose on tip-toe and gave Reed a warm motherly hug.

Geneva stared unabashedly at the evidence of the bond between them. It made her feel even more insecure.

Cora gently pushed him away. "Now, you go on. I'm sure you two have plans for this evening."

Geneva didn't dare look at Reed. Together, the three of them returned to the kitchen and the door leading to the side of the house.

Reed embraced the slight older woman again, admonishing her to eat...or else. Cora made a dismissive gesture with her hand but laughed.

"I'll be over on Sunday," Reed announced.

"I'll understand if something else comes up. But if you come, bring Geneva with you."

Geneva merely smiled, waved briefly in farewell, and got into the passenger seat of Reed's car.

Cora stood in the doorway watching as they drove away. There was little conversation between her and Reed as they crossed the Golden Gate. For whatever reason she remembered his recent promise that they would walk across the bridge together one day.

Thirty-three...

She was certain that would never happen.

"I'd like you to take me home," Geneva said quietly. When Reed didn't answer she glanced at his profile. "Did you hear me? I said..."

"Not yet. I think we need to talk."

Her stomach roiled. "No, I don't want to talk. I want to go home."

"I know what this is all about, Gen."

"Why can't you just do as I ask?"

"Because I don't think it's what you really want."

"How dare you try to..."

"I dare," Reed interrupted bluntly, "Because I know there's something strong going on between us. You know it too, and I'm not going to let you run away from it, or pretend it's not real just because..." He glanced briefly at her face. "Just because I'm younger than you are."

She was horrified, her expression pained as if she'd been insulted. "Oh my God," Geneva groaned. "What...did Trey tell you?"

"A lot." Reed grabbed her hand and held it tightly, even as she wanted to pull away. "Everything he was proud of. Everything he was concerned about and didn't understand. Your ex-husband. Your divorce. Why? Because he loves you so much. Because he doesn't like it when you get hurt or sad and he can't do anything about it. Well, it worked for me."

"My life is not public domain," she said, feeling drained and totally defenseless.

"Of course not," Reed said warmly. "Maybe I did sort of forced my way into your life. I like it there. I want a chance to stay. We belong together, and I'm not going down without a fight."

Geneva couldn't think of anything to say. She certainly hadn't expected this kind of confession. It was so out there and so bold she half believed Reed. But it simply wasn't that easy. They weren't equal. Maybe she didn't have any more to lose than he did if she took a leap of faith, but Geneva didn't think she could take another painful failure. Recovery was too long, and too hard.

Geneva stared straight ahead. "Did Trey also tell you how old I am?"

"Almost forty," Reed said easily.

"Thirty-nine," she corrected breathless, expecting the withdrawal and look of distress.

There was a pause.

"Your point?" Reed asked.

"It's important for lots of reasons."

"Yeah, I know what they are. I don't see any of them as deal breakers."

"What kind of deal are you talking about?"

"Look. I can't predict the future any more than you can. I just know that when I think about the future you're in the picture with me. And I like that. I'm willing to risk a broken heart. Are you game?"

"What do you mean?"

"Let's live together...for two weekends. One in my place, and one in yours."

She chuckled without much humor. "What's that suppose to prove?"

"How much we like being together. Or not. How much we like living apart after that. It's Friday. This is as good a time as any to get started."

She looked at him and saw the flexing of his jaw muscle, the furrow between his brows. He didn't look like he was thirty-three and carefree. He looked like he was in deadly earnest, and that he had a lot at stake.

So did she. Geneva wasn't sure Reed's absurd plan would prove anything. But if she agreed and it failed she could at least say she tried, and then go back to her own life.

"Well?" Reed prompted.

"I think this is silly, but okay," she conceded, already feeling like it was a mistake.

"You first. We'll stay at my place so I can pickup some things."

Whatever expectations Geneva had about spending time with Reed were completely shattered that very night. She didn't think it unreasonable to anticipate that they would sleep together. Of course they did. But they didn't make love.

The evening was less awkward than she would have imagined, for which she thanked the weeks they'd gotten to know each other while working on his office. They'd already had one fight...or rather, she did... over his standing her up. They'd already danced, had dinner, laughed, and he knew she liked red wine. She knew he was totally unpretentious and not given to making a big deal about a lot of things. She knew he was thoughtful, and able to anticipate in a somewhat scary way, a lot of what she was thinking, or even concerned about.

He'd found the quilt she bought at the auction, and had since framed and hung on a wall outside her bedroom. He'd studied it thoughtfully for a while.

"You need a hammer hanging close by so you can break the glass, in case of emergency."

"What do you mean, emergency?" she'd frowned.

He'd glanced at her but actually seemed to be seeing something else.

"If you ever have a baby, you might need that for a crib or carriage."

Security blanket, she'd thought.

So...having successfully gotten through a pizza dinner, familiarizing Reed with her apartment, and watching a DVD of Russell Crowe in 'The Gladiator', a favorite movie for both of them, it was time for bed.

Despite unfounded concerns that it was all going to be about sex, it wasn't. As a matter of act nothing of the sort happened. Geneva liked her showers at night, and when she exited the bathroom, Reed was already in bed. He suddenly seemed to take up a lot of space, and he looked maddeningly comfortable. She tried to be nonchalant as she got in next to him. But instead of reaching for her and beginning a seduction that Geneva knew, from experience, would not fail, Reed merely raised his arm so that she could lay close to him, using his shoulder for a pillow. She did so, sighing at the instant feeling of safe harbor. And when the light was turned out, they did not say goodnight, sleep tight, don't let the bed bugs bite...they began to talk.

"What are you thinking?" she asked.

"About Cora," Reed murmured, his voice gravelly, tired, reflective.

Inadvertently, Geneva pressed closer. "What about?"

For the next hour the conversation was about Reed's concerns for the older woman, and Geneva's offering of advice and support. After a while she felt his steady rhythmic breathing signaling that Reed was asleep. She relaxed and listened to the sounds. When she heard a soft grumble of snoring, it made her smile. Geneva relaxed even more. And fell asleep as well.

She woke the next morning with Reed's body cocooning hers. In seconds he, too, was awake, his body pressing languidly against hers, stroking her stomach, thigh, kissing her neck. He turned onto his back and pulled Geneva into his arms. She went from being conscious of what he was doing to not caring at all, as long as Reed continued to caress her and make her feel soft and limp.

But they didn't make love.

"What do you normally do on Saturday?" he asked, yawning

Frustrated, she sighed and shrugged. "The usual. Laundry, shopping, vacuuming."

"What's the most important thing of the three?"

"I don't know. Shopping for food, I guess."

"Good. We'll go down to the Terminal market." He kissed her quickly and swung his legs from the bed, tossing off the covers.

"I haven't been there in a long time. That sounds like fun."

And it was.

They had brunch at an outdoor café before braving the Saturday morning crowds to find fruits and vegetables, eggs, cheese. Reed insisted on fresh flowers as well. They wandered among the craft stalls for a while, and then headed back to her apartment to wash and store everything, to put the flowers not on the dining table or in the living room, but on her bedroom dresser where the smell filled the air.

She made an early dinner of pasta primavera while Reed fixed a lamp with a faulty switch. And over that meal he somehow managed to coax out of her the painful story of her three-year relationship with an architect, subsequent marriage, and quick flame-out after just six months. Then, putting her life back together.

Reed had listened silently, sometimes looking at her with understanding, but sometimes with a dangerous glint in his dark eyes that made him look fierce. She wanted him to say something, after she'd laid her soul bare. But he didn't. When dinner was over Reed got up, carefully pulled her from her chair, and just held her tightly. It was so caring in a profound way that she felt on the verge of tears.

"His loss. My gain," he said.

He suggested they go out for the evening. Geneva was too embarrassed to admit that mostly she stayed home on Saturday nights. How pathetic was that?

They went back to the club where they'd first spent an evening, more or less, together. It felt special being back with just him. And they danced again, but mostly just enjoyed the music.

By the time they returned to her place Geneva thought she knew the routine. If this was all about being together and being comfortable then she had to term it an unqualified success. There was a flow and rhythm with Reed that she had to recognize seemed natural, and easy. She had given up anticipated when and if they would make love. And when Reed turned out the lights, took her hand, and led her into the bedroom, she so wanted him that her body immediately went into desire mode.

Heat infused her skin. Her breathing quickened, as did his. She could feel the excretions that moistened her, making her ready and impatient for Reed to enter her, fill her, thrust in and against her until she pulsed a release as he lay buried inside. Then he would caress her breasts, sensitive to the touch. He would stroke her and she him, and they'd find another way to lay and pleasure one another.

And that's exactly how it happened.

Chapter Seven

He must have nerves of steel.

That's what Geneva kept telling herself that next week as she supervised the arrival, unloading and placement of the new office furniture for Reed's company. It wasn't that he was ignoring her, but seemed completely focused on the business at hand. That was, trying to maintain some routine in the continuing chaos of deliverymen, boxes being ripped opened, and power tools whirring as things were assembled.

Geneva, more than anyone, understood taking care of business, but would it have hurt Reed to smile at her, call her into his office to make sure everything was okay? Not with Herman Miller chairs and desks, but with her. Or in some other way let her know she wasn't just someone working for him?

She was aware of the contradictions but decided she had a right. A women's prerogative, and all that.

Hadn't she been the one to insist on professionalism? Boundaries, and protocol? A lot of good it had done her.

Suddenly, last weekend was starting to take on the aura of a surreal fantasy. Too good to be true. Saturday night had confused her. It had caught her off guard. After two days of domestic tranquility she hadn't expected the curve ball of passion that Reed had thrown at her, inflaming them both by Sunday morning. An unexpected morning fog had turned into a drizzly day, making it unnecessary to get up and get dressed and be anywhere. So they'd pretty much stayed in bed much of the day. Napping, reading the Sunday papers. Snacking on fresh fruit from the market...and each other.

She was unprepared, late in the day, to awaken to her name being quietly called, to turn over in the tangle of bed linens and see that Reed was almost dressed and preparing to leave. She sat up, dazed. It was almost dark outside.

Reed sat on the side of the bed, leaning over to kiss her.

"I've got to go," he whispered against her lips.

"I know."

"I'm sorry."

"You have things to do."

"I do. Gen..."

She touched his mouth with her fingers. "I'll see you tomorrow at the office. It's going to be a little crazy this week."

He nodded, combed his hair back.

Geneva knew he wanted to say something, but hoped that he wouldn't. There was absolutely nothing that was going to change the moment, or could have changed the weekend for her. As a stand along it had been pure magic. In context to the past or the future, it held possibilities. But she didn't want to talk about it.

All on her own Geneva wanted to be able to take Reed at face value. Not for what he said to her, but for what he did to her that made her want to take that leap, not knowing if there would be a safety net.

She got out of bed and pulled on a robe, followed Reed through the apartment to the front door, where his brown leather duffle was already packed by the door. It was one of the most depressing things she'd seen in a long time.

The goodbye was quick yet tender, but even after she'd closed the door and found herself alone, Geneva felt disoriented, even dizzy, as if her world had just tilted from it's usual orbit.

She was no longer sure of what she wanted from Reed.

"Aunt Eva, are you mad at Reed?"

Geneva was stunned by the question as much as she was by the way her body reacted. She turned her puzzled expression to Trey. "What makes you think I'm mad at him?"

"Man, he's been in a bad mood. He's like, not really listening when you talk to him. And he forgets what he tell you and then he tells you again."

"I don't understand how that's my fault," Geneva said carefully.

"He sure was a lot nicer when I used to talk to him about you. Now...I don't know. But he's just not right."

"I'm sorry to hear that," Geneva murmured.

I'm not quite right, either.

Geneva concentrated on her driving for a moment. She was taking Trey home after attending a basketball game at a rival school. Of course she realized that her nephew was not aware of the subtleties of grown-up relationships, or the sometimes nightmarish maze of emotions that are created when people love each other...or think they love each other. Or when they really hope that someone could love them.

She sighed. How had it come to this?

"Aunt Eva?"

"Ummm?" she responded, distracted.

"You mad at me?"

Geneva considered her nephew. It had been love at first sight from the moment she'd met her newborn nephew. He was a handsome boy, and she could now see his potential as a grown man. He was bright, well-mannered, funny, with an easy ability to switch back and forth between what his family expected of him, and still able to amass an enviable circle of friends of all ages. Like Reed Fairway.

Geneva shook her head. "Of course I'm not mad. Why would I be?"

"Because I made Reed like you."

"Is...that what you're trying to do?"

"Kind of. He told me, my Aunt Eva sounds like his kind of woman.

Do you know what that means?"

"I...I'm not really sure," Geneva said faintly, afraid to put her own spin on what Reed was implying. "But maybe you told him a little bit more about me than you should have, Trey. There are things about my past that I consider private."

"I thought you liked him, too."

"I do like him," she answered.

Very much.

That had been made clear in her mind the weekend it was her turn to stay with Reed, just a week earlier. She went willingly, hoping not to expose her excitement after nearly two weeks of keeping their proper distance at his office. Especially during the open house Reed held when the work was declared done, and his employees returned to find their workplace transformed.

She had been asked to come to the office at a certain time. She'd expected that there was a final check list of details that needed taking care of. Geneva had not been expecting anything more, but had walked in to find, once again, them all gathered near Reed's newly appointed office. Geneva half expected them to burst into song again. Instead, they'd begun wildly applauding and whistling. Off to the side, once again, Reed stood silently watching her with a look in his dark eyes that she easily interpreted.

Taking her by surprise she was made to sit in a chair, and several men lifted her into the air. They paraded her around the room to appreciative cheering as she clung to the sides.

"Hey! Be careful with her!"

"Gen, Gen, Gen..."

The chant went up.

"If you drop her you're road kill."

Geneva laughed with everyone else when she heard Reed's command, although she couldn't see him. Finally, as the enthusiastic employees were about to make a second circling of the huge office with her Reed interceded to lift her to safety. No one noticed that he'd held her longer than was needed, or that they stared silently at one another, or that for a heart stopping second she thought they would kiss, then and there. But they came to their senses as they were each given glasses of mimosas, the drink of choice for the occasion...

In truth, Geneva was sure that she'd moved beyond Reed's challenge. Her feeling had already morphed into a breathtaking desire just to be with him. But it was she, after all, who'd said it wasn't possible for a relationship to work between them.

Then came the weekend at his place. His apartment was a spacious loft in North Beach. There was artwork on his walls in the form of bright and lively exhibition posters. One area was organized with sophisticated electronic equipment, a flat screen TV with surround sound speakers. The bedroom was partitioned off from the living room by a huge Chinese screen, the bed not king sized as she expected, but a more cozy queen, like her own. He had books and CDs and DVDs and magazines neatly piled everywhere.

After she'd arrived, tote in hand, and seen the lay of his place, he'd taken her to explore his neighborhood. It was already mid November and the weather crisp and cool. They held hands, and Geneva enjoyed an odd sense of belonging because they were together and everyone knew Reed. Everyone instantly treated her like visiting royalty, and Reed seemed to get a kick out of that. He kept stopping every hour or so and they slipped inside some local restaurant or café and he'd get her cappuccino to warm up before they continued on.

He cooked dinner that night, a great recipe of baked chicken and vegetables he'd learned from Cora Lambert. And later challenged her to play video games, including one he was developing for PIXAR in L.A. that had the potential to become an animated film. She won.

"I can't believe you beat me! How did that happen?"

"Trey," she'd responded smugly. "You have no idea how many hours I've spent playing with him."

Reed had laughed uproariously.

Saturday morning they had breakfast in bed. They spent the day walking the city finding interesting stores or restaurants or parks. Late in the afternoon they ran into acquaintances of Reed's, a couple who lived in Marin County who invited her and Reed to join them for dinner. It had been stimulating and enjoyable to be able to talk about a wide range of topics, to laugh, to feel so much alive. And the thing that Geneva liked the most was Reed's attitude toward her the whole evening. He claimed her. With his gaze and smile and spontaneous touches he marked his territory.

But by Sunday reality set in like a heavy cloud with the awareness that she would be returning home. Perhaps the most confusing of all for Geneva was that they had not once made love the entire weekend. She hadn't particularly noticed because everything else they'd done together had been so satisfying. Not until just that moment when she was about to leave did it occurred to her that, this could be it.

Their time together had a finite ending by an arrangement that she'd agreed to.

"You don't have to go," Reed told her now, rather than say goodbye.

Her heart jumped at the temptation. "I think I do."

"Why?"

"Because...being with you was so easy, Reed.

"Then, I don't get it."

"I want you to be able to change your mind."

"I'm not going to." He stepped close and took her into his arms, holding her not tightly, but closely. "All I want to do is to love you. To have you love me."

I do. I do.

"I know." She pressed a kiss to his chest, through his Tshirt.

"I thought I was pretty smart. This doesn't make any sense."

"It will," Geneva said, pulling away as she felt her eyes sting with tears.

Without another word she grabbed her tote and hurried to the elevator. Geneva drove herself home, to the memory of Reed's presence, and to a silence that was so profound and dense she wondered how she could ever be alone again.

"Man, grown ups are crazy. If this is what it's like to be in love, I'm not having it."

"I promise you you'll change your mind," Reed said ruefully to Trey.

"I thought it was like, all huggy and kissy and coochie-coo," he said, cackling.

"That's the fun part. But it's more complicated than that."

"How come you don't just call Aunt Eva?"

Reed sighed. Hadn't he thought of that a hundred times himself. The thing was, he had to do this the right way. The only problem was, he wasn't sure exactly what that was.

It wasn't going to be enough for Geneva to hear from him that he loved her. She'd heard that before, from the man she'd married who had crushed her hopes and dreams. So had he, from a woman who'd done pretty much the same. He also didn't kid himself. He thought he understood a lot of what Geneva must be going through. Thank goodness for Cora and his sister who, whether they realized it or not, had schooled him well in the delicate and peculiar nature of the female heart: easily broken; not easily given.

Reed hadn't been surprised when Cora had guessed the cause of his restlessness. But he'd been taken aback by her prescription for what to do.

"Everybody wants to make it so difficult. You don't have to jump through hoops, or change who you are, or shower Geneva with stuff and nonsense. Just love her. Be yourself. Keep it simple and real. And don't have expectations. That's a death knoll for folks in love. They want perfection. They want too much. Remember what drew you to her. That's what you want..."

Reed swiveled in this desk chair, staring thoughtfully at Trey as the teen worked on laptop nearby.

"Do you think I should call her?"

Trey shrugged. "I don't know. Maybe. She'll probably be glad to hear from you."

"Really?" Reed asked, alert.

"Why don't you come to see her," he chortled. "That way she can't hang up on you if you make her mad."

"She might slam the door in my face," Reed sighed in frustration.

"Look," Trey began, as if he was talking to someone dimwitted. "Come to the party on Saturday. Then she'll have to talk to you. I bet she'll even be glad to see you."

"What party?"

"For her birthday. It's really just dinner but we're having a cake and everything."

Reed thought long and hard about it. A birthday celebration sounded perfect. He might only get one shot at persuading Geneva of his serious intentions, and this had to be it.

"Okay, I'll be there," Reed decided, not without a tremor of fear that his future hung in the balance.

"Pssst. Hey, Reed! Come on," Trey hissed into the dark.

Reed got quietly out of his car as the signal was given that it was time for him to come into the house. Following Trey's hand motions he entered stealth-like into the kitchen and was led to the dining room entrance.

"Trey? Where are you? We're going to light the candles."

"Did you have to put so many?" Geneva's voice could be heard. "Ten would have been plenty," she chuckled.

"You wish," Trey's mother said dryly. "Trey!"

"I gotta go," Trey whispered to Reed. "Don't forget. You come in right after we finish singing Happy Birthday."

Reed grabbed his arm. "Did you remember the box?"

"Yeah. It's on the table with the rest of her gifts."

Trey left him to return to the dining room. Reed stood in the dark shadow of the kitchen entrance, the lights behind him turned off and far enough back so that he could not be detected. He could see Geneva and everyone else at the table, sitting adjacent to his position. But he only had eyes for her, his throat dry and his heartbeat tight in his chest. Reed drew in a breath, seeing her for the first time in weeks confirming all his deepest desires.

He still only wanted her. She still made him feel strong and tender and protective of her. Geneva was the woman he was in love with. More sure of himself than he'd felt in weeks, Reed stood ready for whatever was going to happen.

Grace Savage lit the candles on the cake, the gentle glowing flames casting a warm light on Geneva's face. Bradley Savage dimmed the overhead light. They all began to sing to Geneva, who sat in a place of honor at the table, with a pleased if somewhat sad smile.

"Make a wish and blow out the candles," Grace instructed.

"Wait. Aunt Eva's got to close her eyes, too."

"Hurry up. I don't want to eat candle wax with my cake," Bradley groused.

"Alright. I'll close my eyes."

As she did so, Bradley quietly stepped away from the table and against the wall next to the kitchen door. Trey backed away as well, tiptoeing into the kitchen.

"Don't forget to make a wish," Grace said.

She, took walked quietly away, leaving Geneva standing at the table alone, in front of the birthday cake shimmering in candle light. She inhaled a deep breath and bending slightly forward exhaled through pursed lips to extinguish the lights.

Reed felt someone push him from behind, someone pull on his arm. He went through the door into the dining room, standing opposite Geneva on the other side of the table.

Now it was all up to him. And her.

"Happy Birthday, Gen," Reed murmured.

Geneva's eyes flew open! She stared open mouth at him.

"Reed," she got out, her voice barely audible. "What are you doing here? How did you..."

"I told you I had the best present for you, Aunt Eva," Trey boasted.

"Okay, enough. Let's leave them alone," Grace ordered, gathering her family and shepherding them into the family room.

Geneva stared at him, but already Reed was feeling better. Her eyes reflected the truth, and he hoped she could see the same in his. Reed began walking around the end of the table toward her.

"I have a few things to say to you. And then it's your turn." He took her by the shoulder and turned her to face him. "I'm never going to find anyone who makes me as happy as you do. I don't even want to try. I love you, Gen. I want you to be part of my life."

Reed grew confident having said what he had to say, and seeing the light in Geneva's eyes, bright and sparkling with emotion. He put his arms around her drawing her into a gentle embrace.

"One more thing..." Keeping his hold on her, Reed reached to lift a long narrow box from a small pile of wrapped gifts in front of what was her dinner plate. He gave it to her. "Age isn't important to me. Unless you're wine or cheese."

Geneva looked at him and began to laugh gently. She threw her arms around his neck.

"Reed..."

"Aren't you going to open your gift?"

"You are my gift. You're what I wished for."

When she took so long to open the box Reed took it out of her hands and ripped away the paper and bow. He took off the lid and withdraw a silver and mother-of-pearl bracelet. Geneva gasped.

Reed fastened it around her wrist. "You were right about that box of jewelry from the auction coming in handy."

"Now, it's your turn," he said quietly, kissing her briefly.

"I don't have much to say except, I love you. We fit. It works. I'm happy."

"Then it's settled. You have no idea how much I missed you."

"I can tell her," Trey said from the kitchen, turning on the light.

"Are you two finished yet?" Bradley asked, coming back into the dining room.

"Yeah. How about some cake and ice cream?" Trey asked, rubbing his hands together.

"Lord, I don't think they heard a word we've said," Grace chuckled.

The celebration continued around them but Reed felt that he and Geneva didn't need anything else right then but each other.

They ended their two months of abstinence in an embrace and kiss that was better left until they were alone. For the moment their entire world existed right where they stood.

The rest would come later.

Sandra Kitt is the author of more than 30 stories; her titles have been named among the best contemporary books for the year by Amazon.com, and Library Journal. Her first mainstream, THE COLOR OF LOVE, has been optioned twice for film. She is the recipient of two Lifetime Achievement awards, and has been nominated for the NAACP Image Award in Fiction. She is a frequent guest speaker and is an Adjunct Instructor in fiction and publishing. Sandra is a former graphic designer and printmaker, and an Information Specialist in astronomy & astrophysics at the American Museum of Natural History. She lives in New York.

Against Her Better

Judgment

By

Evelyn Palfrey

Acknowledgements

The story was richer because of you. Tina Allen, Chachi, Kitzy Daniels, Sue Coburn, Don and Toby Futrell, Antoine Lane, Delma Lopez, Meredith McKee, Jeannye Polk, Emma Rodgers, and Judge Ken Vitucci.

Chapter One

Judge Beverly Polk read over the letter from the warden again. She looked up at the police chief.

"So?"

"Beverly, this man is dangerous."

"He's in prison, Jack. And he'll be there a long time. How dangerous can he be—to anybody on the outside?"

"That's the thing, Beverly. When we busted him, we thought he was just an up-and-comer in the business. Another wannabe, just moving more weight than most. He wasn't stupid like most of them when they get a little leg up. No flashy cars or house. Didn't hang out, showing off. Turns out, he was smarter than most. He was moving some fairly serious weight. Found out he'd amassed a small fortune in modest rent houses. Fronted several chicken joints. We forfeited as much as we could. I think he'd planned to go legit—"

"But not before he laid waste to the community. Not before he'd made no telling how many addicts, stealing their grama's TVs and microwaves to get him there."

"Well, you put him away for a long time."

"No. The jury put him away for a long time. People are sick of this drug scourge. Sick of living behind barred windows, sick of having their homes and cars burglarized."

"But he isn't making threats against the jury. His threats are against you."

"I get threats all the time. He's not the only one. I'm supposed to be scared? I can't be scared and have this job."

"You saw in the warden's letter that his intelligence says that he may be planning to kidnap you. Even assassinate you. That's serious.

She pushed the letter across the desk. "Now, how exactly is he going to do that—from prison? It's just big talk, Jack. Don't worry about it."

"Come on, Beverly. I know you're a tough cookie. You and I go way back. We've been around this business a long time. I know cons talk tough. But this is different. I'm going to assign an officer 24—"

"You will do no such thing. Whose budget is that supposed to come out of—yours or mine? The City, or the County?"

"This is beyond budgets, Beverly. It's—"

"I will not live in fear." She folded her arms across her chest and leaned back in her chair. "I have a job and a life. I intend to continue to do one and enjoy the other. Period."

They stared at each other, both willing the other to see their side. They had been to this place before. More often since Jack's divorce.

Jack let out a heavy sigh. "I figured you would be this way. I was just hoping that you wouldn't. I guess that stubborn streak got you where you are now." He sighed again.

"You know you could come with me." He raised his eyebrows.

Beverly chuckled. "Right. Spend the next three weeks with you and your grown son, camping and fishing in Canada. I don't think so." She shook her head and chuckled again.

"I could cancel my trip and—"

"No. You will not," she said more harshly than she intended. She softened her voice. "Don't do that, Jack. Go. Enjoy your trip. I'll be alright. Bring me a big ol' fish."

Jack shook his head back and forth. "You're one stubborn woman, Bev." Then, in resignation, he pushed up and out of the seat. He picked up the letter and tucked it in his suit jacket. Then he reached into his breast pocket, pulled out a card and dropped it on the desk.

"If you change your mind, and you still won't accept my help, give this fella a call. He's top-notch. I've been trying to get him to come work for me, but he's too much of a loner."

At the door, he looked back and crimped his lips. His face said 'Please.'

"Go 'way, Jack," she said, flicking her hand at him. "I've got work to do. And you've got to pack. I'll be fine. Don't worry about me. I always wear my big girl panties." She smiled and winked at him.

Jack shook his head and walked out.

By the time Beverly finished reviewing the pile of pre-sentencing reports, the sun had set. She ran her fingers through her hair, and stretched her arms toward the ceiling, arching her back. She felt the creak in her spine. Friday evening was a good time to catch up. Anybody who could, left early and all of the clerks were gone by five. The building was eerily quiet. Or was it? Maybe she was just spooked by Jack's visit. She put on her suit jacket, and got her purse from the bottom drawer of her desk. When she reached to turn off the light on her desk, she saw the business card the chief had left. Devon Carter, PI. She fingered the card, and thought 'Devon. Humph. With a name like that, he must be the age of my daughter.'

She took the judges' private elevator to the basement, and walked through the garage to her car. The tapping of her high heels sounded louder than usual. She glanced over one shoulder, then the other. Was she being more attentive than usual? Damn Jack. He was making her paranoid. But there was a man standing by a column behind her. She didn't recognize him at a glance, and wouldn't take a second look for fear of giving the impression of skittishness. Bracing her shoulders, she boldly strode to her car.

Beverly stopped the car in her driveway near the front door. For the first time, she realized that the tall columns of juniper bushes that flanked her front door on either side, and that she had planted herself when she bought the house, could conceal an intruder. Damn Jack. She changed her mind and pressed the button on the garage door remote clipped to the sun visor.

Once the car was inside and the door had whirred closed, she pulled her purse and briefcase from the passenger seat and got out. She felt rushed to get the key in the door before the light shut off. The switch for the overhead light was inside the house. What was wrong with her? She had never felt this kind of uneasiness. Even at almost 50, she'd felt that if she couldn't out-fight an attacker, she could sure as hell out-run one. She was fit for a woman her age, and over the years had taken short courses in self-defense. Still, she felt a sense of relief when she was inside and had turned the deadbolt.

"Killer? Killer?" Where was that silly dog?

Glancing around for the dog, she dropped her briefcase and purse on the kitchen table then walked to the control panel to disarm the alarm. With her finger poised over the keypad, she realized that it wasn't beeping, signaling the 45 seconds she had to enter her code. She frowned as she tried to remember the morning and whether she had forgotten to set it. There had only been a few times that she had done that. Then she remembered her rush to get to the monthly breakfast meeting of the WIB.

Women in Black was a loosely organized, but long-standing, organization of local women judges. Originally, its purpose had been for mutual support in a then male-dominated field. In recent years, as its original members had begun paying more attention to retirement options, it had shifted to identifying and mentoring younger women who could replace them, and swell the ranks. The invitee for this morning's meeting was way too young and way too ambitious. Beverly opened her briefcase to fill out the form that would reveal her impression of this morning's invitee while it was still fresh on her mind. The forms were to be mailed anonymously to one member who would tally them and report at next month's meeting. But that could wait. She was tired. What she needed right now was a soaking bath. Soak away the aches from sitting all day. Soak away the anger she felt at Jack for trying to make her feel frightened and needy—especially needy of him. She flipped the light switch, shed her suit jacket and walked toward her bedroom in the darkness.

She crossed the den and was at the hallway when she felt a hand clamp hard against her mouth.

Chapter Two

Beverly dropped her jacket and frantically grabbed at the hand against her mouth, digging her nails into flesh. As she pulled hard on the hand that gripped her, she felt herself being jerked backwards and off balance. Her arms flew out and she planted her feet to keep from falling. The assailant grabbed one of her hands and twisted it up behind her back. She struggled to pull away, but his grip was too strong and she couldn't break it. This was nothing like those self-defense classes she had taken, where the contact had been controlled and she had known the instructor would not actually hurt her. This was the real deal.

Fear gripped her hard, but she wouldn't give in to it. Her instincts from growing up in a tough neighborhood, reinforced by those classes, kicked in. She raised her knee, then kicked backwards, intending to stab the jewels with her high heel. She could tell from the feel and from his grunt, rather than a yelped expletive, that she had missed her mark, but he did release her arm. The eyes. She reached behind her with both hands and clawed at his eyes. He must have seen that coming and jerked away. Although she missed the eyes, her nails found purchase in his strong neck. As she ripped downward, her fingers caught on his shirt collar and she desperately ripped at it. Suddenly, he thrust forward, blocking her left foot with his and she stumbled to the floor with him on top of her.

She tried to bite the hand clasped over her mouth, tried to free her arm that was trapped under his.

"Stop it! Be still!" His voice was gutteral and harsh.

Be still, my ass, she thought, as she renewed her struggle. With him lying on top of her, she could hear his heavy breathing, feel his hot breath against her ear. In a flash, she snatched the Waterford crystal bud vase from the coffee table and thrust it back over her head. She missed his head, but hit his shoulder three times before he knocked it out of her hand. He gained control of her wrist, pulled her arm down to her side, and held her still. Then, he rolled them over so that she was on top of him. His hand was still clamped tightly over her mouth, and now his legs were clamped over hers at the ankles. Her body was taut, and they were both breathing heavily.

"Be still. I'm not going to hurt you."

Well, I'm gonna hurt you, mother fucker, she thought.

"I'll take my hand from your mouth, if you promise not to scream. Okay?"

After a long minute while she considered her options, Beverly nodded her head as best she could. She would agree to anything for him to release her.

Slowly, he loosened his grip, but still ready in case she didn't keep her word. Beverly didn't scream. This was so surreal, she wondered if she was having a bad dream. If he wanted to kill her, he could have already done that. Being raped had fallen off her list of things to worry about when her daughter had sprouted breasts.

"Let me go."

As soon as she felt his grip on her arm release, she rolled off of him and scrambled to her feet. She backed up until the wall stopped her retreat. She kept her eyes on him. He sat up.

"How about some coffee?" he asked.

"Are you nuts?" she hissed.

"Okay, tea?"

He was nuts. She'd have to play along. She eased past him and walked to the kitchen. If she could just get to the drawer. He was on his feet with the gracefulness of a cat, and right behind her.

"I have tea. Sit down," she said, pointing to the kitchen table. She was surprised when he did. She took the kettle from the stove, gripping it tightly so that he couldn't see the tremor in her hand. She filled it with water, set it back on the burner and turned on the fire. She leaned back against the counter and watched him watching her.

"You know if I had wanted to kill you, I could have," he said.

She nodded. "Probably."

"I could have raped you."

She shook her head. "I don't think so."

He chuckled. She was wound so tight that when the teakettle whistled, she flinched, then sucked her teeth. She didn't want to show fear or let her guard down.

"Is jasmine okay with you? That's all I have." She pulled the drawer open halfway and ran her hand in it. Then she reached all the way to the back, pushing aside pens, batteries, and miscellany. A frown knitted her brow. She turned toward the drawer and blocked his view. She pulled the drawer open all the way and used both hands to rummage in it.

"Is this what you're looking for?"

She turned and looked at him. He was holding her gun. She looked from the gun to his eyes.

"Tea's in that cabinet," he said, nodding toward the door above the drawer.

Beverly's eyes narrowed as she stared at him. Her lips were tight. She put her hands on her hips.

"Who the fuck are you? And why are you in my house? How did you get in here, anyway?" Beverly's breath came in angry puffs.

His lips curled in amusement. "You want this?" He held the Lady Smith and Wesson revolver toward her.

A look of confusion crossed her face, but she quickly dispatched it, took two steps toward him, and snatched the gun from his palm. Pointing it at his head, she put her finger on the trigger.

"Put your hands on the table. Now."

He gave a chuckle under his breath. "Or what?"

"Or I'm gonna shoot you."

"Shoot."

"I mean it. Put your hands on the table." She lowered her aim to his crotch.

His eyes narrowed. "Shoot."

Beverly squeezed her eyes shut and pulled the trigger.

Chapter Three

Instead of the loud boom she expected, Beverly heard only a quiet rattling. She opened her eyes, looked at the gun, then at him. She counted five bullets in his upturned palm. Near-panic replaced the confidence the gun had given her.

He closed his fingers over the bullets. "Sit down, Judge. Let's talk."

"Who are you?"

"We'll get to that. Sit down."

She drew herself up indignantly, but in the face of his steely stare, followed his order.

"Better. My name is Devon Carter."

Devon Carter? Where had she heard that name? Then she remembered. Jack. That rascal. She wanted to call him and cuss him out for scaring her this way. But she remembered, he was probably on a plane right now.

"You're vulnerable," he said. "I'm here to protect you."

"I do not need protection."

"Well, I'll give it to you. You fight like a wildcat. I didn't expect you to be so strong." He rubbed his hand across his neck, drew it away and looked at the flecks of dried blood on his fingertips. "But I was able to get in your house. And I got the jump on you. If I had really intended to hurt you, it would have been easy. We're going to fix that. Have you ever fired that gun?"

She looked down at the table. "No."

"Didn't think so. So first, we're going to the firing range early in the morning. We'll be there at seven. When was the last time you were hit in your face?"

She drew back, eyeing him warily.

"That long, huh? I guess that's not too bad a thing." He chuckled. "After the firing range, we'll go to the gym. I guess I'm gonna have to hit you in your face."

"Try it. You'll be sorry."

"Well, since we have to be up early tomorrow, I guess you should turn in, young lady."

Beverly stood. She put her finger in his face. "I am nearly fifty years old. I am not a 'young lady'. You may have meant that as a compliment, or flattering. It is neither. It is condescending. Come on, I'll see you to the door."

Devon didn't move. "You must not have heard me. I have a job to do."

"Not in my house, you don't."

"If you won't let me protect you, at least let me teach you to protect yourself."

Beverly thought on how he had breached her security, and rambled through her cabinets—and no telling what else. How easily he had subdued her, despite her best efforts. My God, he couldn't have killed me, she thought.

"I'll accept your offer of the firing range. And I'll be ready in the morning. But right now, you have to leave." She pointed to the door.

Devon stood and shook out his pants legs. "Alright, if it's got to be that way."

Beverly closed the door behind him and immediately turned the bolt lock, then slid the chain into place. Only then did she admit to herself how rattled she was by the encounter. Was she going to give Jack a piece of her mind. She walked to her bedroom and opened the door. Killer ran from under the bed and leaped toward her. Beverly caught the toy chihuahua around his mid-section and held him out for a disapproving look.

"Some killer you are. You let some strange man come in my house, and you didn't even warn me. I outta take you to the pound."

She set the dog on the floor and changed into a nightshirt. Killer followed her, whimpering and staying only inches from her feet. When she got in the bed and turned off the light, Killer sat next to it, whining pitifully. Finally she gave in, picked him up and put him at the foot of the bed.

"You stay there. I'm taking you to the pound tomorrow." Killer wagged his tail and stared at her, hoping for a reprieve. His big brown eyes flitted back and forth from pillow next to hers where he usually slept to her face.

"I dare you." Beverly turned her back to him and pulled the sheet over her. She tossed and turned, and finally fell into a fitful sleep.

She was awakened by the ringing of the doorbell, and Killer's fierce high-pitched barking. She rolled over and looked at the clock. Who the hell could be at her door at four in the morning. It had better not be him. She snatched a robe on and marched to the door. Through the peephole, she saw a police officer. He looked legit, and so did the black and white sedan parked in her driveway.

"Yes?"

"Ma'am, I need you to open the door."

Beverly hesitated, then turned the bolt, and opened the door as far as the chain would allow.

"Are you Beverly Polk?"

"I might be. What can I do for you?

"A neighbor called in a report of a strange man sitting in your back yard."

The other officer pulled a handcuffed man out of the car by his arm, and walked him to the porch.

"Do you recognize this man? He says he knows you," the first officer said.

Beverly stared at Devon. "No. I don't know him."

"Aw Bev, come on. I thought you were over being mad. I didn't hurt you."

"Alright, bud. Back in the car. Gonna have to take you downtown." The officer began pushing Devon away from the door. He resisted.

"Before you take me in, you better call your Chief," Devon said.

The two officers looked at each other and shared a smirk.

"I reckon the Chief's sound asleep this time of morning. You can call him in the morning. You'll get one free call. Now get in the car."

"I'm telling you, you'll be sorry, if you don't call him. His number is 555-3—"

The second officer pulled on his arm. Devon jerked away. The first pulled the Taser off of his belt.

"Whoa, whoa! Stop! Wait a minute," Beverly shouted, fumbling the chain off the door. "Let him go. It's okay. I know him."

"So you made a false report to a peace officer? Are you trying to protect your son? We're just trying to keep you safe, ma'am. If we let him go, don't call us back."

"I didn't call you this time," Beverly said, watching him slip the Taser back on his leather belt.

He nodded to the other officer, who released the handcuffs.

Devon rubbed one wrist with his other hand, as they watched them drive away. Beverly turned and went back in the house. By the time Devon locked the door and got to the den, Beverly was coming from the hallway. She threw a pillow and a set of sheets at him, then went back down the hall to her bedroom.

Chapter Four

Beverly couldn't sleep with the man in her living room, and no lock on her bedroom door. She thought about calling Jack and giving him a piece of her mind. Surely he was in Canada by now. But would his cell phone work? She looked at Killer at the foot of her bed and rolled her eyes. She got up and put her robe back on.

She walked into the living room. Devon was on the floor doing crunches, watching TV with the sound turned low.

"Couldn't sleep, huh?" He sat up.

Beverly sat on the sofa and stared at him. "How long did Jack hire you for?"

"Jack?"

"Don't play stupid with me, boy. I know Jack hired you. I just need to know how long you're gonna be in my house."

Devon's lip curled into a smile. "As long as it takes."

Beverly tried not to stare at his lips. She tried not to think about them.

"How much is he paying you?"

Devon tsked three times. "It would be unethical for me to disclose details of a client's business."

"I'm the client, boy," she said impatiently.

"No," he said slowly. "You're the mark."

That was sobering. Even with her line of work, Beverly had never thought of herself as a 'mark.' It made her feel weak and vulnerable, both anathema to her. She'd decided years ago, in the back seat of a car, to never be weak again. And when her husband left her with a 2-year old and a mountain of debt for a younger, thinner, lighter woman, she had decided to never be vulnerable again.

"And you can stop calling me boy. It's not cute. I may be all that's standing between you and a brushed steel casket. That's not a job for a boy."

The mention of casket was even more sobering. Beverly tightened her lips. She sucked air through her teeth. She folded her arms across her breasts. She crossed her leg.

"What are your credentials? How did you get into this line of work?"

"Oh, I guess I just sorta stumbled into it."

"Not likely. One stumbles into short order cooking."

He chuckled. "I guess you're right. I grew up on a military base. Well, several. My dad was a career officer. Air Force. I joined up as soon as I was old enough. Army—just to goose him. I was in a rebellious stage. The Army sent me to college and I went in as an officer. I did a couple of tours. Got good training with special forces. Did a stint in Afghanistan. Got tired of killing people—and not the guy we should have. Came back stateside. Had a stint doing VIP escorts. Plum assignment. Boring as hell. Dad passed during that time. When it was time to re-up, I declined. Now, I'm in the saving business."

"You should be a police officer. That's what they do."

He gave a short harumph. "Writing tickets? Chasing street-level drug dealers, like a dog chasing its tale? Taking orders from a . . . some dude with less training than I have? Less experience than I have? Not for me."

"That sounds so cocky."

"Didn't mean to. Just stating the facts. I know myself. I know what I'm good at. I work better alone. Listen, it's time for you to go to bed. You only have a couple of hours. Tomorrow is gonna be a long day for you."

She drew her neck back and looked at him as though he had no place giving her orders.

"You're going to need to be sharp. Go on to bed." When she didn't move, he added, "You don't have to worry about me bothering you." His lips curled into another smile.

Beverly tried to look as though the thought hadn't occurred to her.

"Besides, you got that watchdog in there with you."

Beverly looked at her watch, then stood and walked to her bedroom, as though it had been her idea.

The smell of coffee roused Beverly. Killer was at the door doing a low growl. She sat up on the edge of the bed. Then she saw the cup with steam rising from it on her nightstand. Even the indignation couldn't stop her from taking a sip. She looked at the clock, rose and quickly showered and dressed.

In the kitchen, she found Devon standing by the stove.

"Perfect timing," he said, sliding an omelette onto a plate. He held it toward her.

"I usually just eat a cup of cereal with low-fat milk for breakfast."

"That's cool, when you're just gonna be sitting down all day. This won't be that kind of day. You need some protein."

The aroma was heavenly, and Beverly decided not to argue with him.

He joined her at the table. Even though she was only halfway through her omelette, Beverly stopped eating when he finished.

"Do you always eat that fast?"

"Just habit. I've had to eat on the run a lot. Is that all you're gonna eat?"

She nodded.

He picked up both plates and put them in the sink. "You can wait until we get back to do these."

Beverly bristled at his instruction, but then she supposed it was only fair—since he had cooked.

At the garage, Beverly raised an eyebrow at the strange car next to hers. When had he done that? She pressed the button on the wall to open the garage door.

"We'll be taking my car," he said. "Everywhere."

"Not everywhere. I have places to go."

"Not until this is done."

At the passenger side of the car, Beverly stopped before opening the door. "Look, don't take this personal. I'm not used to having somebody all up under me. I can stand that during the day. At work. But I need a lot of alone time."

"You just haven't had the right person all up under you." He opened his door and got in. Beverly threw her hands up and got in the passenger side.

Chapter Five

The car was nondescript. Wasn't big, wasn't small. The silver color didn't stand out. He backed the car out, and Beverly frowned when he pressed her garage door opener now clipped to his visor. He drove carefully, but very fast. Beverly could feel the power of the engine, as he smoothly moved through traffic, and guessed it had been modified.

"Reach under your seat. That's the gun you're gonna practice with first. It's bigger than yours. But once you've learned to handle that one, yours will be a snap."

Beverly took the gun from under the seat and was almost alarmed. It was heavier than the one she kept in the drawer. She set it in her lap and pulled her hands away from it as though it was a snake.

"Do you have a permit for this?"

He looked at her out of the side of his eye and smiled.

Beverly thought of what a pickle she would be in if he were pulled over for speeding. She wouldn't be able to explain the gun. She wouldn't be able to explain him. And Jack was somewhere in Canada fly-fishing.

Devon pulled into the parking lot of a long one-story building. Inside, he bought a box of bullets. The clerk handed them each a set of ear protectors that looked for all the world like headphones.

"Before we go into the range itself, you'll have to put those on. Let's sit over here." He motioned to a wooden settee.

"Okay, press that button and push the cylinder out."

Beverly held the gun as though it might explode in her hand any minute.

"Don't be afraid," he said. "Just do it."

She looked up at him then at the gun, then back at him. He shook his head in dismay. Then he reached down, raised his pants leg and pulled a smaller, but similar gun from the holster around his ankle. He demonstrated the motion.

"You've got to control the weapon. Don't let it control you." He nodded for her to try it.

After a couple of tries, the cylinder rolled out. She looked at him and smiled. He opened the box of bullets and held it out to her. Beverly inserted the bullets into the cylinder. He made a snapping motion with his gun to close the cylinder. She followed suit, but it took three tries before hers clicked into place. With fledgling confidence, she opened the cylinder again, then snapped it back in place. She smiled at him. He shook his head, but smiled back.

"Alright, put on your ear protectors." He motioned toward the door, then put his on.

Inside the range, Beverly wrinkled her nose at the acrid odor of gunpowder. He led her to the end booth. He set the box on the metal ledge, then pressed the button on the wall. The large square of white paper with the outline of a man in black moved away from them. Markings along the wall indicated the distance, from three yards to 25. He released the button at twenty yards.

"Watch," he mouthed to her. He took a stance, legs slightly spread, and braced his hand holding the gun with the other. Standing behind him to his right, Beverly's eye traveled from his feet to his waist to his shoulders. Not bad, she thought. Was she becoming a lecherous old woman? His first shot distracted her attention. Even with the ear protectors, she flinched sideways. By the sixth, she had stilled herself. He looked at her out of the side of his eye and frowned. Then, he pressed the button on the wall again, and the target moved toward them until it stopped just in front of the ledge. Beverly could see that five holes in the paper congregated within a 3-inch diameter, with one outside.

"You wanna do this," he mouthed, pointing at the circle. "Not this."

He pointed at the outlyer. "Your turn," he mouthed, then pressed the button again and the target moved down the track away from them. This time, he stopped it at half the distance.

He nodded to her and moved back. Beverly stepped up inside the partitioned area. She grasped the grip with both hands, hesitated, then pulled the trigger. She wasn't expecting the recoil and she nearly lost her balance, stepping back to catch herself. He put his hands on her waist and held her steady. Then he stepped close behind her, put his foot between hers and nudged them apart. He reached both arms around her and moved her bracing hand from her wrist to cup the other hand. He nodded for her to try again. When her cylinder was empty, she was ready to leave. She knew how to do it. She hated the smell of this place, hated the grimy feeling on her hands, hated the heavy ear protectors. She looked to him for relief. He shook his head, and pointed to the box of bullets. She frowned, tightened her lips and sucked air through her teeth.

Suddenly, a boom so loud it sounded like a canon, even with the ear protectors, reverberated through the room. Beverly instinctively ducked, and crouched beneath the ledge. When she looked up, he was laughing at her. She stood with all the dignity she could muster. He motioned her toward him with one finger, then nodded to the man two booths down. The man's white hair was crew cut. He wore a suit, all black. He looked like an assassin. His weapon looked like something out of a sci-fi movie. Devon laughed again at the look on her face. Then he pointed to the box of bullets.

Beverly filled the cylinder again. Davon gave her pointers, adjusting her sighting, her stance. She didn't like him standing so close to her, invading her personal space, putting his hands on her. She wasn't accustomed to that. By the time the box was empty, Beverly's hand was hurting, but at least there was a hole in the target for each of the last twelve bullets. They weren't in the tight little circle that his had made, but they were all inside the black outline and she felt a little pride. Devon pressed the button until the target was in arm's reach. He unclippped it and motioned her to the door.

Back in the foyer, Beverly jerked the ear protector off and handed it to him. He gave both to the clerk, bought another box of bullets, then led her back to the settee. He spread the target on the seat and pointed to places on it.

"Not bad—for a first time. But not good. You need more practice. We'll do that. But not now.

Beverly rolled her eyes at the thought of returning to the range. "I don't need any more practice. I can shoot if I have to."

He stared at her, then shook his head.

"Come on, let's go wash our hands."

"I'd rather take a shower. I hate this place."

"You can shower later. You haven't even worked up a sweat—yet."

Chapter Six

In the car, Beverly looked at her watch and was surprised. It seemed like they had been in that awful place for hours, but it had only been one. She fumed at his assessment—not bad, not good. She was accustomed to being very good.

He pulled into the parking lot of a gym, then turned to her.

"You've got a lot of want to," he said. "I'm gonna show you how to. Come on."

Inside, he led her to an area covered with wrestling mats. "Sit down."

Beverly frowned at his bossy tone. "I thought we were going to wrestle."

"You've got to learn how to fall first. Sit down."

"Fall? Who has to learn how to fall?"

He put his hands on his hips "Sit down."

When she did, she raised her knees and planted her feet on the floor. She wrapped her arms around her knees, leaned forward and stared at him. "Okay? Okay?"

He knelt in front of her. "Now, fall back. Just let yourself fall."

She let out an exasperated breath, then eased back on her elbows.

"No. That wasn't a fall. Sit up."

She pushed herself up.

"Now fall. Just let yourself go."

She didn't move.

He rocked forward on his knees, she recoiled from him and fell backwards. He leaned on top of her, his body between her legs, planting his hands on either side of her shoulders.

"You're not used to that, are you? You probably haven't fallen in twenty years. You think it's just about the fight. Sometimes, falling is more important than the fight. If you're afraid to fall, you'll push when you should pull, and give your opponent an advantage."

Beverly glared at him, then looked away. "Okay, you can get off me now." She didn't want to think what she was thinking about this stranger. She certainly didn't want him to see what she was thinking.

Devon smiled as though he had. He leaned back on his haunches, reached a hand to her and pulled her back up.

"Do it again. Just fall."

"This feels stupid," she grumbled.

"You want me to help you again?" He raised an eyebrow.

Beverly fell with no further prompting. Then he pulled her to her knees and had her fall from there. He showed her how to fall and roll and get back to her feet. Then, he played the role of attacker to teach her defensive moves, how to break holds, how to disable. She followed instructions, but he felt she was just going through the motions. He needed her to feel strong emotion, as she would during a real attack.

She motioned time out, and sauntered off toward the water fountain. When she returned, holding the pointed paper cup, he pushed her in her chest. Water spilled down the front of her t-shirt. She frowned in surprise, then he pushed her again, hard enough this time to make her stumble. That's when he saw what he wanted. Anger. When he pushed her again—hard enough to make her fall—then straddled her. Beverly showed him that she had learned her lessons well.

Winded and still angry, she turned her back to him, sat on the floor.

"You can't quit. That was pretty good, but you aren't ready."

"I'm ready enough."

When he saw her determined posture, Devon gave up and plopped down on the floor, his back against hers.

"We'll work some more at your house. In a real-life situation, you probably won't have all this space to work in."

"All I'm going to do when I get home is take a hot, hot shower." She dusted her hands against each other, then against her thighs. She pushed herself up to a standing position.

"Let's go. Now." She stalked off to the car.

"Towels and soap are in there." Beverly pointed Devon to the guest bathroom, then went into her bedroom. Killer wagged his tail and gave a happy bark in greeting. She squatted a minute to scratch him behind his ears. He promptly rolled over to expose his stomach. Beverly gave in and rubbed it a couple of times.

"You're worthless as a watch dog, you know. You know it, and now I know it." She braced her hands against her thighs pushed herself up. She shed her sweaty clothes while the water heated up.

In the shower, with her back turned to the pummeling water, she poured her favorite gel on her pink shower puff and began scrubbing her skin. It felt like he had touched her all over her body. She must be losing her mind. Even under the guise of learning to protect herself, she shouldn't have allowed it. She wasn't accustomed to people touching her. No more than a handshake, with arm outstretched. Hugs from her mama, Angie and a couple of other friends. She rubbed her arm where he had grabbed her and tried to take her down. She touched her breast where he had fallen against her, and apologized. Lord, how long had it been since a man actually touched her breast. Several times when she was on the floor on her back fighting like a tiger, and showing him the moves he'd taught her, he'd laid his body across her to control her. As she rubbed her stomach, she remembered how hard his body had felt, and how good it had felt. Without even thinking, she found her hands on her thighs, rubbing inside. She could almost still feel him there, leaning over her, his arm muscles bunched, his strong thighs pressed against hers. Suddenly she clamped her thighs together, leaned back and let the water run over her shoulders and down the front of her body.

Chapter Seven

After her shower, Beverly grabbed the latest Ebony magazine from the dresser and stretched out on her bed. Killer whimpered from the floor beside the bed. Beverly reached down and lifted him up.

"You can't go out there either, huh? Are you scared of him? You don't have to be scared of him. I'll protect you." She pushed him off her magazine. Killer circled around and around and settled down against her. She rubbed his belly absently while she read the article on the young presidential candidate who was taking the country by storm. She paged through the magazine, then lay her head down.

The late evening sun came through the window and fell on her face. Beverly woke with a start. She sat up and dragged her hand across her face. She sniffed the air, then smiled.

"Come on, Killer. Let's go see what's smelling so good." She slipped her feet into sandals and started for the door. When she looked back, Killer hadn't moved. He flipped over on his back, his tail wagging furiously, and looked at her.

"Okay, scaredy-cat. If you're not ever gonna come out of this room, I guess I'll have to bring your food and water in here." She left the door open in case he changed his mind.

She found Devon at the kitchen table reading the newspaper.

"Good nap?" he asked.

She nodded.

"Good. We'll start strength training tomorrow. In the morning, we'll run."

"Listen, I'm a jogger. I'm in pretty good shape."

He looked her up and down, nodding his head. "That may be so. I'm gonna make you a runner."

"Well, not tomorrow morning. I'm going to church in the morning."

"Nope. I'm going to be your shadow until the issue is resolved. You will only be out of my sight when you are at the courthouse. You have protection there. Plus, only an idiot would make a move at the courthouse. A suicidal idiot. Too much firepower around there. I'll take you to work and pick you up. I'll take you everywhere you need to go."

Beverly crimped her lips. Then she lowered her chin, stared at him and smiled.

"I'm going to church. Hope you got a suit."

"Hungry?"

Beverly walked to the stove and lifted the lid on the skillet. "Ouu, that looks good."

"Why don't you sit down. I'll fix our plates."

She replaced the lid and went to the table. "Your mother teach you how to cook?"

"No. She died before I was old enough to cook."

"You said your dad was a career man. He raised you by himself?"

Devon nodded.

"Did you get to live overseas?"

"Oh yeah. Germany. Italy. England."

"So I guess you must be bi-lingual." Beverly leaned back as he set a plate on the table in front of her. She kicked the sandals off of her feet.

"Tri, actually."

"You're lucky. I'm still struggling with Spanish—here in northern Mexico."

"Well, if I'm around long enough, I can help you with that."

"So how long you gonna be around."

"That depends."

"On what?"

He looked at her a moment. "On you."

Beverly drew her chin back and considered the possibility that he might be flirting with her. Had a man her age said the same thing, she would know. And she would know how to react. But here, she was in an uncertain place.

"Me?"

The doorbell rang.

"Are you expecting somebody?" he asked.

"No."

"Then, sit still. I'll get it."

"Oh no you won't. This is my house. You can't answer my door."

"I said, sit still, woman. I'm on duty."

Beverly recognized the voice as soon as the door closed.

"Angela. Come on back. You're just in time. Have you had dinner?"

Angela walked into the kitchen, questions all over her face. She stopped at the chair where she usually sat, then saw that a plate was on the table, and a napkin in the chair. She eyed Beverly with a cocked brow.

"You cooking too, now?" she asked.

"What do you mean, 'too, now'?"

"You know you don't cook."

"Actually, I cooked," Devon said, from the kitchen doorway. "And I'd be honored if you'd join us."

"Oh I wouldn't dare intrude," Angela said, eyeing the pepper steak over rice. "I was just in the neighborhood and thought I'd drop in. I didn't mean to—"

"Oh, I insist," Devon said, holding a chair out for her.

"Well, if you insist." Angela eased into the chair as he pushed it under her. "Just a little. I usually don't eat this close to bedtime."

"I'll set another place," Beverly said, starting to rise.

"Naw, I got it." He quickly returned with a plate and silverware for Angela, but not before she raised an eyebrow at his bare feet. He shook a napkin out and draped it across her lap.

"I can tell you ladies have been friends for a long time."

"Since law school," Angela answered. "We were going to practice together, freeing all of our innocent brothers and sisters. But Bev went over to the dark side."

"The dark side?" he asked.

"The prosecutor's office."

"Oh, I see. And you?"

"I'm still doing what I can to free the innocent."

"Having any luck with that?" Devon asked.

"A little. Every now and then." She gave a wry smile.

"Oh, she's just being modest," Beverly said. "Angela heads one of the top defense teams in the city. If you ever get in trouble, she's the one you should call."

"I'll remember that," Devon said. "Can I get your card—just in case?"

"Look, guys, I hate to eat and run, but tomorrow is another long day. You're a good cook, Devon. Thanks for dinner."

When Beverly stood, Angela looked at her bare feet, and held her eyebrow in check.

"Glad you came by, Angie," Beverly said, as she walked with Angela through the cavernous den.

"Me too. We've both been too busy lately. Especially you." Angela waggled her head.

"Now see, you've got the wrong idea."

"Oh, I got the right idea. You don't have to play it off like that with me. You deserve a boy toy. And one that can cook and hold a decent conversation. Honey, all I want to know is, does he have a brother?"

"Shhh! Don't let him hear you say that. And he is not my boy toy. He's my, uh. . ."

"He's your what?" Angela asked, a big smirk on her face.

Beverly saw it, and knew that nothing she said would change Angela's mind.

"If I tell you now, I'd have to kill you. But I promise I'll tell you later, after this is all over with."

"Okay, that's cool. Here, give him my card—when you're finished with him. See ya, girl."

Chapter Eight

Beverly stepped from her bedroom, dressed to kill—wide-brimmed straw hat and all. Enough of this assassin business. Sunday was her day to nourish and renew her spirit. She had been renewing her spirit at Mt. Moriah since law school. Back then, the current pastor and his wife had been fellow students and had invited her and Angela to services. More than twenty years later, she and Angela were still members.

She changed purses and picked up her keys from the dresser. When she walked through the house, she didn't see any sign of Devon. Just as well. Nothing was going to keep her from going to church.

In the garage, she remembered he had her opener, so she pressed the button on the wall to lift the door. The engine made no sound when she turned the key. What? The car was fine when she parked it just Friday night. The battery couldn't have gone down that fast. She tried again. Still nothing. She slapped the steering wheel and muttered "Damn" under her breath. She got out of the car and started into the house, knowing that in taking a cab she would be late. When she opened the door, Devon blocked her way. He wore a suit and dress shoes. He held up a bundle of colored wires.

"Car won't start without this."

Her mouth fell open.

"You 'bout ready to go?"

Beverly turned and huffed to the passenger side of his car.

At the church, Devon opened the car door for her and held his hand out to her. More because he didn't give her a choice than because she wanted to, she took it and pulled herself out of the car. She tried to walk ahead of him, but he matched her step for step. At the broad cement steps, Devon gently grasped her elbow. The only reason she didn't snatched away from him was the look Mrs. Burney was giving them from the door at the top. Beverly put a pained smile on her face and spoke to her politely when they reached her. She intended to keep going, but the old gossip wasn't having it.

"What a glorious day the Lord has made. Who is your friend, Judge Polk?"

"Morning, Mrs. Burney. This is Devon Carter. He's, ah, visiting."

"Well, we're glad you're visiting us this morning, young man."

"It's my pleasure."

Beverly rushed him into the sanctuary before Mrs. Burney could ask any more questions. She squeezed past the end-huggers on her usual row and sat next to Angela. She rolled her eyes at Angela's smirk. When they rose for the congregational hymn, Beverly held the hymnal open between them. She was surprised at his strong, baritone voice, and that he didn't glance at the book even once.

After the service, Beverly tried to rush off, but the pastor wanted to welcome her guest, and Brother Stanley cornered her about doing a workshop on the law for her teen group. She glanced nervously at Devon and the pastor, while checking her calendar and agreeing with Brother Stanley on a date. No sooner than she rescued Devon and she thought they could escape, Sister Evans caught her to ask for a cash contribution to the seniors dinner, 'because we all know you don't cook.' Why did everybody feel compelled to tell all her business. It felt like the whole church wanted to get a good look at Devon, but maybe she was just being sensitive. She didn't have a good explanation for his presence, and she couldn't tell the truth for fear of alarming them. He carried it all off with a placid smile on his face, being as vague as she was. She cut a mean eye at him more than once. He responded with just the slightest cock of his eyebrow.

Finally in the car, she took off the wide-brimmed hat and slung it in the back seat. A dose of alum couldn't have pursed her lips tighter.

He glanced at her, and suppressed a smile. "You're gonna have to get a better story together by next Sunday."

She glanced at him and sucked air through her teeth.

"So, you ready to go running?"

She turned and looked at him. "You gotta be kidding."

"Not at all."

Beverly crossed her arms and looked out the window on her side.

In the house, Beverly went straight to her bedroom and stripped. She hung her suit from the doorjamb to let it air out, and put the hat back in its box. She slipped out of the pantyhose and wondered why she bothered. She had noticed that the younger women didn't wear them, but she just couldn't do it. She wasn't raised that way. As she put the pantyhose in the bathroom sink with a squirt of liquid soap, she caught a glimpse of her body in the mirror and thought 'Not bad.' She sucked in and held her breath. Not really bad. But no bikini. She pulled on her swimsuit and tied a sari around her waist. Run, hell-y.

Beverly pulled the sari off and draped it over the chaise lounge by the edge of the pool. She stood on the diving board and took a deep breath, then dove in. She was on her tenth lap when she noticed Devon sitting at the table. He had changed into casual linen slacks and shirt. She refused to let his staring interrupt her flow. She finished her laps and climbed out of the pool. When she reached for her sari, it wasn't there. She looked around and saw it draped over Devon's lap.

"I thought we were going running," he said.

"You thought." She held her hand out for her sari.

"I can't give you my best protection if you won't follow my program."

"It's Sunday. No programs. No running. None of that. You do your protection thing. It's my day off."

He stood and walked toward her with the sari draped over his arm. He stopped close to her and looked directly in her eyes.

"You can't have a day off until this is over. Obviously I can't be with you every minute of the day. You have to be on your guard all the time."

"You be on guard," she said.

He stepped toward her. She stepped back away from him. He took another step. She stepped back again, lost her balance and fell ungracefully in the pool. When she surfaced, her eyes were blazing.

Devon held his palms up. "I didn't do that. I told you, you have to be on your guard."

Beverly treaded water until she calmed down. "I guess you're right," she said.

Devon squatted at the edge of the pool and reached a hand to her. Beverly hesitated, then clasped it. She braced her foot against the wall of the pool as he began to pull her up. Then she grasped his arm just above his wrist with her other hand and jerked. As he fought against losing his balance, she released his arm and swam toward the ladder. By the time Devon surfaced, slinging the water from his face and hair, Beverly was seated cross-legged on the deck of the pool, fists at her waist.

"How's that for on guard?"

Chapter Nine

Monday morning, Devon pulled the car into the commercial service zone in front of the courthouse.

"I'll be here at five," he said.

"I don't usually leave that early. I'll call you when I'm ready to go."

"Nope. I'll be here at five. You can't hang around a near-empty courthouse. If you're not here by five after, I'll come to your office."

"I think you're taking this too seriously. You're making me feel like a prisoner. You're interfering with my life." She gave him her most intimidating judge look.

"I'm just making sure that you have a life."

There was no arguing with the man. He was stubborn as a mule, she thought. And he would not be intimidated. Beverly crimped her lips, opened the door and got out.

At five, Beverly emerged from the courthouse, her briefcase stuffed with files to review later. Accustomed to taking the back way, she was surprised to see so many people in front of the courthouse. Most were waiting for the bus, but some, like her, were expecting other rides. She spoke to the three young women who worked on her floor, and followed their gaze to the curb.

In khaki pants, a knit pullover shirt, baseball cap and trooper shades, Devon leaned back against the car, his arms folded against his chest, one leg crossed casually over the other at the ankle. When he saw recognition register on her face, he smiled and pulled himself off the car. He opened the door and held it for her. When she approached, he took the briefcase from her hand and put it in the back seat.

As she buckled her seat belt, she glanced back to see the questioning looks. That bothered her. She would have felt better if they had looked stunned—stunned that at her age she could catch a fine, young man. Instead, she saw them calculating—too old to be her son, too young to be her brother. Was he a relative? Would she give them his phone number? As he pulled away from the curb, Beverly pushed the high-heeled shoes off her feet and wriggled her toes.

"Those ladies were sure checking you out." She said it light-heartedly, as though it didn't make her any difference.

Devon just smiled. He didn't respond. Beverly didn't know what to make of it, or of the thought that if he were just ten years older. . .

Devon unlocked the door and let Beverly go into the house ahead of him. She sniffed, then cut her eye at him.

"Yeah, I did that," he said.

Beverly tried to suppress a smile. His cockiness got on her nerves, but in this case, maybe it was deserved.

"We'll . . . jog, then have dinner," he said.

When she passed by the stove, she couldn't help but lift the lids on the pots. How could she stay pissed with the man? She changed into her swimsuit, a pair of shorts and a t-shirt. When she came back in the den, he was doing stretching exercises. He followed her out the door and onto the sidewalk. Beverly felt his eyes on her in a way that he shouldn't have been looking. Or was it just her imagination?

They jogged through the neighborhood, him following her lead, allowing her to set the pace. Beverly felt as though each neighbor watering grass or puttering in a flower bed did a double-take. She wanted to stop and explain. Maybe she was being just a little ridiculous. They were accustomed to seeing her on her daily jogs. Maybe they were looking twice because they were accustomed to seeing her alone, and not because of his age. Maybe it was just her imagination. She gave her usual wave—and a sheepish smile.

Back at the house, Devon sprawled on the couch. Beverly went to the patio door to get in the pool. When she reached to open it, she jumped back at the sight of the huge black dog, sitting at attention just beyond the door. She looked back at Devon.

"What the hell is this?" she asked.

"Oh him? That's Bruiser. He's an attack dog. But you don't have to worry. He won't bother you. He only bothers the bad guys. You can go ahead and have your swim. Then, we'll have dinner."

Beverly looked back at the Rottweiler. He cocked his massive head, staring at her. When she slid the screen door barely open. The dog stood on all fours, its stub of a tail still as a statue.

"You don't know who the bad guys are. How does he know who the bad guys are?"

"Oh trust. He knows."

Beverly felt no assurance in his answer. She rubbed her thumbnail back and forth across her chin until she decided not to go outside. Instead, she showered and donned a caftan. When she crossed the den on her way to the kitchen, she cast a glance at the patio door. Bruiser was back in his sentry position, staring at her.

When she sat at the table, the plates were already there.

The next day, when he picked her up from work, he insisted that they do more practice shooting.

"In this suit? And high heels?"

He nodded. "If someone comes after you, what you gonna do, say 'Wait until I change into something more comfortable?' You've got to be ready, no matter what or when."

Instead of the indoor range that she dreaded, he drove out of town, twenty miles past the last new subdivision and turned on a graveled road. A mile or so later, he turned into a driveway nearly obscured by overgrowth and rumbled across a cattle guard. At a clearing, he parked, handed her a box of bullets and got out. He leaned back in the car and said, "Put your shoes on."

Square bales of hay were scatted around the grassless clearing, some single, some stacked double, and some triple high. He walked off and she watched him setting up targets that looked like the one at the indoor range. Finally, she reached under the seat for the gun and put bullets in it. The sooner she did this, the sooner it would be over with, she thought. She put her shoes on, grabbed the box of bullets and got out of the car. She looked down at her multi-colored fabric shoes and frowned. She decided she'd rather get her feet dusty than the shoes. She raised one foot to remove the shoe.

"Leave 'em on," he shouted.

"I am not—"

"Leave them on, I said. If you normally wear heels that height, you need to be able to handle yourself in them."

Beverly slowly put her foot down, glaring at him.

"Come on over here."

He started her ten feet from the target. "Aim for the torso—the stomach, the heart. You have a small caliber weapon. If he's a big man, it may not kill him, but it'll stop him."

When she hit the mark twice, he put his hands on her waist and backed her up two feet.

"Again." He repeated the sequence until she was twenty feet from the targets.

"If you get this much distance, you'll have the opportunity to find cover." He pulled her behind one of the double-stacked bales. "Crouch down. Get down on one knee. For stability. Pretend this is a car," he said, patting the hay bale. He knelt in the dust beside her. "Now, lean out just enough to spot your man, fire twice, duck back. Quick as you can."

She felt silly, but she did it. When he was satisfied, he held his hand out to her and pulled her to her feet, then pulled her toward a triple stack. Beverly wanted to brush the dust off her knees, but oddly she didn't want to let his hand go. Was she losing her mind? She wasn't used to being touched. Maybe she needed to be touched.

"This is a tree," he said. "Or a building. Take your pick. It's cover."

He put his palms against the front of her shoulders and pushed her back against the stack. Beverly felt the stubble of the rough-cut hay against her back, and the warmth of his hands too near her breasts.

"Same, same. Quick, quick." Then he stepped out of her way.

She took a deep breath to clear her head of thoughts she shouldn't be having, stepped out and fired. He grabbed her around her waist, jerked her back and pushed her against the bale. He got in her face.

"No! You'll get yourself killed like that. Just ease out enough to see your target. You've only got a second. Remember, he's gonna be trying to shoot you too. And there's no doubt he's got more experience, and his aim will be better. Now, do it again," he ordered.

Beverly stared at him. No one had used that tone of voice with her in years. She pushed him off of her. She quickly leaned out, took two shots and jerked back. She crouched on one knee, eased out, took two shots and jerked back. She stood, slammed the gun in his hand and strode off toward the car. "Enough," she yelled back at him.

Halfway there, she heard him coming up behind her, but she kept going. Suddenly, she felt herself falling. She couldn't believe he had tackled her until she hit the dirt, face first. And in her good suit. Using the moves he'd shown her, she scrambled away from him, then suddenly turned, knocked him over and was straddle him, her knee at his groin. "I said, enough. And you're paying my cleaners bill, too."

Devon smiled. "I'll be glad to."

Chapter Ten

By the end of the week, Beverly was growing accustomed to having a chauffeur, and home-cooked meals waiting for her after work. She was surprised that she wasn't gaining weight. She wasn't getting her usual swim but her exercise program had been stepped up a notch. Without her realizing it, Devon had eased her past jogging to all-out running. He had taken her to the high school stadium and dared her to run up the steps to the top of the bleachers. Never one to shirk from a dare—and even though it almost killed her the first time—she made it.

She still had mixed emotions about Devon being in her house, but she didn't find it objectionable. In fact, even though she certainly wouldn't admit it to him, and hardly wanted to admit it to herself, she was enjoying the company. Even Killer had ventured out of the bedroom, tentatively at first. By Friday, he once again had the run of the house, but he would dash past the patio door like the devil was after him. She wasn't the only one unnerved by Bruiser's presence. Beverly noticed that Killer stayed close to Devon. Maybe it was the fact that they shared her house all day while she was at work.

Friday night after dinner, Devon presented her with `a stack of movies he had rented. Beverly picked a comedy, and settled on the sofa to watch. When Killer approached, eager to jump on the sofa, but too far a reach for his stubby little legs, Beverly reached for him. Devon pointed his index finger at him, then pointed down. Killer sat down—so eager to please Devon that his tail almost wagged him.

Beverly looked from Killer to Devon, then back to Killer and reached for him again. Devon pointed his finger again. Killer stayed on the floor, cutting his eyes from Devon to Beverly and back. Beverly frowned.

"How did you do that?" she demanded.

"You just have to show them who's in control."

All those weeks they had attended puppy training classes before they flunked out, came back to Beverly. Killer followed instructions when he wanted to, but when he didn't want to he would just sit and stare at her with his big brown eyes. No matter how the instructor urged her to be 'in control,' to be the pack leader, Killer wouldn't cooperate. She wanted to tell the instructor that she was in control all day long and that her 8-to-5, more like her 8-to-7, used it all up. Control wasn't all it was cracked up to be. Instead, Beverly had concluded that Killer was untrainable, and they would be something more like roommates. As long as he didn't mess in the house, she was cool.

Beverly got a few laughs out of the movie, but she kept looking from Killer to Devon. And he kept looking from her to Devon. She wondered if Killer felt like a prisoner too.

She had tried to call Jack a few times during the week, but couldn't get through. Maybe the area was so remote that it lacked service. Or maybe he had turned off his cell phone. She remembered when Jack had carried two beepers, a radio and a cell phone, and was in constant communication with his commanders. The last year or so he'd reduced to one Blackberry, and sometimes, she noticed, he turned it off. He'd been talking about retiring more and more lately. Police had a great retirement package, and he was way past eligible. Sometimes she sensed that he'd lost his snap, his love for the job. Off and on, he'd suggested that she look at retirement too. He even offered to have his broker look at her portfolio to show her how she could do it. He'd hinted that, even if she couldn't quite stretch it, together, they could save expenses. She had laughed it off, saying she didn't think she'd enjoy fly-fishing. She wished she could see a future with Jack. But try as she might, the feeling just wasn't there.

When Sunday rolled around, one look at Devon in tailored pants, and she knew she was going to give that ol' gossip more fodder.

"You don't have to go, you know. You could just drop me off. I can catch a ride back with Angela."

"No. I enjoyed the service last week. I'm actually looking forward to it."

Easing past the end-huggers, Beverly saw that Angela's smirk was even broader than last Sunday. During the announcements, Angela scribbled something on her bulletin and passed it to her. "He must be really good."

Beverly quickly folded it and glanced at Devon. One corner of his mouth was turned up into a smile and she knew he had seen it. She stuffed the folded bulletin in Angela's purse between them, and rolled her eyes at her. The visiting minister's message was on resisting temptation.

On Monday, like every morning, Devon insisted she remain in the car while he came around and opened her door. He said it gave him a chance to make a visual sweep of the area. When he dropped her off, Beverly's secretary was walking up.

"Morning, Judge."

"Morning, Esther." Beverly felt odd, even after all these years, calling Esther by her first name. It went against her home-training to call a woman ten years her senior by her first name, but Esther insisted. Beverly held the courthouse door open for her. On the elevator Esther said not a word, but Beverly could hear the question loud and clear.

"He's my—uh—cousin. He's in town for—uh—a couple of weeks, looking for a job. "

Esther's smile and shrug said 'I don't believe one word of that.' The elevator stopped on their floor.

"It can be kinda nice having someone around for a while. Best not get too used to it, though. Makes it really hard when they leave." From the wistful look on her face, Beverly knew Esther was thinking about her last husband. He'd died a few years ago, after two years of mostly marital bliss.

"I don't think he's gonna be around that long. He'll be able to find something pretty soon. He's smart. And he has education. And skills."

"That's good," Esther said. Her smile made Beverly want to explain some more, but she decided to quit while she was ahead.

"Don't forget, I'm taking the afternoon off. For my mammogram. Have you had yours this year?"

Beverly's brow wrinkled as she strained to remember.

"I don't believe you have. I'll check and schedule it for you if you haven't."

As Esther turned to go to her office, she called out. "Judge, you didn't mention that he was handsome. You thought I'd miss that?"

"Why no, Esther, I just didn't . . . I didn't think that was important."

"Welll, I'd say looks aren't as important as, shall we say, build and skills." She winked at Beverly and walked off.

Beverly closed her mouth and went to her own office.

Chapter Eleven

Beverly blamed it on Esther, the fact that she found herself more and more noticing Devon's build. And sometimes she caught him looking at her too. Maybe that was just her imagination. The steady and hard exercise was sculpting her body in a way that pleased her. She determined that even after he left, she would keep it up.

It seemed that Esther took an inordinate interest in Devon. "Your, uh, cousin find a job yet?" Or "What kind of work is he looking for?" Thursday, out of the clear blue, she said "You know, my Arthur, rest his soul, was younger than me." Before Beverly could answer, Esther walked away.

That night, Devon worked her harder than usual. She managed to keep up, but was almost hobbled when they got back to the house. She collapsed on the sofa and began rubbing her ankle.

"I pushed you too hard. Let me do that for you." Devon sat next to her and pulled her foot into his lap. He held her leg just above her ankle and rotated and flexed her ankle. Then he did the same with the other one until she sighed with relief.

"Feel good?"

She nodded.

"I can make you feel real good."

She cut an eye at him. "Ah, that's alright. I think I feel good enough. I think I'll go shower."

"Not yet. Lay down. Turn over."

She didn't move, so he helped her. He straddled her and started at her shoulders, kneading, pressing and massaging. "You know, you are really tense."

"What would you expect? I deal with criminals, lawyers and cops all day. And to top it off, somebody is supposed to be trying to kill me. Wouldn't that make you a little tense?"

He pressed his thumbs against the muscles in her neck until they released. He spread his fingers, pushed them into her hair, and massaged her scalp until she groaned. With an elbow, he kneaded the long muscles in her back. Then he pressed his thumbs into the small of her back. He didn't touch her buttocks, but he twisted his knuckles into the backs of her thighs. She hadn't been touched in so long, and never like this. Beverly decided she was going to put massage on her schedule.

He raised off of her and leaned back on his haunches. "Now turn over."

When she did, he leaned forward and massaged her temples and the place just above her ears. She was surprised when he touched his lips to hers, and then touched his tongue to hers. He lay his body against hers. Beverly knew she should push him away but the weight of his body felt so good. Still, she pushed against his waist with the heels of her hands. They both knew it was a feeble and useless attempt. Beverly embraced a pleasure she hadn't known in a long time. In fact, the pleasure was so intense that she wasn't sure she had ever experienced it before, and she let him know that. When it subsided, she was embarrassed. She pushed him off, ran to her room and closed the door.

The next morning, Beverly dwaddled in her room until nearly time to leave. Finally, she couldn't put off facing him any longer. She found him in the kitchen whistling.

"You're late for breakfast."

She looked away. "I don't have time. Let's go." She walked to the back door.

He set the plates down on the stove. "Alright."

In the car, he looked at her, as he turned the key in the ignition. She looked away.

As he pulled out of the garage, he said "You're acting like they say men act, afterwards."

When they were near the courthouse, Beverly took a deep breath, then expelled it. "Devon, I can't explain my behavior last night. That should never have happened. I owe you an apology and—"

"Isn't that usually what the man says?"

She jutted her chin up, summoning as much dignity as she could. "I want you to move out of my house. I want you to put my car back together. I want you to go away. If there is an assassin—which I doubt after all this time—I will take care of him. This won't ever happen again. We won't ever do that again."

He pulled to the curb, went around to open her door. When she stood, he didn't back up.

"Yes, we will." Then he stepped back and let her pass.

The first thing she did when she got to her office was call Angela and leave a message on phone to come by her office asap. Beverly was sharp and impatient with the defense attorney and the prosecutor all morning. They both looked at her and at each other. The morning dragged on with Beverly continually checking her watch. She recessed court at 11:30.

By the time Angela showed up at 12:15, Beverly wore a deep scowl.

"Who ate your breakfast?" Angela asked.

"Nobody. That's who. I didn't have breakfast. It's past lunch time."

"Hmmm, a little edgy, huh. A little trouble in paradise?"

"No! Yes! Let's go. Come on. I can't talk about this here." Beverly snatched her suit jacket from the coat rack. "Let's go to the sandwich shop across the park."

Outside the courthouse, Angela said, "So, what's up?"

"I don't know what got into me," Beverly started.

Angela laughed. "Well I do." She laughed again.

"Not funny, Angela!" She grabbed Angela's sleeve. "Don't look now. See that guy at 3 o'clock? Black shirt. Do you know who he is?"

Angela took a casual sweep to her right. "Nope. Been seeing him around the courthouse lately."

"Is he a lawyer?" Beverly asked.

"I haven't seen him in a courtroom. Just kind of around. Every day, now that you mention it. Maybe he's a new bondsman."

"He's been watching me. I've been walking to the sandwich shop for lunch since I haven't had a car. He's always around. Just watching."

"He looks aw'ite. Doesn't look like he's watching you, to me."

At the sandwich shop, they got their orders and found a table. Beverly felt Angela watching her.

"What? What?"

Angela looked at her. "Beverly, are you alright?"

"Of course, I'm alright."

"You know you can tell me. You've been acting kinda strange. It's not like you to take up with a young man. Move him in your house. Now you think a man is watching you?"

"No. It's worst than that. See, last night, I . . . we . . . well, shit Angela. I can't believe I did that."

"Did what?"

Beverly tightened her lips and frowned at Angela. "You know."

Angela looked at her with a raised brow. "Last night? You mean that fine boy's been living in your house three weeks and you just now jumped his bones?" Angela chuckled. "You really expect me to believe that?"

"Of course I expect you to believe me. You've known me, what, twenty years. You know I'm not that kind of woman."

"Damn near thirty years. And you ain't had a piece in . . . years. I just have one question. Was it good?" A twinkle lit Angela's eyes.

Beverly drew in a sharp breath. Then her lips tightened into a smile. "It was aw'ite."

"Aw'ite, my ass."

"Okay, okay. It was good." Beverly saw the expectant look on Angela's face. "Okay, it was great."

"So, I'm trying to figure out what was so asap that I had to leave a long-winded client—a rich one at that—with an associate, to rush over here. You just wanted to rub it in?" Angela rolled up the paper her sandwich had come in. "Where'd you meet this guy anyway?"

"It's a long story, Angela. I'll have to tell you about it later. But it doesn't matter. Devon is moving out today."

"Oh, so that's why you're so out of sorts. Well, you knew that was gonna happen. It couldn't last. That's just the way it is. What's he, like twenty years younger than you?"

"Only fourteen." Beverly replied, defensively.

"Only fourteen. Humph. Well, at least you've got some good memories. Listen, I've got to get back. You wanna go to happy hour later and cry in a beer?"

"Thanks, but no. I'll just be glad to have my house back. I'm just going to enjoy a nice, quiet evening."

Chapter Twelve

At 4:30, Beverly called a cab. Austin wasn't a cab kind of town and she knew it would be half an hour before one came. While she waited, she called Jack's cell phone. It was time for him to be back. No answer. She called his office. His secretary told her that Jack had sprained his ankle and wouldn't be back for another couple of weeks.

When she walked out front at five, Devon was waiting at the curb. He opened the door. She intended to ignore him, but when she glanced around, she noticed the women watching her. She walked to the car and got in. She didn't say anything for a couple of blocks.

"You've packed, right? And got that big-ass dog out of my yard? And fixed my car?"

"No."

"No?"

"No. None of the above. I still have a job to do. I'm not leaving until it's finished. If you don't want a relationship with me, I'll get over that. I feel a little used, but I—"

"What kind of relationship can you and I have? The age difference is too wide. Or hadn't you noticed that? I'm thinking about retiring. You're trying to build a career. My friends have grandkids. You don't have any kids yet. You're—"

"I don't want any kids."

"Every man wants a son."

"I'm thirty-five years old. I know what I want, and don't want."

"And just for the record, I didn't use you."

He cast a side-long glance at her. "It sure feels that way."

"Let's just say that I lost my mind."

"Okay, you can say that."

In the house, Beverly went straight to her bedroom and closed the door. Killer sat in the hallway a minute, then went looking for Devon.

Sunday morning, Beverly intended to demand the keys to his car, but when she emerged from her bedroom, Devon was dressed and waiting. Neither of them spoke all the way to the church. When she sat next to Angela, she ignored the curious frown on Angela's face. The minister's sermon was on forgiveness of sin.

Monday was the start of jury week. The trial ran over. A long-winded witness and an attorney who objected at every sentence wore Beverly's patience thin. When she finally found a convenient spot to call a halt, it was 6:15. She found Devon sitting in her chair, his feet propped on her desk, reading a magazine. Her lips tightened.

"I wish you had waited outside," she said.

He pulled his feet down. "I wish you had come out at five, like I told you to. I had hell parking in all that traffic."

"I wasn't alone. I had a courtroom full of people."

"Did you know that courthouse security ramps down at 6? Now, come on let's go."

Beverly stopped putting on her suit jacket. " You know, all this bossing around is getting a little tiresome."

"Let's go," he said in a firmer voice.

Beverly decided right then, that whatever it took, she was gonna raise Jack and insist that she call this guy off. Even if it meant calling the police in that area and reporting him missing, she had to raise Jack.

Nothing had happened. No mad assassin had appeared on her doorstep. In fact, the only disturbance of her peace had been Devon. She pulled the jacket on and snatched her purse from the coat rack. Not another word passed between them, out of the building and the two blocks to the car. As they pulled out of the parking space, she glanced at him. His jaws were was tight as hers, his breathing as measured.

On the freeway, he said, " I know you're pissed."

"Got that right," she answered.

He pulled a greeting card envelope from under his thigh and handed it to her.

"I found this on your desk."

Beverly looked at it, then rolled her eyes at him. "You opening my mail now, too? That's a federal offense, you know."

He looked at her, then cut his eyes back to the road. " There's no postmark."

Beverly turned the envelope over and looked. He was right. She pulled the card out and read it.

Be careful. I'm watching out for you.

Devon had nixed running, stating they couldn't afford to be in the open. Dinner was a somber affair. He was unusually quiet, his face almost grim. He ate even more quickly than usual, left his plate on the table and went to his bedroom. Killer followed him. Beverly heard the door close. Then Killer came back and sat at her feet. She cast him a glance.

"Traitor."

He slumped back on his haunches and whined.

After Beverly cleaned the kitchen, she started to her bedroom. She met Devon in the hallway. He carried two long guns, the likes of which she'd only seen in the movies. Her eyes widened.

"You thought this was a game, didn't you?" he said.

She opened her mouth, then closed it.

"Well, no. . .actually, I didn't know what. . .actually I'm a little scared now. Just a little."

Devon saw the vulnerability in her eyes, heard it in her voice. He set the guns down and leaned them against the wall. Then he took both of her hands in his.

"Actually you don't have to be as scared as you should have been before."

She looked up at him, questioning.

"We didn't know who it would be. Now we do," he said. "This isn't a hit and run guy. That's good news."

Somehow that didn't feel to Beverly like a big ol' birthday present tied with a bow.

"Doesn't mean he's any less dangerous," he said. "Or less determined to harm you, just that he's going to take his time and toy with you. But that gives me time. Now I know who I'm dealing with. And if I find him first—"

Beverly looked relieved. "So you know who he is? So you can just go get him? And that'll be the end of it?"

Devon gave a wry chuckle. "Well, not quite. But I will protect you. You don't have to worry—as long as you do what I say. Exactly what I say, when I say it. Understand?"

She nodded. He pulled her to him and put his arms around her.

"It's gonna be okay. I'm gonna take care of you. You have to believe me, okay?"

Beverly slowly nodded against his chest. She almost believed him, she wanted to believe him.

Chapter Thirteen

Beverly was at her bench, scanning through the sheaf of documents the defense attorney had handed her when the alarm sounded. She looked up to see Neal, her bailiff, marshalling spectators out of the courtroom. Another drill, she thought. Damn. Why now? The drills were quarterly, and the judges were generally given a heads-up a few hours before. She didn't know how she missed this one. She was certain that she had checked her e-mail before going in the courtroom this morning.

"Court's in recess," she announced and went straight to her office. She slipped out of her robe, picked up her purse and went directly to the stairwell. She was glad she was in good shape, since her courtroom was on the fifth floor and she felt sorry for a couple of the judges on the eighth floor.

The sheriff normally kept the doors to the stairwell locked, citing security reasons, and it was dusty from lack of use. Now, as Beverly entered, it was crowded and noisy. There was an almost festive air among the workers, who received a respite from the grind of being tied to a computer screen all day entering data, updating cases. Lawyers, however, wore annoyed looks and grumbled at the disruption in their schedules. Defendants were just glad to be free one more day. Beverly could tell which ones were jurors because they looked confused and disoriented.

When she emerged on first floor, a deputy directed traffic, rushing everyone out of the building. Other deputies were posted every twenty feet or so, steering everyone to the square block of park adjacent to the courthouse. Grumbling as they shuffled off into alleyways, the chronic homeless who had in recent years claimed the park as home, ceded it to the better-dressed crowd.

According to the protocol for fire drills, Beverly went directly to the oak tree on the other side of the park that was the assigned meeting place for fifth floor. Her staff was already there, milling around, making jokes. Neal was the captain for fifth floor, and it was his responsibility to see that everyone was accounted for. When he saw Beverly, he gave her the thumbs-up sign and checked her name off on his clipboard. Over Neal's shoulder she saw the man. He made eye contact with her, and held a minute before he turned and walked away.

After an hour, the deputy came over and announced that it was safe to re-enter the building. Beverly moved along with the crowd back toward the building. Halfway there, she saw the sheriff and walked up to him.

"Hey, Dan. Couldn't you have done this drill at 4:45?"

"Just between you and me, it wasn't just a drill," he said, his voice lowered. "There was a small fire on the ninth floor. Someone set this fire on purpose. My guys are on it."

"Small fire. Ninth floor. You evacuated the entire building. Nice going, Dan."

She walked away from him and joined three other judges in the judges' elevator. They commiserated about how they were now behind schedule. Beverly got off on her floor, went back to her office and donned her robe. Out of the corner of her eye, she saw a large gift box on her desk. It was tied with a ribbon in red—her favorite color. Jack knew it. She wondered how the courier delivered it in the midst of the drill, but she smiled in anticipation. The folk in the courtroom could wait just a few more minutes.

She untied the bow and lifted the top off the box. Then she pulled out layers of tissue paper. When she took the last sheet of crumpled paper off, she recoiled at the sight of a small dog. Then she looked closer and saw that it was a Chihuahua and that it was dead. She stifled a scream, grabbed her chest in reflex, and stumbled backwards. From across the room, she realized it was a different color and wasn't Killer. Still, she was shaken. She pulled her cell phone from her purse and with shaky fingers dialed Devon's phone. There was no answer. Then she called her home phone. Still no answer. Where was he? Why wouldn't he answer the phone? Her legs felt like rubber as she walked to Esther's office. She was getting re-settled at her desk.

"Esther, where is your car?"

Esther looked at her puzzled. "It's in the lot at 9th street. Why?"

"I need you to drive me to my house. Right now."

Esther took one look at her and said, "Sure, Judge. Okay." She hit the screen saver on her computer and reached into the drawer for her purse. "But what about the trial?"

"I'm through for the day. Neal can handle it. I'll let him know. You just go. Get your car and pick me up behind the courthouse."

As Esther left, Beverly started dialing Jack's number, then stopped. She remembered that he wasn't back from his trip. Even if he had been, what was Jack supposed to do about a dead dog in her office? That was a job for building maintenance. She couldn't make herself go back in her office, so she looked through the folders on Esther's desk until she found the number.

By the time she was at the back of the courthouse, Esther drove up and pulled to the curb. Beverly got in the lime green Beetle and gave her directions. Esther made small talk about the drill and how disruptive it had been. Beverly could hardly sit still. She could feel Esther glancing at her curiously. When they pulled into the circular drive in front of her house, Beverly had her hand on the door handle.

"You want me to wait?" Esther asked. Beverly could see the concern on her face.

"No. Why don't you go on home for the day. No point in you going all the way back to work."

Beverly closed the front door behind her, and called "Devon? Devon?"

When she got to the den, she gasped. There was a large bloodstain on her ecru suede sofa, another on the carpet, another on the fireplace hearth. She turned to go to her bedroom to look for Killer. Then, she froze. What if the killer was back there waiting for her? He surely would have heard her come in, and calling Devon. Then she heard a noise in the kitchen. Devon walked into the den, his shirt spotted with blood.

"He must have come in while I drove you to work," he said, walking toward her. "The attack dog was poisoned, but may survive. I just took him to the vet."

"Where is Killer?" Beverly asked in a frantic voice.

" I'm sorry Beverly, Killer didn't make it. He was cut up real bad. Butchered." The muscle in his jaw pulsated. "He was already dead when I got here. I didn't want you to see him the way he was. I left him at the vet for cremation. Listen, we have to leave now. Right now. This guy is closing in. You're in danger. I've already talked to the police and arranged to secure the premises. Hopefully they can get prints. Make an identification. But we have to go now." Devon pulled the shirt off over his head, walked to his room.

Beverly stood there, almost in shock. She was truly frightened, and she couldn't believe that Killer was dead. That was so pointless. Killer never hurt anybody. She clasped her arms around herself to stop the shaking. Before she could sort it out in her mind, Devon came back wearing a clean shirt on, and carrying a small duffel bag. He took her by the arm and steered her to the car.

He drove to the open-air practice range. At the back of the property, he pulled alongside an RV and stopped.

"Come on," he said urgently. He opened the RV door for her, then opened the trunk of the car. He took two long guns and a silver metal briefcase out and put them in the closet in the RV. Instead of going back to the main road, he drove county roads that twisted and turned through farmland so much that Beverly lost her sense of direction. They passed through towns that were no more than a spot in the road. Despite her doubt and confusion, the farther away he drove, the safer Beverly felt.

Just as the sun began setting, Beverly saw the ocean.

Chapter Fourteen

Devon drove along the road that paralleled the beach. Then the road ran out and he drove on hard-packed sand. He slowed down and positioned the vehicle to take advantage of the breeze that blew off the gulf. He pulled a curtain across the front windshield, then checked the doors to make sure they were all locked.

"I'll fix you some dinner."

"I'm not hungry."

"You need to eat. It's nothing fancy. Just a frozen casserole. It won't take long to heat up in the microwave."

Beverly picked at her meal and only ate a few bites. He ate quickly, then took their plates to the galley.

Beverly moved to the couch, took her phone out of her purse and began dialing.

"What are you doing?" he asked, coming from the kitchen galley.

"Calling Angela."

He snatched the phone from her hand. "Don't be ridiculous. You'll compromise our safety. Maybe her safety. I don't know what his tech skills are, but I do know that he was able to disarm your alarm system. He may be able to trace your calls. You think he won't hurt Angela to get to you? Look what he did to your little dog."

It was finally too much. Beverly's face crumpled and she burst into tears. She didn't know where she was. Her dog was dead. Her whole world had spun out of control. She covered her face with her hands and wept. Devon stopped short. He sat on the sofa next to her and put his arm around her, pulling her to him. Once the dam broke, Beverly let it all go. Her body shook with sobs. Devon didn't say anything, just rubbed her back and held her.

Just before the sun rose, Beverly woke. She tried to ease away without waking him. When she stood, she heard him say, "I put some of your stuff in that bag." He pointed to the bed over the cab. Beverly unzipped it and found the essentials—toothbrush, underwear, two pairs of shorts, a pair of jeans and a couple of t-shirts.

They spent the day inside with the blinds drawn. Devon disassembled the long guns, cleaned them and put them back together. Beverly shied away from them. She had found an old novel in the bathroom and took it to the overhead bed to read. She dozed off and on. There was nothing else for her to do.

"Let's go for a walk. You look restless."

"I am. I can't stand being cooped up like this." She looked at her bare feet. "But there's just . . . all that sand out there."

Devon stepped out of his flip-flops. They were obviously too large for her, but Beverly slipped her feet into them, then followed him down the steps.

They walked a while in silence. He walked at the edge of the surf where the water lapped at his bare feet. The full moon reflected off the ocean and lit their way. He took her hand and pulled her toward the water. She resisted.

"No. Wait. I don't want to get my feet—"

"Aw come on. It'll feel good." He pulled her to where the water just grazed her ankles. Her steps were awkward, the sand sucking the flip-flops. Then she stumbled. When she tried to catch herself, her foot came out of the one stuck in the watery sand. He caught her and held steady.

"My shoe!"

He snatched it just before the tide carried it away. Then he knelt down, pulled her other foot up.

She braced her hands against his shoulders. "What are you doing?"

"Making it easier for you," he said, as removed the other one. He hooked both sandals over the fingers of one hand and caught her hand again with the other.

"Come on," he urged.

"Ouu yuck. I hate this."

"No you don't. You just think you're supposed to. Just feel it. Not what you think. Just what you feel."

"I feel like a shark is gonna bite me."

He chuckled, but didn't break his stride. "It'd have a be a mighty skinny shark."

Soon, her gait met his. And before she knew it, the water was to their calves. His hand, clasping hers, felt so strong, yet so gentle. She could have pulled her hand away, should have pulled her hand away, but she didn't.

"We'd better head back," he said.

This could all be so perfect, she thought, with another man. A man her age. Except that a man her age probably wouldn't walk in the surf. Probably wouldn't be as fit as she was. What would it be like to feel his hard body next to hers again?

As though he had heard her thoughts above the low roar of the ocean, he stopped and turned to her. His eyes held hers a long time. Then he pulled her toward him and kissed her. She didn't resist. He put his arm around her waist to pull her closer. His other arm rested around her shoulder and she could feel the flip-flops hanging between her shoulder blades. She stretched her arms up his back and held him. And he felt so good. Then he dropped his arm to her bottom and pressed her to him.

"You said we wouldn't ever do this again," he whispered against her ear. Before she could answer, he covered her mouth with his and kissed her until she was breathless.

Suddenly, he released her, held his arms out, the flip-flops dangling from his forefinger." He smiled and backed up two steps. "You want this? You gotta come get it."

Beverly didn't move. How dare he.

"You don't want to be seen with me." Devon backed up two more steps.

"You don't want your friends to know." Then he backed up two more.

"I'm not that kinda guy. You can't have this unless you want all of me. It's just you and me that's important. So, you want this? You want me?" He backed up again.

Beverly saw the distance between them growing. Her better judgment told her to let him go. But she couldn't. She started toward him. He grinned and quickened his backward pace. Then he turned and loped toward the RV. She caught up with him at the door and they tumbled onto the floor of the RV. In the urgent tangle of arms and legs and discarded clothing, Beverly decided he could stand the carpet burn better than she could. She maneuvered herself on top and had her way with him. Spent and sated, she lay against his chest. He rubbed her back. They rose together. Devon pulled the sofa into a bed, and reached into the overhead cabinet for bed linen. Beverly helped him spread the sheets, slipped between them and curled into her usual sleeping position. He climbed in behind her, spooned against her and fingered her until she clamped against his hand. Then it was his turn.

The next morning, Beverly eased from the bed and quietly dressed. When she got to the door, she heard him stir.

"Where you going?" he asked, sleepily.

"I thought I'd take a little jog."

"Good. I'll go with you," he said, sitting up.

She held up both palms. "No. I need some time to think."

"Well don't think too long. And don't go too far. I'll be here when you get back. I'll have breakfast ready."

Beverly went down the steps and closed the door behind her. She needed time alone. She was accustomed to being alone. She walked a while, then stopped and did stretching exercises. His constant presence in the confines of the RV had her mind all cloudy. That was surely the explanation for her behavior last night. Then she took off in a trot. She could feel the rush of the wind on her ears. She ran faster, trying to drown out the thoughts of 'What now?' She'd crossed a line, and didn't know how to go back, how to get back to her old life, where Devon didn't fit in. But she couldn't out run it. She was getting winded. So she slowed her pace. She heard him behind her, but wasn't ready to face him yet.

"Slow down. I need to talk to you."

She frowned. It wasn't Devon's voice.

Chapter Fifteen

Beverly saw the old couple ahead, sitting in beach chairs guarding their fishing lines. She glanced over her shoulder and saw the man's face. The same man she'd seen before. She hadn't been imagining things. He had been following her. She wished she had told Devon about him. But she hadn't wanted him to think she was paranoid and crazy. The man reached out to grab her, but she jerked out of his reach and sped up.

When she was within six feet of the couple, she stopped abruptly. She turned to face him. She saw the edge of the holster where the thin jacket he wore was open.

"Hey. I'll bet they can tell us where the bait store is." She walked between the couple and the water. "Could you tell us how to get to the bait store?"

The couple looked startled. "Watch out for the line," the woman warned.

Beverly caught one of the taut lines in her hand.

"Harry, tell 'em how to get there."

The man came and stood at Beverly's side, feigning interest in what Harry was saying, but keeping his eye on Beverly.

"He's not good with directions," Beverly said. "Can you draw us a map?" She pointed to the sand.

The old man struggled to his feet, bent over and used his fish-gutting knife to draw in the wet sand. He motioned with his hand.

"Okay, lean down here, sonny. This here's the park road. Then you turn left—"

As soon as the man leaned over, Beverly yanked hard on the line, wrapped it around the man's neck, then released it. The pull of the tide tightened the line. He looked surprised, clawed at his throat, but couldn't grasp the thin filament. Beverly pushed him into the old man, so that they both fell on the woman. She snatched up the knife the man dropped and took off. She didn't look back as she sprinted away. Fueled by fear, she ran faster than she'd ever run in her life. Halfway there, she could hear him behind her. She didn't dare look to see how close. When she got to the RV, the door was open. She stumbled up the steps and fell backwards to the floor as she pulled the door closed behind her. The knife fell from her trembling hand, and she quickly flipped the two locks. She held onto the door lever and gulped for air, calling "Devon. Devon. Devon."

But he didn't answer.

She reached up and pulled the shade to cover the window in the door. The blinds in the living area were closed. Why wasn't Devon answering her? She stayed low and crawled toward the back. When she reached the kitchen, her hand slipped and she fell flat on her stomach and her chin bumped on the tile. When she raised her hand to cup her chin, she saw blood on it. She held her hand away from her and shook it. Then she saw the trail of blood that ended at his leg extended from the bathroom door. She scrambled across the kitchen floor to the door. She had to push the door against his leg to squeeze through it.

Devon was lying on the floor. The front of his t-shirt and his hands were covered in blood. His eyes were closed. Beverly knelt between his legs and shouted his name. He didn't respond. She grabbed his wrist and pulled and shook him. His eyelids raised, but she could only see the whites of his eyes. She bent to put her ear to his chest, but jerked back. She didn't want any more blood on her.

She pulled a towel from the rack on the door and wiped her hand. She touched two fingers to his carotid artery and held them there. She felt a weak pulse.

Her mind ran in all directions. She tried to tear the shirt away from him, but it wouldn't give. She scrambled back to the door and got the knife. She got on both knees, held the t-shirt taut and jabbed the knife into it, pulling it down, viciously ripping the fabric. Then she saw what she really didn't want to see. Blood was oozing from the hole in his side. In her head, she was screaming and running around with her hair on fire. But on the outside she was almost calm. "Devon. Devon. Devon."

She balled the towel and pressed it against the wound. She didn't know if it would do more damage with the bullet still in there, but she did know that she had to staunch the bleeding. In her first aid class, the instruction had been to stop the bleeding, then call for help. But that had been for cuts, not bullets. She needed help. Where was her phone? In her purse. On the sofa. She lifted the towel, saw that the flow had slowed, but not stopped. She clamped it back again. "Devon. Devon. Devon."

He moaned and his eyes squeezed hard. Beverly took that as a good sign. She pulled his hand to the towel.

"Hold this, Devon. Hold it tight."

His arm was limp, and his hand fell back to the floor. She had to get to the phone.

"Devon! Devon!" She grabbed his cheeks and shook his head back and forth. No response. Then she slapped him. She slapped him again, hard. His eyes opened wide. He strained to focus. She grabbed his hand again. "Hold this!"

Beverly crawled to the living room and turned her purse upside down, dumping the contents on floor. She grabbed the cell phone and dialed 911. Something like a busy signal came from the phone, but not quite. She scrolled through the numbers until she reached the one. The phone rang 4 times, then went to voice mail.

"Shit! I'm in trouble here! I need your help! I'm at . . . shit, some beach. By. . . never mind. Fuck it!"

She pressed the button. Then thought of Angie and pressed her number. After three rings, she heard Angie's sleepy voice.

"Angie, Angie, Angie. . ."

Beverly heard her name. She took the phone from her ear and looked toward the bathroom. Then she heard it again and turned toward the door.

She set the phone down and crawled to window by the door. She raised the slat of the mini-blind just enough to see outside. She could only see his shadow.

"Beverly, open the door."

"What? Who the hell are you?"

"I'm Devon Carter."

"You're not Devon."

He nodded his head. "I'm Devon. I've been looking out for you. I'll explain it all later. Come on out. I'll take you somewhere where you'll be safe from him."

"You're not Devon."

"Yes, I am, Beverly. You've got to believe me. I was sent to protect you. But he got to you first. I've been here all along. I can explain it all. You just need to come on out of there now. I've got a swat team waiting to move in. But I've got to get you clear first." He pulled on the door handle.

"I don't see any swat team."

He gave a half chuckle. "That's why they're called swat, Beverly. You're not supposed to see them. But trust me, they're in position. As soon as you come out of there, they can do their thing."

"How do I know you're who you say you are?"

"You just gotta trust me. We're wasting time. Come on, Beverly. Just open the door."

"No. Why should I trust you?"

"Because he is a cold-blooded killer. He's not satisfied just to kill. He likes to toy with his victims first. Tells them some sad story to get them feeling all sorry for him. Plays on their emotions. Sometimes he says he's an orphan."

Beverly remembered Devon telling him about his mother dying.

"He always has sex with them."

Beverly could almost feel his hands on her.

"Most times he tortures them. He tortures animals, too. He killed your dog, Beverly."

Her eyes went wide. Oh, Killer. She was reaching for the door when she heard his voice.

"Don't listen to him, Beverly. He's the killer."

She turned and saw him pulling himself toward her with one forearm, holding a gun and pressing the towel against his stomach with his other hand.

"Don't open the door!" he huffed through a grimace.

She looked from him to the door, and back. She flashed back to coming home and finding Devon covered in blood, her dog missing, then him rushing her off in the RV.

"Did you kill my dog?" she screamed. "Did you kill my dog?" Beverly scooted back against the sofa. She ran her fingers through her hair and rubbed the heels of her palms against her temples.

"No, Beverly, I wouldn't have killed that sorry-assed dog. He killed your dog. Believe me, Beverly."

"Sorry-assed dog? Killer?"

He was still pulling himself toward her, grimacing in pain. The man outside jerked on the door latch. One of them would be her savior. The other intended to kill her. But which one? She had to decide, and time had run out. She reached through the mess she'd dumped out of her purse.

She picked up her gun and aimed for his torso. She pulled the trigger three times.

Chapter Sixteen

The lights were bright and harsh. Beverly paced the corridor, wrinkling her nose at the antiseptic smell. Earlier, two detectives from the sheriff's department had escorted her from the scene, to a private room in the hospital and taken her statement. They also took her gun. Then they left.

She assumed the older couple on the beach had called the sheriff when they heard gunfire. But maybe they had called as soon as the old man had pulled himself out of the sand. She had seen them being carried away in a deputy's car. She wondered what statement they gave.

Now, in this strange place, and alone, she again questioned her judgment. Two men were in surgery from gunshot wounds. Both were there because of her. Could any of it been prevented? Had she made a mistake? Had she shot the right one?

Finally, she sat down on a sofa. She felt tired all the way to her bones. She had been up since sunrise. Pacing the corridor for hours had tired her out. She hadn't eaten since yesterday. The enormity of what she had done almost numbed her brain. She nodded off a couple of times, then pulled her feet up and lay down. She put her forearm under her cheek for a pillow. When she woke, the sky was very different from when she'd been brought here. There was a different lady at the nurses' station than before. She wondered if this one would give her information. The other one wouldn't--since Beverly wasn't next of kin to either man, and probably since she was the shooter. Beverly ran her tongue over her teeth, and felt the fur. She found a ladies' room and used a paper towel wrapped around her finger as a toothbrush. She combed her hair with her fingers into something fairly presentable, and pulled at her clothes to try to straighten them. The deputies had been kind enough to let her grab a pair of jeans.

Behind the lady at the nurses' station, there were so many people that it seemed more like meeting. As she approached, one or two eyed her, while continuing their conversation. The others ignored her, their eyes focused on computer monitors or metal clipboards containing patient charts or passing instructions. Beverly decided to try to the new lady.

"Excuse me. Can you tell me about the two men who were in surgery this morning?"

"Are you family?"

"Sort of."

"Sort of? We can only release information to next of kin. Which one are you related to?"

Beverly went back to the sofa and sat down. She was still a prisoner. She now, at least, knew she was on the Gulf coast, 200 miles from home, in Corpus Christi where she knew no one, and no one knew her. She searched her mind for the name of a colleague there, but none came. She didn't have her purse, her phone, her id, nothing. She had no money, not even any lipstick to soothe her dry lips. She hoped one of the deputies had her purse and that it wasn't in the RV on the isolated beach. She was sure she looked like a homeless woman to the nurses and doctors.

Just as she was plunging into the depths of despair, she saw the one person who she really needed to see. Leaning on a cane, Jack hobbled down the corridor with a surgical boot on his leg up to his thigh. She rushed up to him so fast, she almost knocked him off-balance. He put one arm around her, while leaning on the cane with the other.

"I'm so glad to see you," she breathed against his chest. And she was. He was like a pair of old house shoes. Comfortable and dependable. They had history. Tears of relief sprang to her eyes and she let them flow. Jack was the only man she had ever let see her cry. She thought about Devon. No, Jack was not the only man, but the first man.

"Girl, what have you been doing? I send a man to protect you, and you almost killed him. I should have taken you with me. You're dangerous." He rubbed her back, and felt her chuckle.

"How did you get here? How did you know to come here?" she asked.

"Well, I am the Chief of Police, you know." He gave her a smug smile.

She crimped her lips, balled her fist and gently bumped his chest. "Serious, Jack. I didn't tell them. I didn't give them your name. There was no reason for you to be mixed up in this."

"I know you didn't. Devon did. Before he went into surgery. The Sheriff called me. I had Flyboy bring me down in the copter. I'm sure I'll take some hits for that when it makes the paper in Austin. But what are they gonna do, fire me?" He sucked air through his teeth. "Come on. Let's go see how Mr. Carter is doing. The other one didn't make it."

At the door, Beverly hesitated. What if the man inside the room was the man who had been outside the RV door? What if she had fallen in love with the man who had tried to kill her, who had killed her Killer?

She held the door open. "You go ahead, Jack."

Jack hobbled to the bedside. "Devon. Remind me not to hire you to protect anybody else. You might not survive another one."

Still loopy from the anesthesia, he gave a weak smile. "I'll be aw'ite."

Beverly walked to the other side of the bed and forced herself to look. She did her best not to grin.

The End

EVELYN PALFREY is a native Texan, a graduate of Southern Methodist University and the University of Texas Law School. Besides working in the criminal justice system, she is an avid motorhomer and gardener, and is active with the Writers League of Texas, the Austin Romance Writers of America, the Travis County Bar Association and the Links Inc.

"I write stories that have middle-age heroes and heroines because I believe that romance is just as beautiful with a little grey at the temples."

"There is challenge--and joy--at every stage of life. Enjoy the one you're in now. It will last too long going through it--and not long enough looking back on it. Look forward to the next one. It will bring its own challenges--and joy."

Evelyn was nominated for Career Achievement Award, Romantic Times Magazine

Stormy Weather

by

Laura Castoro

Dedication:
To the Pleiades and the Harbor City Book Clubs!

Chapter One

The moment her car left the blacktop, all Beverly Freeman could think about was that she was going to miss the birth of her first grandchild.

"Ma'am? Ma'am!"

Beverly opened her eyes. At least she thought her eyes were open. She couldn't see a thing. What was going on? Where was she? She felt strangely suspended, floating. Was this a dream? No! Something had happened! Something she would begin to remember in a moment.

"Are you hurt, ma'am?" It was a man's voice, carrying the command that she answer.

"I—I don't…" The darkness about her exploded in light and then thunderous sound that vibrated her world. Adrenalin shot through her system. She whipped her head in the direction of the stranger's shout. "Where are you? I can't see!"

"Okay, hold on."

She heard some scuffling, as if someone was scraping shoes over gravel, and then another bright flash of lightning lit the space around her. That's when she realized something was covering her face. For the first time, panic edged into her thoughts. "Help! I'm stuck!"

"It's okay, ma'am. I'm right here." His voice was much closer. "I'm going to touch you. Okay?"

Confused, Beverly drew back instinctively from the idea of a strange man touching her. "Why do you need to touch me?"

She heard his quick grunt of amusement. "I need to move the air bag away from your face. Okay?"

Air bag? Why would there be an air bag over her face?

As he tugged the fabric away a bright halo of lightning stabbed her eyes. It took a second for her vision to adjust before she noticed the face of her rescuer. It was a very nice face, brown like hers, but something about him was very wrong.

She squinted at him. "Why are you upside down?"

His smile was as gentle as his touch had been. "It's not me who's upside down, ma'am."

"What?"

His smile should have reassured her but it didn't. It made no more sense than her situation, which wouldn't come right in her mind.

"Can you remember what happened?"

"I was… flying." The words surprised her even as she said them.

He nodded a little. "You've been in a car accident."

"Accident!" It all came back to her in a flood of detailed memories.

Cliff, her son-in-law, had called at the crack of dawn to say that Angelique's labor had begun. Angelique was terrified of pain, had been since a child. Not even having her husband by her side was going to keep her calm for long.

Prepared for the 'baby's coming' call Beverly had grabbed her already-packed travel bag and not even bothered to check the weather until she was on the road. She wasn't particularly concerned when her iPhone pinged an alert concerning a major storm system moving in from the Gulf. Thunderstorms were a regular part of spring weather in Arkansas and Louisiana. A little rain wasn't going to keep her from the birth of her first grandchild.

The only portion of trip she was the least bit concerned about was the stretch where she had to leave the Interstate highway. The state roadway she took as a shortcut through southern Arkansas narrowed to a two-lane blacktop without shoulders as it snaked through piney woods. But with a little luck she would reach the next Interstate before the rain struck.

Beverly sipped Chai tea from her thermos and willed herself to relax.

She had plenty of time to get there. Birthing took time for women in her family. Angelique, her only child, had been a nineteen-hour long labor. She had made this four-hour trip from Little Rock to Shreveport often since Angelique and Cliff relocated there six months ago. Bless her, Angelique needed help selecting everything from an apartment to curtains, and leaving her to unpack a household in her pregnant state just wouldn't do.

"She should have stayed in Little Rock until after the baby was born," Beverly murmured under her breath, and not for the first time. That's what everyone said. But who could really argue with a first-time mother who wanted to be with her husband, even if his relocation had come at a bad time for the young couple?

Everybody's mama! That's what Denise, Beverly's business partner in their medical billing service Med-Cap, called her. Denise like to rag on her about the fact that anytime family members or friends were feeling needy or neglected or wanted kindhearted yet practical advice, they turned to Beverly.

"Damn! Even strangers come to you for help," Denise had said just the day before after Beverly had given directions to a motorist. "

Maybe so. But somebody had to be in charge. In business Denise deferred to her. So today, she was doing what she had always gone, making it happen for her baby girl.

Beverly glanced at the large diamond ring on her right ring finger. That stone, in a different setting of her own design, was the only reminder of a marriage she had left two decades ago, at age twenty. No need to throw out the baby with the bathwater went the old saying. So she'd kept the good things, Angelique and the diamond. That's what she'd always done in her life. If being a single working parent meant she had been too busy to take seriously a relationship with a man, that's how it was.

After Angelique and Cliff and the new baby were settled then she'd think about her personal life again. Though, Lord Jesus! How Angelique was going to cope alone with a brand-new baby didn't bear thinking about. The girl was book smart and good-hearted, but she didn't seem to have a common sense bone in her body. She would need lots of help with a new baby. So, Beverly would get a life as soon as she found the time.

Laura Castoro

When she reached that dicey stretch of back road, the first jittery flashes of lightning brightened the edges of thick purple clouds swallowing the once bright sky. Even so, she made a quick call, to reassure her daughter that she was on the way,

"Now you just have to pace yourself, Angelique. Remember your birthing class instructions. Babies come in their own time. You have to have patience and take each pain as it comes."

All at once, straight-line winds began shoving her car like a linebacker trying to break through. She had thought she had time. Time had just run out.

"I got to go now. You and Cliff just concentrate on having that baby. Love you. Bye!"

Not wanting to worry Angelique, she didn't mention the wind, or the approaching storm. Gripping the wheel, she cast an eye upwards. It didn't look encouraging. A thick wedge of a wall cloud had swooped low, catching its raggedy edges in the treetops. By the time her gaze dropped back to the road a solid sheet of rain had drowned out the ribbon of blacktop ahead.

A frighteningly close burst of chrome-white lightning lit up the gloom a split second before an earsplitting crack of thunder lifted her in her seatbelt. One moment it was daylight, the next her car was enveloped in a downpour that came so thick and fast the windshield wipers couldn't clear her view of the road.

Instinct urged her to pull over. But she was an experienced driver who knew that it was more dangerous to pull off into God-only-knew what kind of ditch or risk being rear-ended by a rain-blinded driver. Slowing to a near crawl, she clutched the wheel until her knuckles hurt, and began to pray

She thought she was alone on the road. Then the enormous cab of an eighteen-wheeler in the opposite lane came roaring over the top of a slight rise, its high beans piercing the curtain of rain.

Gritting her teeth in horror, Beverly watched as the cab veneered off the blacktop on the opposite side, its tires churning up great clods of mud and water. Despite the pounding rain she heard the hydraulic roar as the driver slammed on his brakes. Resisting those brakes, the heavy trailer it hauled jackknifed behind the cab, swung across the highway and into Beverly's lane. The momentum of the entire truck sent it skidding straight at her.

She didn't have time to do anything but brake and jerk her wheel to the right.

The moment her car's tires lost traction, she knew she was in serious trouble. She felt the car leave the slick road, rising for an instant toward the angry gray sky, and finally she was tumbling and jerking and--.

"Dear Lord!"

"Ma'am!" Someone was shaking her shoulder, and not gently. "Ma'am, stay with me!"

Surprised again by the sound of a man's voice so close to her, Beverly swung her head toward him. This time she could see clearly the face only inches from her own. It was wet with rain and marred by streaks of red mud, and still upside down. No! She was upside down. "My car!"

He nodded. "You've been in an accident."

"Yes." She swallowed. She remembered that. Now.

The hair lifted on her arms, a second before lightning forked down around the car. "Oh, my lord!" escaped her in a whisper.

"Take it easy." The man reached out and touched her arm more gently this time. "You're doing fine."

No, she wasn't! She was stuck inside her overturned vehicle, the one she had just made the last payment on. This car was supposed to last her another four years if she took good care of it. Now it was lying in a ditch like an overturned turtle. But that wasn't her fault.

With sudden suspicion, she turned her head back toward the stranger. "You ran me off the road!"

"No, ma'am. The eighteen-wheeler that did is piled up about a quarter of a mile down the road." She watched his expression dim for an instant, as if he was remembering something terrible, but the dark emotion was quickly gone. "I didn't know e another car was involved until I saw your headlights off in the —."

A deafening clap thunder cut him off.

Beverly felt the car tremble in response. She could have died, just like that! Through no fault of her own!

A rush of anger poured through her, willing away any concern for her own safety. She had other more important things to think about. More important than her car or herself. She needed to get to Shreveport. Angelique would be worried if she were late.

She tried to free herself from her seatbelt but couldn't. Her left arm was still trapped by her side. Anger warred with a returning fright as she began twisting frantically in her seat. "What's wrong with me? Why can't I move?"

The man scooted closer by crawling on his elbows. "Now take it easy, ma--. What's your name?"

She took a deep breath, trying to will away a helplessness she'd seldom known. "Beverly Freeman."

"Can you look at me, Beverly?"

Slowly she turned at looked at him, really looked. He was sprawled on his belly, his legs stretched out behind him through her broken passenger side window. He was young, and looked big and solid. Just the kind of man one would want around in an emergency. Even his eyes, a golden amber in a darker face, seemed to glow with confidence.

When he took her free hand, she felt proof of reliability in his touch. "My name's Will, Beverly. I'm going to get you out of here safely. Promise. But you've got to help me, too. Can you do that, Beverly?"

"Yes." Funny, she didn't usually like it when black people took liberties of familiarity with strangers simply because the strangers were both black. But this time she wouldn't have minded if he had addressed her as 'sister lady' or even 'sister.' He was so formal, using 'ma'am and even her name in that impartial way professionals used when talking to a client, or a serviceman speaking to a civilian.

It took her moment to realize that the only warmth she felt came from the fact that he was still holding her wrist.

Embarrassed, she pulled her arm away.

He released her. "I checked your pulse. It's good. Can you tell me if you're hurt?"

"I'm not quite sure." Self-consciously, she reached up to touch her cheek. It was slick. Was she crying? No! She didn't ever cry. She swallowed hard then felt another deeper touch of fear. "I--I think I'm swallowing blood."

He stretched out a hand to her face. He touch was gentle, his fingers barely skimmed her brow and eyes then felt carefully along her left cheek, lightly across the bridge of her nose to her right and then up to her chin. "The airbag broke your nose on impact. I'm sorry."

"Is that all?" Relief flooded her. A broken nose was nothing. "I'm fine except my left hand is stuck."

"Let me check that." He scooted in closer until his cheek was practically against hers and she could smell his aftershave, something light and citrusy. Then he aimed the beam of a flashlight she had not known he had up her body. She tried to follow its path, but the seatbelt kept her from moving much. Thank goodness she always traveled in jeans.

As he continued to gaze upwards, she found her thoughts strayed against her will to other details about him, like the way his ears lay so nicely against his head. He must have been to the barber recently since his close-cropped hair still retained its razor-line perfection.

Finally he turned to her. "I'm sorry but I'm going to have to get a bit personal, okay? I need to feel around to see where you're stuck."

The heat coming off him as he pushed in against her upside-down body in the tight confides of the car made her realize again how cold she had become. Though his t-shirt was wet and muddy, beneath it his body radiated heat everywhere they touched. He quickly felt up her arm from shoulder to where her hand disappeared between the seat and the driver's side door.

As a new barrage of heavy rain drummed down on the car, she wanted to lean her cheek against his warm for reassurance. Without him she would be trapped and totally alone. But she wouldn't embarrass either of them like that. Instead she whispered a prayer of gratefulness and protection for this young rescuer.

"Can you shift away from the door, Beverly?" he shouted down between them.

She tried, but—"The steering wheel's in the way!"

"Ok! Relax!"

Relaxing was impossible. The strong winds shaking her vehicle were making her nauseous from being suspended head-first so long. It took several seconds before she realized that the faint music she heard was her phone. It must be Angelique!

She felt for her cell phone ear bug but it was missing. Will would have to find it. "Do you hear my cell phone?"

"Don't worry about that now." She heard him curse under this breathe as he shifted her weight with one hand while feeling with his other hand up along the side of the door.

She jerked on his shirt. "I need my cell phone. Now!"

Not bothering to answer her, he released her weight back to the harness and bent down close to her face. This time his expression was tense. "I could release your seat belt but I don't want to risk breaking your hand or dislocating your shoulder unless I have no choice. So I'm going to get help. Understand?"

Leave her! Beverly swallowed what felt like a frozen milk carton of fear. "Fine. Just find my phone before you go."

For the first time, she saw impatience flick through his expression. "This car is in a ravine and the ravine is filling with rain." He splashed his hand in the shallow pool of gathering beneath her head for emphasis.

Beverly hadn't paid attention to the water gathering in the roof of the car even though he'd splashed it into her face as he moved around. Now the significance of this struck her with full force. She could drown before he freed her!

She sucked in a quick breath. Suddenly his youthful positive solid determination didn't seem enough to get her through this mess.

As he started to shimmy backwards out the window through which he'd come, she reached out and gripped his arm. "Do you have a cell phone on you?"

He nodded. "Right. I'll call the Highway Patrol again."

"No! I need to call my daughter. She's having a baby. Today. She's expecting me. I don't want her worried about where I am while she's in labor."

He stared at her for a moment then reached into his jeans and pulled out his cell and offered it to her.

Instead of taking the phone, she pulled him closer until she was staring into his honey-brown eyes. "Now listen to me, Will. My daughter can't lose her mother on the day her first child is born. You got to get me out of here."

She saw in his expression that she had surprised him by her calm but he covered it very quickly. Then he smiled that confident, just short of cocky, smile that had been the first thing she noticed about him. "I promise, Beverly."

She drew in a slow breath to ease the fear she felt as she watched her rescuer – Will -- shimmy back out of sight.

"Hello, Randal? No, I'm fine. How is she doing?" Cliff's voice was an octave higher than usual with excitement. "Now listen carefully, Cliff, and don't let Angelique see your expression change. I've been in a fender bender. I'm fine! But it's slowing me up. If Angelique asks, tell her I pulled off the road because of the weather. That's right. I'll be along shortly. And I expect to see my grandchild when I get there."

As she spoke she felt the chill touch of rainwater on her scalp. "I got to go now, Randal. Take good care of her."

Beverly closed her eyes and let the cell fall from her hand, suddenly too weak to hold it. She heard a splash by her ear but it barely made an impression. She was tired, more tired than she'd ever been in her life.

Will Solomon had seen enough death to last him two lifetimes. A firefighter by profession, and a recent veteran of the Iraq war, he'd spent his adult life saving lives, though he had lost a few. Sometimes he came upon the deed after the fact. The latest was unlucky truck driver who had died instantly, ejected through the windshield when his rig hit a stand of pines. He was not about to lose the woman whose car had tumbled into a ravine trying to avoid that truck.

When he'd made his way through the mud and weeds up to the top of the embankment, he found two state troopers in parkas standing in the whipping rain watching him.

"Anybody alive down there?" one shouted against the wind.

"Woman! Trapped in her car! And the water is rising!"

The men seemed to understand without conversation what action was required. Each ran to his own vehicle and returned with cable and jacks and wire cutters, anything anyone had that might help free the victim.

They descended the embankment quickly. Will, who got there first, aimed his heavy duty flashlight through the windshield at the woman. She wasn't moving and her eyes were shut.

"Is she dead?" shouted one of the troopers coming up behind him.

"No." But Will knew that was possibly a lie. She'd seemed fine when he left her but life had a way of betraying itself when trauma was involved.

His heart beating thickly in his chest, he shouted over his shoulder to the two men. "You get on the other side! If she's ok, we're going to have to right this car!"

He knelt down and slid into the passenger window once again. The water was noticeably deeper. She was hanging there, so still, her hair trailing out in the muddy rivulets flowing by the top of her head. He reached out and shook her. "Beverly? Beverly? You still alive?"

She opened her eyes. She looked angry but that was fine, better than fine, because it meant she was still fighting for her life. Then she offered him the first smile he'd seen on her poor battered face. "Are you going to just stare or can you save me?"

Will felt as if he'd been given a gift. "Okay. Sure, I can do that."

Chapter Two

Beverly had been medevac-ed back to a Little Rock hospital the day before and was still groggy from the anesthesia she'd been given for the procedures to set her broken wrist and realign her broken nose. Both her mother and her Aunt Casa had flown in from Chicago to offer their support. She appreciated their presence but didn't feel like making the effort to speak. So she kept her eyes shut to keep them from knowing she was awake.

"If you're not more careful with your outfits, you're going to start folks commenting on your age." Erica Burns, Beverly's mother, perched on the edge of her daughter's hospital bed.

"What do you mean? I look good!" Casa's laughter was as edgy as her outfit of peep-toe heels, skinny jeans and a leopard top. "I may be fifty-six and had two boys, but I never let my figure go."

"You let those boys go wild, is what you did," Erica responded.

"After Leon died, I had no choice but to work hard. But I did my job at home. You ever see any babies' mamas running round my house? That says something."

"It says you were lucky."

Beverly sighed to herself. Her mother and aunt were sisters but they were about as alike as peaches and okra. They couldn't hold a conversation for more than two sentences before one was on the other about something.

"When Jourdan and Beverly were born, I took a full semester of maternity leave each time from my teaching position."

"That's because you were all they had." Casa snapped her gum. "For all the time Hayden spent in your lives, you might as well have been—."

--A single woman with a ring on her finger, Beverly finished in her thoughts. That was Aunt Casa's way of expressing her opinion of her sister's husband's frequent absences during their marriage.

"I've asked you not to talk about Hayden," Beverly heard her mother say in a tight voice.

"You bought him up." Casa sighed. "Fine. I'll take the man out of it. No woman should stay in an unhappy situation. Get up, get out, and get on with the next good thing! That's what I say."

"I left Hayden."

"Not until after Beverly jumped up and married his protégée just to please him. Eighteen years old! And a baby nine months later. What did she know about life?"

Beverly winced. I knew nothing!

"Hush, Casa! Beverly might hear you." Beverly held her breathe as her mother stroked her cheek to see if she got a response. Finally she moved away.

"All I'm saying is Beverly may have got up and got out quick after she realized her marriage was a mistake. But the girl never got on with finding the next man."

"Beverly's too smart to think a man can solve her problems. She'll find someone when she's ready."

"You've got to be looking to find one. You see a man in her life? No. She spends all her time living through her daughter."

"Now, sister, don't…"

"What? Tell a truth?"

Beverly's eyes opened a slit as Casa pulled her sister's arm to draw her away from the bed to the corner. Yet Beverly heard every stinging word when Casa spoke again. "You ever wonder if Angelique moved to Shreveport to get breathing room away from her mama? But still Beverly's ripping and running up and down the highway to see to every little thing for a grown woman with a perfectly good husband!"

That wasn't fair! Angelique asked me to come for the birth.

Her mother echoed her thoughts aloud. "Angelique asked her mother to come the Shreveport each time."

Casa sniffed. "Then maybe Angelique needs to do some growing up, too."

Beverly swallowed carefully. That was something she had begun to think herself, but then Angelique seemed to need her. For everything.

Casa was on a roll, speaking her mind as she usually did. "Beverly might not be twenty but if I had her looks and talent I'd have more self-respect than to almost die trying to get to the birth of a baby that didn't need me in the delivery room. My niece needs to live her own life for a change!"

Hurt by her aunt's criticism, Beverly turned her head away. Is that how my relatives see me? Pitiful and over-bearing?

So what? They had no right to pick her apart like a fried chicken wing! What she did in her life was none of their business…even if they are right.

The fire went out of her and Beverly sank deeper in her pillow. Who was she to argue in favor of her sorry old life? Aunt Casa was right. I haven't really lived in years, and now my life almost ended on a rain-slicked highway!

That realization hit Beverly hard, as if the airbag were exploding against her once again. She squeezed her shut eyes to keep tears from escaping with her thoughts.

A that moment the plastic surgeon swung through the door at a pace that surprised the three women. "Well, how are you doing?"

Even though both her mother and aunt tried to answer for her, Beverly noticed the surgeon kept his gaze on her, waiting for a reply. "I'm okay." Her voice felt thick in her mouth, as if she'd been to the dentist.

"That's good." He patted her foot. "The procedure went well. We were able to relocate your nose without extensive invasion. You'll have two black-and-blue eyes for a couple of weeks. Then you should be as good as new."

"Does that mean she won't have a scar?"

The surgeon looked at Erica, who'd asked the question. "No

scarring, no permanent swelling.

"What about her hand?" Erica pointed to Beverly's cast.

"That's not my department," he answered with the smile. "I'm sure her orthopedic doctor will be happy to answer all of your questions about that." Again he patted Beverly's foot, this time adding a little squeeze of her toes. "I heard they had to pry you out of your overturned vehicle."

"Yes. A young man stopped and saved her life." Casa sounded as proud as if she knew him personally. "I don't know what would have happened if he hadn't come long. God is good, all the time."

The surgeon nodded noncommittally as he looked at Beverly. "I've seen the results of other accidents like that. You were lucky."

"Lucky." Beverly smiled though she wasn't sure it registered behind the bandages. Yes, she had been lucky.

She didn't remember much about the accident. Her doctors assured her that once the trauma subsided, much of it would come back to her. She'd been told by the state patrolman who came by the hospital for her account of the accident that she owed her life to the man that had crawled through the broken window of her auto.

"They say he was like a one man demolition squad, getting help to right your vehicle before the flashflood swamped it." Aunt Casa beamed at Beverly. "Then he pried you out in the middle of the stream. You don't remember any of it?"

"No." What she could recall was a smile. Warm. Real. A hand on her face. Tender. Assuring. And feeling safe, really safe, for the first time in a long time. She wasn't about to tell that to the freckle-face trooper. But it was enough to remind her that her life was far from over. And that some changes needed to be made.

What was the punch line of that old joke her uncle like to tell? Something's got to be did about the status quo, which am Latin for the mess I is in.

The firehouse in Conway was quiet for a change. Two of the men on active duty were relaxing and eating a meal of spaghetti and garlic bread.

"It was the damndest thing." Will wagged his head at the memory. "Here's this lady suspended upside down in a car she's rolled into a ditch filling with rain water, and she's trying to give me orders!"

Eddie bobbed his head in time to the rhythm of the hip hop music playing nearby. "That's a woman for you. Always trying to tell a man another way to do his business."

"No, it wasn't exactly like that. It was more like she thought no one else could or would do anything for her." Will cocked his head to the side, thinking. "It was kinda sad, like she didn't trust anyone to look out for her."

"That's another reason to steer clear of that type." Eddie grinned, showing some of the food still in his mouth. "A woman who doesn't want a man's help when she's about to die ain't never going to thank him for anything else he might do for her."

"I wonder." Will sopped up the last of the red sauce on his plate with a thick slice of bread. "There was something about her, you know? Kinda sticks in my mind."

"It's been two weeks and you're still talking about her. A body would think you're--." Eddie's fork paused halfway to his open mouth. "Oh hell no! Come on, bro! You're young, okay looking and got a job. You could be running a stable of women and you're hung up on the one that showed you her behind?"

Will shook his head. "I'm telling you. It wasn't like that. She was hurt and scared but she wasn't even thinking about herself. She was thinking about her daughter. She could have been dying. She just didn't want her daughter to have to deal with the knowledge that her mother died trying to get to her."

"What was wrong with the daughter?"

"She was having her first child."

"Whoa! Hold up and roll back a few. The woman you're all strung out on is a grandma? You got to be outta your original mind!"

Will just grinned at his friend. "I hadn't really thought about that. She looks young."

Eddie reared back in his chair, the slight bulge at his waistband the only thickened part on his wiry body. "She can't be but so young. 'Course with all the babies having babies these last years. She could be a grandmother at thirty-two, which is two years younger than you!" He held up his hands, pretending to count on his fingers. "Let's see. Sixteen years plus another sixteen, that's some rough grandma-mother-daughter math."

"The daughter is grown and married. To a pharmaceutical rep."

"How you know all that?"

Will avoided his friend's eye because he suddenly decided that maybe he was revealing too much about something he hadn't thought enough about. "You know how it is. Sometimes you have to keep a person talking while you're trying to work out how to save them."

"Yeah, that's true." Eddie reached forward and snatched the final piece of garlic bread off Will's plate and took a big bite. "But I don't ever remember what the victim said. You were all up in her personal business."

Will casually ran a hand across the table to within a finger's reach of Eddie's bowl of peach cobbler. "I wasn't on duty, remember?"

"Even more to the point." Eddie slammed a palm down across the path of Will's wandering reach. "You crawled into an overturned car to save a stranger who almost drowned, and you weren't even on the clock." He pushed Will's hand away. "The Good Samaritan thing is frowned on by us professionals. No uniform equals less skilled judgment. You came up a hero in Iraq. I salute that. But do you see anyone hanging a medal on your chest for this last act of bravery?"

Will hunkered down over his own dish of cobbler, as if protecting it. "I didn't do it for that."

"No. You're into that noble sh--whoa! Hold up!"

Eddie lifted both hands in defense when Will half-jumped to his feet as though to attack his friend. Instead, Will reached out and palmed Eddie's cobbler while Eddie had eyes only for him.

Snickering, Will settled back into his chair with both bowls of cobbler and placed them between the walls of his forearms. After a moment, he picked up a spoon and began eating without another glance at his friend.

Eddie went and dished up another bowl for himself, and then waited until Will had swallowed a few times before speaking again. "I know you don't like to talk about that went on over there. But being a hero's a dangerous thing. It busted up your marriage and your life. You're just getting it back together. You don't need some hungry old cougar prowling around your sweet young body. What you need is some double-jointed, nubile shorty hanging on your jock."

Will turned his head and stared mildly at his companion. "That's disrespectful, bro. Women are complicated."

"Now that's your problem!" Eddie stabbed the air with his spoon for emphasis. "You don't see the simplicity in life. Get paid, get laid! That's my motto."

Will chuckled. "You're supposed to be a happily married man."

"Did I say I didn't take my paycheck home? Clarice loves her some man what brings home steady money. Awite?"

The men shared a laugh and settled in to do serious damage to their dessert.

The sound of the station house alarm brought both men to their feet at the same time.

"Damn! I was looking forward to that game about to come on," Eddie grumbled as they both scrambled into gear.

"It's a medical emergency," Will replied, having checked the dispatch. "Maybe the EMTs will beat us there and we can get back in time for most of it."

"Or maybe the emergency is a sweet young thang dying from lack of a certain kind of attention that only a hero can provide. Peep your technique."

Will gave him skeptical glance as he zipped up his coat. "What, you think you're gonna see something you haven't seen before?"

"Not unless you got a twenty-four carat dick in your drawers." Laughing, Eddie slapped Will on the back as they swung into action. "Let's do this!"

Later, lying in his bunk at the fire house, Will once again found himself thinking about Beverly. He couldn't say why. Maybe it was that she had tried so hard not to appear afraid. Or maybe it was that despite her reluctance to express her fear she had clutched him so tightly after he pried her out of that car that the EMTs had had to coax her to loosen his t-shirt from her grasp in order to lay her on the stretcher. She had looked up at him, seeming so fragile at that moment.

Will rolled over on his side and looked at the night beyond his window. He had saved a lot of people in his years as a fireman. He had done his part in Iraq, at some cost to himself. Yet no one had ever held on to him like that, as if her very being depended on him.

Maybe Eddie was right. Maybe he needed to be a hero. But that wasn't the feeling he got when he remembered Beverly Freeman. The feeling was how she felt in his arms, and how his body had behaved very unprofessionally as she clung to him.

Will smiled and adjusted himself on the narrow bed. At thirty-four, he still considered himself a young gun. Yet he hadn't felt that level of immediate and lowdown urgent interest in a woman in a while.

Or maybe he just needed to get laid.

For the first six months after his divorce, he'd hooked up here and there, never with the intention of anything serious. Serious was what had gotten him in trouble in the first place. Sherrae had just been in view when Uncle Sam called his reserve division to active duty. Until that moment, the future had not required him to think about it. But then he was leaving for war, and nature pressed him to leave a bit of himself back in the old U. S. of A. Marrying Sherrae was to make whatever might develop legal.

He pulled out his cell phone and studied the wallpaper photo of his son Mykel, and smiled. The boy was six years old, and growing like he had a deadline to meet. He knew Mykel was his child the first time he laid eyes on him four months after his birth. They shared the same high round forehead and golden gaze. He might have caught a shade of Sherrae's nose but the full lips and chin, that was all his father's, via the Solomon line.

Will slung an arm over his head. Maybe he'd made a mistake marrying a woman he no more than liked at the time, but when he thought about Mykel it seemed like something greater had had a hand in that plan. Still, he'd not been able to stop after one tour of duty to look after what he'd promised God to love and cherish. Two tours became three with stop-loss kicking in. By the time he exited Iraq and the service, he was another man in another place, and it wasn't good. Not for a long time.

Will punched his son's number.

"Hey, Mykel!"

"Daddy! Where you been?" Mykel sounded relieved. "Momma said you wasn't gonna call."

Will breathed through his nostrils. "I was out on the engine tonight. But you know I had to holler at my little man."

"Momma! Daddy was on the engine tonight!" Mykel's voice held a note of triumph that made Will glad he had called though it was past Mykel's bedtime. His ex had a way of putting him in the wrong with his son anyway she could. But his son mustn't know how much that angered him.

"Whadaya know that's good?"

"Nuthin." Mykel giggled, which his dad knew meant he had a surprise. "Only guess what? I got a B in Art. And one in Reading, too."

"Two Bs. That is good. Proud of you. We need to celebrate that."

"When?"

"This weekend."

"You picking me up?" Mykel's excitement made his tone sharp. "Can I can stay with you all weekend, too?"

"Yeah. We're good." If Sherrae didn't come up with some last-minute excuse! He could hear her shouting at Mykel to get off the phone. No, he wouldn't allow that. He needed to be with his son and his son needed him. "Time to dive under the covers."

"Ok, Dad." He could hear a muffled sound and then the whisper, "Love you."

Will's felt his throat tighten with emotion. "Love you, too. Nite, son."

He rubbed a hand over his face. Things hadn't gone his way in a while. Time to change that. He was ready to fight for partial custody of Mykel so they no longer had to beg and barter for time together.

After a second he scrolled through the rest of his messages, stopping only at one. He felt the heat of a blush touch the backs of his ears. He thought he'd deleted all text messages from Shreveport.

He had used the phone number Beverly had punched into his cell from her overturned car to get in touch with her next of kin. With her belongings spread over God's half-acre of a field in pouring rain, he'd had no other way.

Will checked the message. It was a week old, from Cliff, Beverly's son-in-law, saying she was okay and being released from the hospital. He'd included Beverly's business information, and a photo of his new baby girl.

Will shook his head. The son-in-law was a trip! He'd had to tell a stranger all about his brand new daughter's birth before he let a man tell him his mother-in-law was on her way to the hospital. He'd been reluctant to say more than he'd been a part of the rescue. But then, he'd texted a couple of times to make sure Beverly was okay.

It came as a bit of shock to learn that the woman he's saved on the Arkansas-Louisiana line lived practically on his doorstep. Little Rock, to be exact. A thirty minute drive, or less, depending on the part of town. That's where Sherrae and Mykel lived. He finessed a few more tidbits from Cliff, like the fact Beverly Freeman was single and unattached. He kept thinking that maybe Cliff would say something to his mother-in-law about Will's call and texts, and then she'd get in touch. But she hadn't.

Will wiped a hand across his mouth, feeling tense for no reason. At the time he wasn't sure he even wanted her to contact him. Might even have acted standoffish if she'd called. What if she was nothing like the woman he'd put together in his mind? He or his body might have blown things all out of proportion. So he had waited.

But now, knowing that he wasn't going to stop thinking about her anytime soon, it was time to find out what the hell was the matter with him.

Just to make certain his mind -- and most especially his body -- weren't playing tricks on him.

Chapter Three

"You're back!" Denise fell on Beverly's neck with the hug one gave a long lost friend.

"Easy, girl." Beverly laughed and gently pushed her off. "I just saw you yesterday."

"True. But that was at your house." Denise slipped a finger under the edge of her half-moon reading glasses to swipe away a tear. "You haven't been to work in two weeks. It's so good to have you back."

Beverly smiled. "It's good to be back." Except for the cast on her left hand and the unusual amount of concealer worn to cover the last traces of her black eyes, she knew she looked like her old self, too.

"Is that a new bag?" Denise pointed a French manicured nail at the zebra print purse hanging in the crook of Beverly's arm. "Don't tell me you up got up off some cash for something for yourself for a change?"

Beverly nodded, feeling a little sheepish. "Just couldn't resist."

"All right then, Ms. Freeman." Denise took the purse and held it up to herself. "How do I look?"

She was five inches shorter than Beverly with a compact body. To compensate she wore her hair in a halo of standup twists and dressed in one color at a time with spiky heels in some look-at-me hue. Today bright peacock blue heels punched up her cream blouse and slacks.

Beverly laughed. "The bag's working for you."

Denise handed it back. "Just you remember you said that when I come by to borrow it. I have a hot date with Jerdell this weekend." Jerdell was her steady man friend of three years and counting. "So tell me again about Miss Mia."

"Mia Bashelle. She's perfect, like her grandmother predicted." Beverly opened her new bag, and pulled out her digital camera, and began scrolling through the more than six dozen shots she'd taken of her new granddaughter and her parents.

After a few days at home recuperating, Beverly had flown to Shreveport to meet and spend time with her new granddaughter. She tried to pretend that the accident had been blown out of proportion. Yes, her car was a complete loss. But it was insured. No, she wasn't in any pain. How could she be when she held this beautiful bundle of joy? If her bandages alarmed Mia Bashelle, it didn't show.

"Angelique is adjusting, I hope." Denise glanced up from the camera.

Beverly nodded. "Surprisingly, Angelique is copying well with motherhood."

In fact, Angelique had frowned at any advice her mother had offered. Maybe Aunt Casa was right. She had decided to back off and wait to be asked before offering to do another thing for her daughter. It was simply bad luck that she'd caught a flu virus on her return home that kept her in bed for a few days. Now it seemed like a year since she'd been in the groove of her life.

Finally Beverly shut off her camera. "Let me get to my desk. Working from home was beginning to work my nerves. How do people do that, stay cooped up day and night in the same place?"

"I'd like to find out." Denise laughed. "Working in pjs has its appeal."

"Uh huh." Beverly reached for the mail stacked on her absent secretary's desk.

Thank goodness she ran the kind of office that could operate without her in place every minute. While many of their competitors favored big flashy marketing budgets and extravagant office accommodations, Med-Cap's offices were modest and low-key. With a B.A. in accounting in hand, Beverly had built her medical services business by word of mouth from her clients, and spent resources on keeping up to date with the latest technological assistance available. As she told Denise, who had a B.A in finance when she joined what had been a one-woman operation five years ago, their job was to save money and convert their clients' medical services into cash. The business relationship turned into friendship where they trusted one another unconditionally.

Still, she was very glad to be back in her physical world where she could keep an eye on things. Even the best team had a tendency to wind down when the boss was gone too long. For instance. "Where's Wanda?"

"Getting coffee. The machine broke. Nothing else has changed," Denise assured her, as if reading Beverly's mind. "I finished the monthly reports last night. We met all our objectives. Check it out."

"I will." All it took was a glance at Denise's posture for Beverly to realize she sounded critical. Impulsively, she hugged her friend. "Thanks for being there for me."

As she walked toward her office space, Beverly noticed that her desk was as neat as she'd left it. However, something she definitely hadn't left there was the vase of fresh pastel pink roses sitting on one corner.

She leaned down to smell them. "Oh, they're lovely! And smell good, too." She turned to Denise. "Thank you."

"You're welcome. But all I did was put them there this morning." Denise arched a brow. "Do you have a new admirer you haven't told me about?"

"You'd be the first to know." Beverly reached out to finger among the stems with her good hand to reach the card tucked into the middle of the bouquet. Using her thumb, she tried unsuccessfully to open the little envelope.

"Let me do that for you." When Beverly hesitated to hand the card over Denise made a wiggling 'gimme' gesture with her fingers. "There's no shame in needing help. You have an injured hand. What else can you do until it heals?"

Beverly eyed the envelope, murmuring, "Manage."

"You always try to manage. Won't ask—." She paused in astonishment as Beverly lifted the envelope to her mouth and withdrew the card inside it with her teeth.

Denise shrugged. "So, who are the flowers from?"

Beverly flipped the card over then frowned. "It doesn't say."

"What do you mean it doesn't say? What does it say?" When Beverly didn't answer, Denise snatched it from her. "Ha! Now I'm going to find out for myself."

Beverly refused to compete for it. She held out her hand as a silent command.

Denise stood her ground, fanning the card just out of reach. "I love you like a sister. Well, better than my sister if we truth-telling. But you are too stubborn for your own good. Someone needs to see to it that you don't miss out on the fun in life. F-U-N. You do remember the word?"

Denise held up the card to the light, as if she were studying an x-ray, and read aloud. "Welcome back. Hope you like roses."

Denise tilted her chin down and glanced at Beverly over the tops of her half -glasses. "Well, well. Ms. Freeman has got herself an admirer."

"I don't know what you're talking about. They're probably from a client."

"To begin with a client wouldn't drop fifty dollars on flowers and not sign the card. They'd want you to know who you're beholden to."

"Beholden?" Denise laughed. "Sometimes you sound like you're just up from the country."

Denise struck a pose with a fist on her hip. "Don't be calling me country when your people are still picking cotton bolls outta their nappy heads!"

It was a long-standing joke between them, since they were both Arkansans. They both laughed and hugged one another, happy to be together again.

"What did I miss?" Wanda, their twenty-two year old secretary, stood in the front door with a cup holder with three steaming cups in it.

"You missed Beverly's return for one." Denise swooped in to relieve her of a cup. "And the reading of the card that came with the flowers."

Wanda's eyes got big. "Oooh, I knew I shoulda told that barista to stop macking and brew those shots. What did it say?"

"Nothing." her companions answered in unison and turned toward their desks.

"I thought you talked to her about professional dress," Beverly said with a backwards glance.

"I did and she was doing better." Denise rolled her eyes. "At least she's wearing leggings."

Beverly shook her head. Wanda liked spandex short skirts. The one she has on today was short and tight enough to have been used as a tube top.

It was just about lunchtime when the door opened again. Med-Cap seldom had walk-in traffic. The business of medical billing services was done mostly by phone, pick-up, mail, computer hook-up, and online messaging. So all three women looked up when the door buzzer sounded. They all saw variations of the same thing: Young African American male, loose athletic build, easy stride, really nice smile.

Wanda noticed he had big hands and a wide forehead. She liked a man who could really hold on to a woman. Her grandmother told her a wide forehead meant a generous nature. What he had he'd share. Pleasure and generosity packaged like that? Yummy!

Denise eyed his shoes, real shoes, not expensive sneakers. Then her gaze traveled upwards over slacks that fit slim hips and a firm butt to his tucked-in shirt that revealed the contours of a trim muscular build. In a world of baggie pants and oversized shirts, she as a sucker for a trim fit.

Beverly was the last to react. Tall, dark and handsome was a cliché for a reason. But more than that kept her staring at their visitor instead of switching immediately into business-with-potential-client mode. There was something uncomfortably familiar about this man that she couldn't quite place.

When he saw her, his eyes widened slightly in that sign of recognition one can't fake. And then his smile widened into a confident curve of pleasure. That's when her mind locked into place with the realization of who he was.

He was her rescuer!

Chapter Four

Beverly felt her body flush hot, then cold, then extra hot! He was coming toward her with a purposeful stride she couldn't mistake. And a smile she couldn't forget. That self-assured smile arrowed through her middle and lodged in a more private area, lower down.

She rose to her feet. She hadn't been certain she'd remembered the face of the man who had saved her life. Now she knew she did. This golden-eyed man with the was the one she had been dreaming about recently. And -- lawd a' mercy -- they weren't the kind of dreams she wanted to share, even with her girlfriends.

"Ms. Freeman?" He held out his hand. "We met before but let's make it formal. My name's Will--."

"William Solomon. I remember." Beverly took his hand reluctantly. Touching him was like setting foot in her private Wonderland. Afraid he would notice her embarrassment, she glanced nervously past him. "How are you, Mr. Solomon?"

He cocked a brow at her and then followed her gaze back two the two other women in the office who had left their desks and were staring openly at him. "How are you ladies doing today?" he asked them with a nod of greeting.

"Better now you're here," Wanda answered, grinning, and received an elbow dig from Denise. "What?"

"Come on, Wanda. I need to show you something in the back." Denise hooked her arm through the secretary's and practically dragged her toward the room that served as both office kitchen and file room.

"Do you know who he is?" Wanda asked loud enough for Will and Beverly to hear. Denise shushed her but Wanda was on a roll. "Well, I know he don't look like a doctor but you never can tell…" Her voice trailed off as Denise gave the rear door a shove with her foot.

When Beverly's gaze came back to Will, she couldn't think of anything to say. The wonderland she'd been sucked into also had a nightmare underground. Without any warning, she was once again upside down in a totaled car, shivering, while Will Solomon's attractive face was the only hopeful thing in view.

He was studying her with an intensity that made her want to scratch. Then he nodded slowly. "Your nose looks fine, considering I didn't see it before."

He looked down at her cast. "How is that healing? Giving you any pain?"

"It-I'm fine. Thank you for asking." She couldn't believe how panicky, how jerked out of her own skin, she felt standing before this man. Her mind went blank, a stupid no-coins-in-the-box kind of empty. When an idea did rattle down the chute she said the first thing that came with it.

"Why did you find me?"

He grinned. "Don't you mean how did I find you?"

"No. I can see that you did." She could feel reality returning, and with it came an automatic withdrawal that was second nature to her. She folded her arms before her chest, right over left as if to protect her cast. "So my question is why?"

He held out a package she hadn't noticed he had with him. Pretty paper covered it in shades of pink and cream stamped with the words 'Welcome Baby" all over it. "For your grandchild, Mia. I hope she and your daughter are doing well?"

"Why yes. How did you know her names?"

"I was the one who called your son-in-law to tell him about your accident."

"No one told me." Beverly frowned and reached up, about the rub the bridge of her nose until she remembered that she was still tender there. "To be honest, Mr. Solomon, I don't remember a lot." Liar, lair, pants on fire! "I guess I was operating on adrenalin. Trying to stay alive."

"That's a good thing." He placed the package on her desk and folded his arms across his chest, looking relaxed. "You kept your head. I admired that about you."

Beverly felt a blush sting her neck at his compliment. "If I wasn't rattled I'm sure I would have called 911 instead of my daughter."

He nodded. "You did worry more about your daughter than yourself."

"I had cause. Angelique and Cliff lost a pregnancy in her fourth month last summer. I wanted to be there to assure her that everything would be fine this time."

He whistled. "You got that kinda pull? Knowing beforehand how things will turn out?"

Beverly had to smile. She sounded like a micro-managing fool.

He nudged the box on her desk.

She picked it up, feeling awkward. "You really didn't need to do this."

He only smiled and refolded his arms.

She took her time opening it, sliding a nail under each piece of tape so she wouldn't tear the paper. "It really should be Angelique opening a baby gift."

He didn't respond.

It was a complete layette in pale pink. She lifted out a sleeping sacque, two onesies, matching booties and a hat, two bibs, and a receiving blankct. Each was embroidered with Mai Bashelle's name the softest cotton she had ever touched. She looked up at him, "How did you know her name?"

He bit his lower lip and grinned. "I got pull, too."

"This is too much. It must have coast a small fortune." She covered it quickly, trying not to damage the paper. "It's beautiful. But I couldn't possibly—."

"Say thank you?"

His comment was right on the money, and she knew it. "You're right. I haven't thanked you for all that you did for me. Thank you."

"Is that all?"

For a second Beverly couldn't imagine what he might mean. And then, with a thud in her middle, she thought she did. She reached for her purse. "But of course. You've earned some sort of reward."

"I hope you're not about to insult me after you've already injured my good will."

Her head jerked up in his direction. "What are you talking about?"

He spread his arms and flexed his shoulders. "You refused my gift after I put a considerable amount of pressure on my sister to complete it before I drove all the way to Little Rock to see you."

"Your sister made this?"

"She designs and sells infant clothing under that label "Karibu BeBe. It's out of Memphis."

"I've heard of her." Beverly fingered the edge of the receiving blanket. He came in from out of town to see her? He said see her, not bring the gift. There was a difference.

"The gift is truly lovely." She looked up, allowing herself really to look at the handsome man before her for the first time. He seemed sincere. "I accept. Thank you."

"That didn't hurt too much, did it?" The smile, the one that had saved her life, again spread across his face.

She smiled back. "I'm sorry. This is such a shock. I didn't think I'd ever see you again."

He shrugged. "I gave you my contact information."

"It was lost at the hospital."

"Why didn't you ask the state police for my information?"

Beverly blinked. He was being awfully persistent. "I didn't think of that."

He didn't call her a liar but somehow she knew that he knew that she wasn't being completely honest. To give herself something to do, she quickly gathered up the present and placed it on the credenza behind her desk.

"Now about that reward."

Her head swiveled in his direction. "Yes? What do you want?"

"I'm glad you asked. I think I deserve a pleasant memory of you to replace my – ah, first impression."

Her guard went up. "I made a bad impression?"

"Let's say you were at your best, under the circumstances. I'd like to see what your best is like when you're really trying."

She couldn't mistake the challenge in his tone. He was flirting with her! How did he know she couldn't resist a challenge? "How long are you in town?"

"How much time do you need?"

"Not that much." She glanced at her calendar on her desk, pretended she didn't know her schedule. "How about dinner tonight?"

"How about dinner in two weeks?" He laughed at her expression. "Now hear me out. This is your first day back on the job. You must have lots of catching up to do." He glanced around the office. "I can see you are a woman with a business life. I respect that. Miss Independence. Nice."

"Yes, I am busy." She tried not to let her disappointment show. "And behind."

"Besides, I prefer Friday night dining. I'm off duty in two weeks." He pulled a card out of his pocket and laid it on the desk beside her. "That'll give us the whole evening to get to know one another."

I don't know…" But he wasn't listening. He was backtracking toward the front door.

When he got there he gave her a little wave. "A pleasure to see you again, Beverly. Two weeks. I'll call you." Just like that, he was out the door.

"Well, well, well!"

Beverly turned. Denise now stood in the doorway to their filing room. How long she had been listening to their conversation was anyone's guess.

"I thought you didn't know the name of your savior."

"I didn't remember it until he walked through the door." Beverly picked up the card he left. It was a blank business card in which he had neatly penned his name and cell phone number. He had come prepared to leave his digits. What did that mean?

Wanda pushed past Denise. "Lordy Jesus! I'd jump off the Big Dam Bridge if I knew a man that fine was gonna save me."

"Don't blaspheme, Wanda. Isn't that your phone ringing?" Denise leaned against the door jamb, while Wanda hurried to answer the call at the front desk. "Tell me why you didn't introduce us?"

Damn! She'd been so caught up in confronted her own fantasy that she'd completely forgotten to do even that!

Beverly looked away from her friend. "I didn't know what to say." The lie was so big she could have driven a Hummer through it. "I thought he was much older. He's just ah – young." No woman in her right mind would think of that much male as a boy.

She stole a glance at her friend to see how this was going down. "He just wanted to make sure I was okay."

"He already put his life in danger to do that." Denise raised her brows at Beverly. "If someone had done that for me, he wouldn't have had to look me up afterwards. I'd have tracked him with a big ole bundle of thank yous!"

Beverly cringed at the thought of how ungrateful she must seem. "I wasn't sure what the protocol was."

"The protocol? It's, 'Hello. Thank you for saving my life.' How hard is that?"

Beverly hunched a shoulder, trying to sound offhand. "A woman can't be too careful these days. He might have been the kind of person who expected a generous reward." She glanced at the expensive lovely layette set. Did he really have a sister who made those things?

"That's right. Any man who seems interested in Beverly Freeman has to have an underhanded motive." Denise threw up her hands and came marching into the room.

"Girl, get real! It's been more than two years since you allowed a man to walk through your door. And here one tracks you down after meeting you on the worst day of your life. You've been praying for a better way. This could be it. Don't refuse the gift."

Beverly looked at her curiously. "What do you mean?"

"That man didn't come here today to bring a baby gift. That's a man who knows what he wants. And what he wanted was to see you, if you need clarification."

Beverly couldn't keep herself from glancing at the door Will had just stepped through. "What do you think I should do?"

"When a man that fine says he wants to have dinner with you, you accept."

"He asked you out?" Wanda had returned and spoke to Beverly. "I didn't hear the part about him asking you out. Denise was blocking the door."

"It's not a date. It's a thank you dinner. He's… well, he's too young for me to consider dating."

"Too young?" Wanda looked between them. "How young do you think he is?"

Beverly didn't want to encourage them. "Oh—twenty-eight."

"I don't think he's that young." Denise gave Beverly the fisheye. "I'd say he's in his thirties. And cute. With a great body. I can see how he pulled you out of that wreck without any help."

"Ooh, I like a man that can handle business!" Wanda tried for a high five with Denise but got left hanging.

"If you ladies will excuse me, I have half a day's work piled up and waiting." Beverly gestured in dismissal with her fingers.

She heard Denise mumble as she turned her back, "I just hope you will follow up with that man."

Once behind her deck Beverly plugged iPod buds into her ears, as she often did when she needed to get a lot of work done without distractions. The song that came on was one calculated to completely destroy her train of thought. It was Ne-Yo, crooning about his new interest in "Miss Independent." That's what Will had called her!

Beverly hit the forward button on her iPod. Next up was John Legend singing, "Give me the Green Light." The tunes were stacked against her.

She propped her chin on her hand. So she had remembered Will, remembered every little thing about him in the weeks since the accident, but hadn't allowed herself to admit who he was.

Her family doctor remarked repeatedly on how well she was coping with the aftermath of her accident. She kept asking Beverly if she felt any anxiety or suffered irrational fears. No, she didn't. She was even driving again, a loaner until she could decide on a new car. Once her memory began returning, it was not about the accident but about her rescuer Will Solomon.

Beverly bit her lip. In the beginning, only vivid impressions came and went, like the warmth of his smile as he kept her calm. Then the honey color of his eyes lit from within began to preoccupy her daydreams. The solid feel of his hand grasping hers let her sleep through the night. His strength as he scooped her out of the wreckage when she was finally free made her feel safe alone in her bed. Those impressions and more played over and over in her mind until they gradually transformed her rescuer from object of comfort to object of her desire.

Beverly crossed her legs under her desk and glanced around, to check that her colleagues were no longer watching her. That was the problem!

Even when the dreams turned steamy, she indulged them. She was a single healthy woman, and alone. It seemed safe to create erotic fantasies about a man she was unlikely to meet again. No harm, no foul.

But then there he was this morning, in the flesh, looking better and more real than any dream. It was pure unexpected lust that had made her act so strangely.

In her ears, John Legend sang about being ready to go right now!

She hated to admit it, but she had secretly hoped against every rational reason to the contrary that they would meet again. Yet she hadn't planned to seek him out. It was scary, and thrilling, to look at a man and feel the rush of carnal hunger other women opened joked about but that she had long ago decided she was not capable of feeling.

…checking your smile…

Could a man that fine, that young, really be interested in her?

Beverly found herself smiling. He had found her. He had traced her down and sent her roses. She just knew now they were from him. He might not even have noticed the age difference. Men were often generous in their assessment of a woman, as long as she kept herself up. She was tall and slim, what her ex called a 'tightly wrapped package' but it wasn't meant as a compliment. He meant she was reserved and dignified, two things he found toward the end of their brief marriage to be the two things he disliked the most about her.

Beverly began twirling her pen round and round on her desktop. Yet there was no reason in the world to think Will might not be interested… until she remembered that he'd called her "ma'am" right from the moment he'd crawled into her car to try to save her.

"Ma'am" was how younger people in the South referred to an older woman.

She had turned forty a month ago, an event she would not allow anyone, including herself, to celebrate. Thirty had whizzed by so fast she couldn't remember it. No, that was the year she began building her business. In those days the men she met were more of a disruption than a comfort. They demanded her time when she didn't have enough for eating and sleeping properly after hustling at work and then caring for a daughter at home. She didn't chase them away, they left.

A decade later when the Big 4-0 jumped up before her eyes she wasn't ready to accept that she had been single for twenty years, with no prospects in sight. She wanted to pretend she had more time before the calendar pointed out the fact she was no longer really young. Perhaps aging stopped for those lucky "Sex in the City"- type singles but she was an ordinary woman. Time in the real world had a way of outing a person. She was now a grandmother of a seven-pound thirteen-ounce baby girl named Mia Bashelle.

I'm ready to go right now!

Beverly snatched off her earphones and put the iPod in the drawer. Enough of that!

She took a deep breath and deliberately uncrossed her legs. She had to honest with herself. There might only be a few years between them. But those years would seem like a generation between a single man and a grandmother.

So, she would keep her distance. She had promised him a thank-you dinner that he seemed eager enough to have. Two weeks should give her enough time to tame her dreams, and her libido. The last thing she wanted to do at this point in her life was make a fool of herself over a man, especially a younger man.

Even so, at the end of the day, she picked up the card and the roses, and took them home with her.

Chapter Five

Will ran his tongue over his teeth as he checked out the trendy Kavanaugh Boulevard restaurant Beverly had chosen for their dinner. It was an upscale place featuring lots of dark polished-wood surfaces, exposed brickwork, and strategic lighting that gave customers the feeling of seclusion even through he and Beverly sat at a table near the front window.

A substantial bar, running the full length of one wall of the long narrow space, formed the spine and hub of the venue. From where he sat he could see the crush of professionals vying for that first Friday evening letdown-to-get-down drink. Black, white, Latino and otherwise, they had one thing in common. They were still dressed for business in a place that in another hour or two would likely turn urban casual. That wasn't the only thing out of sync. It was six p.m. What the hell kinda time was that for a celebration dinner? It was senior-citizen early-bird special time.

Will casually eyed his table companion, who was busy re-arranging her napkin in her lap. He should have known she was up to something when he called and she already had a time and place, and insisted on meeting him there. The second he saw how she was dressed, in a buttoned-up trouser suit more fitted for a business meeting than a Friday night out, he knew he'd made a mistake in pushing this date. One of the Sisters of the Traveling Pantsuits! She was some kind of uptight.

"Would you like a drink?" The waiter gave them an indifferent glance, as if he was accustomed to a woman trying way too hard to look like she was not with the man with her.

"I'll have a white wine, house wine will do." Beverly said this while barely moving her lips. Maybe she couldn't, Will mused. With her hair slicked back so tight it seemed painted on her head, she might have lost all feeling in her face.

"What's on tap?" Will grinned at Beverly who didn't respond in kind.

The waiter ran through the beer list. "We're very proud of our wine list, too. Perhaps you'd prefer to peruse it first."

Will waved away the wine card. "Dos Equis Amber, por favor."

"You speak Spanish?" It was the first personal question she had directed at him since he sat down. He wasn't late but she had been there ahead him, as if he had kept her waiting.

"Un poco. In my profession it helps to speak a little of whatever you can pick up."

Her eyes flickered. "Your profession?"

Okay, so that's what she wanted to know. "I'm a fireman. Have been since college. It's a family tradition."

"Oh. That explains your expertise in rescue missions. Interesting."

He could tell by the way she said it she didn't even begin to mean it. It annoyed him that she seemed to be trying to find reasons not to like him. It reminded him of Eddie's teasing him about always wanting to play the hero.

He tried again. "So, what do you do when you're not working?"

She glanced up from her lap. "Not much. I work a lot."

"I work hard. But I like to play, too."

She seemed to consider her response a long time before she said, "What do you do when you're not working?"

In a split second Will thought about and rejected three answers. They went from bad to worse and, truly, why was he here if only to antagonize her? "I like to swim. I play handball at the Y. I play a little guitar."

"Seriously?"

"Well, not entirely seriously. I hacked a few chords for a hard rock band back in the day. But mostly now I sit in on a local session when I'm asked."

She stared at him. "You and Jimi Hendricks?"

"More like Me'Shell Ndegeocello." She stared blankly. "Gnarls Barkley? Living Colour?"

"Wasn't that a TV show?"

"Yeah." Will stroked his upper lip to hide his smile. In Living Color was the correct name of the Wayans brothers' TV show, but why argue? The woman was not into hard rock.

"Your beverages." When the waiter set a beer before him, Will didn't wait for her before taking a swig. This whole evening was getting hard to swallow.

"Are you ready to order?"

"Yes—no--." They looked at each other.

The waiter smiled. "Why don't I give you a little more time?"

"No, that's all right." She looked at Will, who had said no. "Unless you're not ready."

"No. Fine. I'm ready." He flipped open the menu and smiled at what he saw. "I'll have the burger and fries."

Her eyes widened. "Oh, but this place is known for its seafood and steaks. Maybe you should reconsider. After all, this dinner is your reward."

For the first time the waiter's expression brightened in interest as his gaze swung between them.

Will could guess what the waiter was thinking. "I'll save my reward for later." He let a lecherous grin ease into his expression. "After all, we have all evening."

He saw her withdraw behind her eyes, as if it was possible for her to retreat even more from him. But she asked for it, sitting there like a poker with an I-smell-something expression on her face. She'd asked him out, sort of. He might not have been her type. But damn! He wasn't something she should be ashamed to be seen with.

Jaw tightening, he glanced up at the waiter. "Burger. Fries. It is on the menu."

"It certainly is." The waiter looked at Beverly. "Ma'am?"

"I'll have the Ahi tuna specialty." Her voice was only a breath.

Will took another long pull on his beer. Over the end of his bottle he noticed a Miss Dark and Lovely with long soft waves eyeing him at the bar. He held her gaze a second, registered her interest, and then looked away. Another time he might have smiled. That was how he was wired. Southerners smile at shee-allt, a New Jersey brother in his division liked to say. But Will didn't like it when a woman openly tried to poach another woman's man.

He looked down at his empty bottle and wondered where the beer went. He was drinking much to fast on an empty stomach. Tension was gonna make him sweat in a minute. Got to handle that!

"So, what types of music do you like?"

He tone must have startled Beverly, who had been gazing out of the window. She turned toward him, her eyes wide. "I like lots of different types."

He leaned back in his chair and stretched out a leg. "Is it a secret?"

"Oh, I like Floetry, Alicia Keyes, Beyonce, some Mary J. Blige…"

"That's a nice grouping." But was she trying to tell him something he hadn't even considered? That was an all-female line up.

"Outkast, well, I buy the censored version of their albums at Walmart. And John Legend." Her voice turned soft. "I really like him. He's romantic but not mushy."

Will fingered his empty bottle. "Not mushy. What else do you like about him?"

She smiled. "His songs are about the kind of man who would make a woman smile a lot when he's around. Funny. Smart. Not so serious. Listening to his lyrics. If he's anything like them."

Listen to this! She was talking and smiling. "Give me an example."

She suddenly looked nervous again. "Why?"

He shrugged. Talking to this woman was like picking a pecan! "We've got to talk about something." He leaned forward until both forearms rested on the table. "Or I can pay the bill and we can go home, alone." He quickly shook his head. "No, that's not right."

He licked his lips and then trained a steady gaze on her wary expression. "I came out prepared to enjoy a lady's company tonight. I don't know how or why things got off the tracks right at first. If you are truly miserable, we can go our own ways. No harm, no foul. Just tell me how it needs to be."

He watched her regroup behind her bittersweet chocolate gaze. "I'm sorry if I'm such unpleasant company—."

"--No harm, no foul." He reached out and touched her arm with just one finger. "I'm going to take a little stroll. And when I come back you can be here and we start over, or not, and I'll understand. Understand?"

To his surprise she seemed to shrink in her chair, looking suddenly younger and softer and more vulnerable. "Fine."

He added a second finger to the one on her arm, his voice quiet. "I really hope you're still here."

He headed toward the back of the establishment, where he heard musicians warming up, and where he expected to find the john. As he passed the bar, a shoulder bump and a smile checked his advance.

It was the Miss Chocolate Drop. She smiled coyly at him from beneath two pairs of fake eyelashes. "Bring your aunt to dinner?"

He smiled slowly, leaned into her, and whispered.

She jerked back with a startled expression before he continued his stroll. Sometimes it had to be said.

Watching Will walk away, Beverly wrestled the shame and anger and anxiety warring within her. She was acting as if a combination of Godzilla and Diary of a Mad Black Woman had jumped in taken her over, mind and body!

She reached for her wine but her hand was shaking so badly she didn't pick it up. She hadn't wanted white wine in the first place. She'd wanted a pomegranate martini. But then she'd thought he might think that she was…

A light bulb when off in her head illuminating the sorry trail her thoughts had gone down. She had fallen headfirst into the 'what if' trap.

Two weeks ago she had been certain she could handle tonight. She'd been out to dinner so many times with a potential client she knew little or nothing about, and charmed them by the end of the meal. She knew just what to say, how to be interested without being nosy, how to flatter without it sounding like a come-on. Having a pleasant dinner with the man who'd saved her life should have been more than easy.

When she called Angelique the evening after Will's visit to her office, her daughter said she was relieved that her mother finally knew about his calls to her.

"He asked us not to tell you he was checking up on you. He said he didn't want to intrude on your privacy. He sounded sincere so Cliff and I tried to honor that. However, Cliff can tell you I wasn't entirely happy he gave Mr. Solomon your business address. Still, I'm glad to hear he's the real deal. So, what's he like?"

Beverly wanted to keep her opinion of Will Solomon to herself. To change the subject she mentioned the gift.

"A complete Karibu BeBe layette? Oh my! They're so expensive. Cliff said we couldn't even think about wanting one. Now my Mia Bashelle has the whole layette!" That settled, Beverly thought she knew how to proceed. She called up a favorite upscale eatery in midtown for a reservation. Not wanting to presume she would dominate his entire evening in town, she made it early in case Mr. Solomon had somewhere to go later. She even called him to make sure he knew when and where to meet her. No need for him to have to escort her home if he had another appointment.

The dreams had stopped, cut short by the reality check of his appearance. Life got back into a rhythm she was accustomed to. Everything was copacetic. Until she woke up this morning.

The more she thought about the evening ahead, the more nervous she became. Nothing in her closet seemed appropriate. What if he thought she dressed too conservatively? Or worse. What if he thought she had tried too hard to look like a sweet young thang when it was clear she couldn't pull off that kind of look?

She hadn't had a chance to keep her hair appointment the day before because a meeting ran late with a new client, a large medical clinic that had just opened its doors on the far west side and wanted to parse every sentence in their contract. She pulled it back and up into a French twist. But the ends around her face weren't cooperating. By the time she gelled and sprayed them into submission, her head looked Symonized.

As for her outfit, she'd put on a feminine halter-neck top with a ruffled front under her business suit. It bared her shoulders and a good portion of her back. It was the kind of top that changed any pair of pants into a dressy casual evening look. But then at lunch, Wanda had run into her with a cup of tomato basil soup in hand. No amount of rinsing could save those ruffles. There was no time to go home and change so she'd buttoned up her jacket and come on.

She thought it would be okay until she saw the look on Will's face.

No man she'd ever known could successfully hide his reaction to the way a woman was dressed. Will was smoother than most, shifting his gaze away from her pantsuit to her face as he smiled in greeting. But his first disappointed expression was enough to put her back up, and she'd not been able to smooth herself down again, mostly because he looked better than she did. Dressed in nicely creased slacks, a thin v-neck sweater, and caramel leather jacket, he turned every head when he walked in. They must all have wondered by he was with her.

Looking over the women at the bar, it was easy to spot the single ladies. It wasn't only the absence of a certain kind of ring on a particular finger. They looked single, in sophisticated yet flirtatious outfits. At ease with themselves as they perused the gathering, they could tense a fraction when they spied a man looking back at them. She had always been good at judging other people. That's why she hadn't missed the obvious interest in Will by a young woman at the bar. Psychology might have been her field, if she hadn't derailed her life by marrying at eighteen.

That glass of wine looked really good all of a sudden. Beverly picked it up and took a thirsty swallow.

They say every girl wants to marry her father. I did, Beverly mused.

It certainly explained her rush to the altar at eighteen, despite everyone's objection but her dad's.

Her father was in the diplomatic corps. He wasn't home much while she was growing up. She was thirteen when she learned that he wasn't faithful either, but he was discreet. Her mother looked the other way and they maintained a life until her brother Jourdan left for college, and she decided to marry. Her parents lived apart after that, not divorced but not exactly married either.

Beverly twisted the diamond ring on her right hand as she stared out the window at a darkening sky brightened by a bank of clouds turned amber in the sunset. That usually meant that rain was on the way.

She had wanted to be married because her father thought it was a good idea. He offered so few opinions about her life that when he introduced her to Marlon, she wanted to please him. Plus, she thought she was in love. Marlon Freeman, eight years older, seemed the ideal mate. Dad's protégée at the State Department, he was sophisticated, already in a career, and headed for better things. The kind of man every woman would admire. And admire they did. Turned out he was like Dad in everyway; self-interested, on the lookout for the next big break, and not above cheating on his wife.

Beverly stopped twisting her ring, and picked up her wine again. She wasn't her mother. She had gotten up, gotten out, and gotten on with her life after only two years and the birth of Angelique.

She set her glass down a little hard and looked around in the direction Will had taken but he was nowhere to be seen. A new thought struck her. Maybe he was giving her enough time to pay the check and--."

No, there he was, coming toward the table with a determined stride.

"You came back—."

"You stayed—."

"I'm glad." They had spoken together and after a second's hesitation they both expelled a little embarrassed laugh.

Will slid into his chair, an eager expression on his face. "Okay, so here's how I see it. What happened before is getting in the way of now. So let's just say we are two people who've just met, maybe at the bar, and decided to get to know one another over dinner. No history, no promises. You cool with that?"

"I'm cool." Beverly picked up her wine glass only to discover it was empty.

He picked up and shook his empty beer bottle. "How about another round?"

"I'd like to order a pomegranate martini, instead."

A slow smile spread across his face. "So you do take chances."

"That's taking a chance?"

"Vodka on top of wine? That's a challenge to my stomach these days. I have to pick a liquor and stick to it for the night."

"I hear that. Acid reflux comes with --." She blinked, she'd nearly said with age.

He signaled their waiter. "I chew through a roll of antacids a day, some days. Two tough alarms in a row, I can feel my stomach grinding on itself."

At that moment the wait staff arrived with their plates. Hers was a lovely display of pan-seared tuna slices and grilled vegetables. Will's plate contained two tall narrow burgers, stacked up side-by-side like twin high rises. Twisty orange fries swirled over the edge of a fancy martini glass the waiter set beside the plate.

Amused, Will glanced up at the waiter. "I ordered a burger and fries."

The waiter nodded. "That's our menu item. Twin charred sirloin burgers, served with white Cheddar, arugula, onion marmalade, and chipotle mayo."

"And the fries are orange because...?"

"They are sweet potato fries with sea salt. We cook them in duck fat."

"Duck--!" Will chuckled and fell back in his chair.

"If you don't like it, sir..." The waiter looked doubtful.

"No, no, man. I'm liking it. Well, mostly. We'll have to ease up on the fries. Duck fat. Okay." He nodded. "Bring my companion a pomegranate martini." He looked at Beverly. "Straight up? And I'm going to definitely need another beer."

Beverly eyed his burger challenge in doubt. "How do you eat something like that?"

"You sneak up on it." He picked up a fry and swirled it in the red sauce served with it. "Sweet and sour, kind of," he said after a taste. "Don't suppose they know what a ketchup bottle is in this place."

Beverly laughed and she could feel her whole body ease out of the tension of the past hour. Just like that. The evening had changed.

She didn't care what they talked about after that. But they talked, not about their lives, about everything but that.

He talked about music. She talked about buying a new car. He knew someone who was trying to sell a late model sedan she might be interested in. They talked about movies. He liked SF and thrillers. She had seen enough of the more recent ones to hold her own, though he didn't follow up on her interest in foreign films. He liked non-fiction; biographies, and political and social history. With time on his hands at the fire station, he read a lot. She read Oprah books, and cookbooks, and lighter fare. Magazines, and three daily newspapers online.

Yet at the back of every question she asked and every reply he made, she was searching for clues about his life. She had no reason to ask him outright without revealing more than a casual interest in him. So things like, are you dating, married, seeing someone stayed off the menu of subjects.

He did manage to eat both burgers, after un-stacking the salad parts from the buns and eating them as a side dish.

The crowd thickened inside, as the sky outside turned inky with distant glimmers of lightning. It was spring, after all. Showers often bloomed late in the day.

Finally, Will leaned forward and placed his palm fully over her hand, and squeezed a little. "I think we've covered all the safe subjects. What do you say we get out of here and find something more interesting to do?"

Beverly blinked. She was feeling rather good on one wine and one martini but was he…? "Are you flirting with me?"

"Is it that obvious?"

Beverly froze in thought. This was the moment. She was interested. He was interested. No doubt about it. But she had to know if it was a pipe dream. "How old are you?"

He turned her hand over until they were palm to palm. The current that jumped between them seemed to hum in the air. "Old enough to date. Why?"

"I think you know. I'm older than you."

He grinned. "I kinda figured that. Not on your looks. Just you have a grown daughter."

Beverly looked toward the window and saw lightning sketch the sky. He wasn't going to make this easy. "I'm forty." She glanced back at him.

He nodded. "Forty's the new thirty. That's about right."

She sucked in a breath. "You're thirty?"

He shook his head, the curve of his lips deepened.

"Not thirty?" Oh lord! He was a child.

He wouldn't let go of her hand when she tried to pull away. Instead he laced his fingers between hers. "If you were thirty and I was forty, would you care?"

She shrugged. "No."

"You're a modern woman who believes in equality for women, equal pay for equal work. That kind of thing. Am I right?"

"Yes. But this is different."

"It's different because you are prejudiced."

"What are you talking about?"

He laughed at her expression. "Figure this. A man can have a good job, take care of his business. Looks okay. Will do when he needs to save the woman's life. But he isn't good enough to take her to dinner, let alone to bed. Now tell me how that doesn't stack up as a big-ass bias against him if it's all because of his age?"

Take to bed! Where had that come from?

Beverly pulled against his grip and this time he freed her. She put the hand to her cheek, feeling the warmth of his fingers still residing in hers. "Listen to me, Will. I'm more than just forty. I'm a grandmother. What would your friends think about that? Seriously."

He leaned back, and folded his arms. "Have I asked you to marry me?"

"No, of course not."

"Until it gets that kind of serious I don't see how anyone can get in my face for any reason about a woman I'm seeing."

The waiter appeared, setting the check down exactly between them. "I'll take are of this when you're ready." He moved away too quickly for either of them to reply.

Beverly didn't hesitate to reach for it.

"If you pay for this meal, you won't see me again."

Beverly looked up at Will to be sure she'd heard him correctly. He nodded. "But I invited you."

"That's not how I see it. If we'd just met at the bar, I, being my mother's rightly brought up male child, would offer to pay. You could suggest, since this was a chance meeting, we split the check. Then I could agree."

Beverly put the bill down. "How about we split the check?"

He smiled.

Chapter Six

"I don't know the place but I'll follow you in my car." Beverly had to shout as they exited the restaurant because wind had come up and thunder rumbled in the distance.

Will pulled the zipper up on his jacket to keep out the unexpected chill. "Where are you parked?" She pointed in the opposite direction of where his truck stood. "You can come with me and we'll swing back by later for yours."

"It's a loaner. I don't want to leave it on the street." Two fat raindrops struck her on the shoulder. "See. It's beginning to rain. I'll be fine."

"Then I'm walking you to your car."

"No, No. You'll get soaked." As she said this thick drops, so heavy each one made a separate smacking sound, began pelting the sidewalk and nearby cars. She pushed him. "Go on! I'll wait for you to pull along side." She turned and hurried toward her vehicle.

Will stood with hunched shoulders and watched her go, moving quickly past couples arriving with umbrellas open. He couldn't worry about a little rain when his mama's voice in his head was scolding him about not acting the gentleman she'd taught him to be. At the very least he could watch until she was safely inside her auto.

He heard the squeak of her alarm unarming, and saw her pull open her car door.

The breeze went stiff. Then the hair on his head and neck lifted as gnats seemed to swarm his skin. A stream of jagged light arched out from a distant thunderhead and came straight toward him. His reflexes understood long before his conscious brain did that that lightning was seeking contact with the ground. He hit the pavement, going low to keep from being that contact point.

The crack of thunder was a physical force holding him in place as the top of the telephone pole across the street exploded in a white-and-blue fury of sparks.

He was up and running before any other person moved. Heart pumping what felt like pure adrenalin, he skimmed the sidewalk where pieces of the exploded transformer rained down, headed for Beverly's car.

"Beverly! Beverly!" He didn't see her. And then he realized her car door was still open. She was crouched down low by the driver side door, cringing, as she pressed her hands over her ears.

He reached down for her. "Are you okay?"

She didn't respond to his touch but she was whispering something he had to bend low to here.

"Make it stop! Make it stop!" She was whimpering. "Oh Lord, please make the car stop!"

He recognized at once what was going on. She was having a flashback, reliving her accident.

As stinging rain hailed down on them he grabbed her by the arm to pull her to her feet. She was shivering hard but she let him guide her so he hurried her around the car, yanked the passenger side door open and pushed her in, slamming the door after her. People were spilling out of the nearby suddenly-darkened buildings into the rain swept street.

"She hurt?" a man called out to Will.

"No. Just shook up. Thanks."

Will swung back round the front vender, slid in under the wheel, and turned to Beverly. She was huddled with her back to her door staring at him, her eyes so wide he could see lightning reflected in those depths. "What happened?"

He reached up and touched her face very gently. "Lightning struck a transformer near your car."

She frowned, looking confused. "No, before…"

"Before was a memory. Only a bad memory."

It broke his heart a little to watch understanding dawn in her stricken expression and then tears well up in her eyes. As annoyed as he had been at the beginning of the evening, thinking her controlling, snooty, and aloof, he realized seeing her brought low was the last thing he needed to witness. Wanting to protect them both, he leaned forward and pulled her into his arms, and kissed her.

He was wet, rain ran in rivulets from his face and head onto his leather jacket and over her fingers clutching him by the shoulders. Beverly didn't care. It had been a long time, a long long time, since a kiss felt this good, this right, this urgent and necessary.

And when he went deeper, slipping his tongue into her mouth something broke open inside her, spilling heat and shivery happiness into her blood.

She clung to him for a moment after that kiss, her head on his shoulder. His arms stayed about her, strong, comforting, a protection even against her own tumbling thoughts. Finally he slipped a hand under her chin and brought her face up to his.

He smiled at her, skimming her cheek with the back of his fingers. "I kinda thought it might be like between us. Didn't you?"

She didn't answer. Fair enough. He must see the answer in her glow.

"So, let's just see where it takes us."

He released her and slipped the car key he'd picked up off the street into the ignition.

He had put the car in gear before she thought to ask, "Where what takes us?"

"This." He leaned over and kissed her very very softly this time. And then he turned and pulled away from the curb.

She grabbed for her seatbelt and locked in. "Where are we going?"

"I'm driving you home, after you give me directions. And then I'm going to call someone to come and get me."

"You know people in Little Rock?"

"My son and my ex-wife."

Beverly opened the door to her modest bungalow, located in the Hillcrest area of the city. It was small on a street containing more substantial homes but well-kept. Most of the time she was proud of her little oasis, enjoyed the moment when she opened the door and saw all the things in her view that reflected her choices. But tonight she was too tense to really see anything beyond the haven it offered out of the storm.

She rushed over to turn on a light. Then she turned to her guest. "Let me get you a towel. You're soaked."

"No, I'm good." Will shrugged out of his leather jacket, streaked dark in places by water. "I'll just put it here for a moment." He laid it over a wicker ottoman that formed part of the causal seating area in her living room. As he continued to stand, she realized she hadn't actually invited him in.

"Come. Sit. Would you like something? Tea. Coffee. I may have a bottle of wine…" She trailed off, distressed that she couldn't remember the contents of her own kitchen.

Will watched her for a moment longer. "I don't have to stay. I can just make a call and be out of here in a minute."

"No. Please don't go. Unless, of course, if you want to." She bit her lip and waited. Ever since he'd kissed her she hadn't known what was coming next or what she wanted to come next or if he…she didn't know.

He walked over and sat on the wicker chair that was a companion to the ottoman. "Don't you want to get out of your suit?" Beverly blinked. "You're pretty wet."

She glanced down at herself. She was more than wet. The shoulders of her suit jacket were squishy and her pants legs were streaked with mud from where she'd fallen on her knees in the street. "Yes, I should change."

She put down her purse and unbuttoned her jacket, turning away from him as she did so. "I'm so embarrassed. To breakdown like that in public. I don't know what happened."

"It's called a flashback."

She glanced back over her shoulder at him. "What?"

He was sitting forward with his forearms resting on his knees and his hand loosely clasped. "Something happens, something innocent. One minute life is wonderful. The next a man or woman is cowering, or crying uncontrollably, or raging mad for no good reason anybody can guess." He looked away. "It's happened to me."

"You?" She stripped off her jacket and hung it on the wrought-iron hat rack by the door. "Why…I mean, you're a fireman." She kicked off her squishy heels. "Danger is your job."

"Yeah. I can handle my job. But I was in the reserves and got called up to serve three tours in Iraq."

"I didn't know."

She saw his eyes widen as she turned toward him and then remembered the halter top she wore with the big pink stain on the front. At least now he knew she'd tried to look nice and what had happened to that effort. He smiled and patted the ottoman for her to come and sit on, removing his jacket to the floor.

"It's something different when you're sitting in a Humvee, riding down the same road you travel every day, twice, four times a day, every day, until the sameness stretches out even in your dreams. You know the danger in here." He pointed to his head. "You've seen the bad days reflected in other soldiers' eyes. But that ain't you. Not yet, anyway. There's only so much preparing a man can do when disaster is an everyday thing."

He paused, looking at her sitting before him. When she didn't move, didn't even blink, he went on.

"A fireman chooses to go into danger, knowing what it is and where it is. Iraq is a fun house with no fun. Distortions. Danger. The freakiness seeing you before you see it. Guard up or guard down, you can't get it right every time."

"What happened to you?"

He hunched his shoulders. "Everyday thing. Roadside bomb. The vehicle ahead of us hit it." He shook his head. "The world exploded. Shrapnel cut through the air like burning slivers of molten glass. Two friends gone. Concussion and some cuts for the rest of us."

Beverly swallowed. "You hear about these things. See them on T.V. But as awful as it is, and as sick as it makes you feel, it's not the same."

"'Til it happens to you." He added softly. "You know?"

She did know. She thought she had conquered all her fears about the accident, even driving again. But a little storm knocked it all out from under her. "I'd never been in an auto accident before. Not even a vender bender."

"I'm not surprised." He moved to run a finger down her bare arm from shoulder to elbow. "You're a careful woman." He sketched a smile in her direction and dropped his arm to his side. "It ain't about careful in a war. That was the worst time, but not the only time in the funhouse."

"You were injured again?"

"Not like that again, not so it showed." He looked way. "I came home, thought I was fine. Got on with my life. My wife --." He cut his eyes to her. "My ex-wife and I should never have married but I was ready to man-up, do my part. Had a child by then." He smiled. "My Mykel. Do anything for that boy."

Beverly absorbed this information without comment. He'd been through more than she had imagined. He wasn't a carefree single man, macking on every woman who passed through his range of vision. He was a vet and a divorced father.

"—killed him that day."

"What? What did you say?" Beverly's wandering thoughts slammed on the brakes. "You killed your son?"

"I said I could have." His face changed, his expression losing all warmth. "It was my fault. I won't lie about that. And I can't say the judge was totally wrong to award custody to my ex. But I think I deserve a second chance now that I've proved myself."

Beverly's thoughts ricocheted off each other as she tried to process his admission. "Do you want to tell me what happened?"

"Tell you?" He cocked his head to one side, considering. "Yes, I'll tell you. Because you're you."

He took a deep breath. "I'd been home, permanently, about three months. We went to a Fourth of July celebration. My wife got tired and left early with some friends. But Mykel, who was three, wanted to see the fireworks, and I wanted him to see them." He shook his head in memory, a smile playing on his face. "They were just about the most beautiful ones I'd ever seen. We stayed to the very end.

"After it was over, we were walking back across the park to the far side where I'd left my car. I didn't see the boys with the fireworks. Mykel was riding on my shoulders. Next thing I know the world exploded at the corner of my vision. I don't remember anything after that for about a minute. They say I picked Mykel up off my shoulders and tossed him into some bushes, and then I threw myself on the flames." Will blinked rapidly for several seconds. "I broke Mykel's arm."

"You thought you were protecting him."

"I thought I was in goddamn combat again. For that instant it was night in Fallujah, and I was protected my ass!"

"No, you were protecting your son. You were ready to sacrifice--."

He held up a hand. "It didn't matter. Not to my wife, or the judge. I'd had a couple of problems leading up to that, argument in a restaurant after a few too many. Three speeding tickets. I was getting outta control." His mouth formed a compressed straight line. "She filed for divorce and took my son."

Beverly looked down and then up, straight into his face. "Did you assault anyone?"

He held her gaze. "Never laid a hand. On anyone. In my civilian life." He said the words slowly, giving her time to fill in all the spaces with all possible meanings.

"So how have you proved yourself?"

He smiled. "I got help. Fast. Two years in therapy got me balanced. I learned that denying stress can make it worse. I learned that talking about things with people who understand, been there, helped. The lesson that helped most? Every day is not a given, so you have to take it as it comes." He looked suddenly embarrassed. "I learned to be good to me."

Beverly nodded. "That's what everyone told her needed to do, be good to herself. Pamper herself a little bit and let the rest of the world take care of itself for a while.

She watched him visibly work to relax, flexing his fingers again and again as if to relieve the pain of holding on to something too tightly. She admired the fact he had not tried to spare himself in the telling of his story. He didn't ask for pity or understanding or forgiveness. He was still working out how to forgive himself.

She laid a hand on his arm, feeling the need to comfort him. "So you think what happened tonight, with me, was a flashback? Because of the accident?"

"I'm not a shrink. But, yeah, possibly."

"You think I need help?"

"I think you need to ease up in your life." His smile was a little dim.

"You hold yourself to a high standard, Ms. Freeman. I don't have to tell you that. You don't like flaws, especially in yourself. When you think you've failed you clamp down even harder, refuse to ask for help. Want to tell me why?"

No! That was her first thought. There were things she never wanted to talk about, like her father, her marriage, her....

He reached for his jacket. "I guess it's about time I found myself a way home."

As he started to get up, she held on to his arm to halt him. "No, you're right. I try to cover up things I don't like about myself. And I have a thing about control. But it's because I've had no choice. I reared a daughter alone because the man I married, much too young, wasn't anyone I wanted my daughter to admire. I'd admired my father and it almost ruined my life."

He fisted his jacket in both hands. "You don't have to talk about it. This isn't a therapy session. I'm all up in your business with my business, but I don't need you to bleed for me. Understand?"

Beverly smiled. "You say that a lot. 'Understand?' You don't seem to have any trouble getting your points across."

He nodded. "It's a work habit. In a stressful situation it's important that everyone involved knows what's going to happen, in what order. Mistakes can be fatal."

"I understand."

It wasn't funny but they both burst into laughter, deep hilarious belly convulsing laughter that bent them over until their heads were touching.

And then his arms were sliding around her, this time finding her naked shoulders and exposed back. His mouth sought out hers, swooping in hot and heavy. Not like before. Beverly knew this wasn't the kiss of comfort. This was an act of desire.

Chapter Seven

They continued to kiss for a long time.

After she moved off the ottoman and into his lap.

After they both decided without conversation that the chair was much too confining for what was on their minds.

After the rug gave them a comfortable surface to lounge on.

They lay side by side, his arm cushioning her head as he halfway lay over her, each kiss promising more, suggesting another thing, and yet offering enough interest on its own to keep them from wanting to hurry on to the next thing. The man could kiss!

When his palm started moving up and down along one side of Beverly's body with caressing slowness, she sighed joy at the warming sensations left everywhere he touched. It was going to be all right. She could feel herself relaxing, giving in to the moment.

His hand moved lower, found the edge of her blouse and slipped underneath. When his fingers eased the hooks from her bra and then traced her breasts they left little tingling impressions on her skin that connected directly to her spinal column. She had been chill from the rain, now she was catching fire.

She touched him back, his neck, his shoulders, feeling out the dimensions of his body that until this moment had been a stranger to her. Yet his heat was familiar. And the citrusy smell of his skin. It was going to be fine. She needed to not think for a while. It had been a long evening, a longer month. She just wanted to be for a minute, with Will.

He slid a leg up and across both of hers. There was no hurry, no sudden moves, just the gradual urge building into more contact. He took her hand and slid it down between them until they reached his belt buckle. Then he pushed her hand up under his sweater, flattening her fingers against his bare stomach.

She skimmed his skin tentatively, causing him to laugh into her mouth. "You like to tickle, huh?" he said against her ear and then stuck his tongue in it.

She pressed her hand more firmly against his stomach and added her other hand lower down. He sucked in a quick breath at her touch and then he moved over her, his knee finding the natural divide between her knees.

Oh, not yet, she thought in sudden anxiety. Just let the kissing go on a little longer. That would be enough. Just a little longer, please. Just a little!

He moved between her thighs, the weight of him and the pressure of his hips a signal that playtime was turning serious.

What had been slow and leisurely had shifted into third, no fourth gear. She tried to keep up but she could feel herself being pulled away, from the pleasure, from desire, from him.

"Wait. Stop." Stiffening, she pushed against Will's chest.

He rolled back on an elbow to look at her. "What's wrong?"

"I—I." She took a breath. Confession time. How could she have not known it would come? "Listen, Will. I like you. I do. But I'm not very good at this."Horizontal lines formed his frown. "At what?"

"Sex."The lines smoothed out as his lips spread in amusement. "Oh now, I can take care of that." He offered her that half-aroused wolfish grin she'd seen before when a man was willing to say anything to keep things moving forward. It bothered her more than usual because she suspected he was about to be more insulted than a man her own age.She pushed away the hand he tried to slip back under her blouse and sat up. "No. I'm serious." Pulling in her legs, she wrapped her arms around her knees, not looking at him.

"Is it the weather?" He glanced at the drapes closed over her front windows. Beneath them the pale flash of the retreating lightning could be seen. "Because, if it's the weather we can empty ourselves a dark closet and—."

"No." She's totally forgotten about the weather. "It's about me." She looked at him, thinking how sexy he looked with a well-kissed mouth. But it didn't help. "I just thought you should know, beforehand. I don't, well, erupt."He looked totally mystified for a second. "You mean climax?"

"Yes."

He relaxed. "Okay. You're shy the first time, with a new lover. I'm feeling that." She didn't answer. "Or is this just too fast? First date, and all?" She could tell he was trying to wrap his head about an excuse that made sense to him. But his efforts weren't making it any easier for her.

She nodded. "Yes, this is too fast. I'm not into hooking up. I'm old-fashioned. Sex needs to mean something."

She saw caution enter his gaze. "I knew that. I can respect that." He adjusted his hips a fraction in an unconscious response to a need he'd just discovered was not going to be met. He touched her arm. "But a man can hope."

Beverly looked away. Her hope, and oh she had hopes, had sunk back to reality. "What I'm trying to say, Will, is even if we were in a relationship, I don't…can't…" God, she was beginning to sweat.

"You don't climax." His brows shot halfway up his forehead. "Ever?"How to put this delicately? Feeling herself blush she shot him a sideways glance. "Not with company."He looked as astonished as he'd been told she'd never had ice cream, or been to church or something else equally ordinary. "What kind of sorry men have you been with?"She tried not to wince at the memory of those who had come and failed before. "The usual kind."

He grinned slow and seductively. "Well, you haven't been with me." Her thoughts must have shown in her expression because his grin went weak. "You've heard that boast before, huh?""Once or twice." He nodded. "Ok, but you were married. Had a child. Surely with your husband…?" His face fell as understanding dawned on him. "Damn!"She decided his opinion didn't need further comment.She pushed her mussed hair back from her face, a nervous gesture meant to smooth away her own internal discomfort. She wasn't trying to warn him off entirely, just advise him not to expect too much from her. "I don't mind sex. If I like the man I like the man to be happy."His expression intensified. "And these men were happy with being satisfied by themselves?"She dropped her gaze. "Not always." Why did some men think she was a challenge that needed to be conquered like Mount Everest? And when they failed, they made it her fault, as if she had insulted their manhood.

She lifted her chin and turned back to him. Looking at Will made her feel as if she was holding it to the fiery heat of a July sun. "Let's just say if they weren't it was their own doing."He studied on that a minute. Then he levering himself into a sitting position, pulled in his knees and adopted her position, resting his chin on his shoulder as he looked at her. "Okay, so you'd be doing me like this big favor having sex with me?"

When she didn't answer immediately he added, "It goes without saying I'd be grateful." He cocked his head to one side and for several long uncomfortable moments watched her beneath his lazy lids. Finally he drawled out the word, "Okay."She gave him a doubtful look. "Okay, what?""I'm okay with the deal. Okay?"

From the businesslike tone of his voice, she half expected him to put out his hand for her to shake. Then she noticed the expression in his gaze. There was uncertainty over whether she would reject his offer and the hope, more than simple lustful desire that she would.She offered him her hand. "Deal."

He shook it, solemnly, and then--. Nothing! He didn't try to kiss or embrace her. He just sat beside her, silently.

She could hear him breathing through his nose and wondered if he were trying to get his interest back, or figure out how to leave without hurting her feelings."So what now?" His voice startled her.

"I, I don't know." She chuckled. "You're free to leave. No harm, no foul."

He smiled at her slyly. "I'm talking about next time. What are we going to do next time?"

Next time? He was actually thinking about coming back for more… or less?

"How about we go out next weekend? The movies. And then some dinner." He tossed off the words casually as he rose to his feet and adjusted his sweater back over his slacks. "I'd kinda like to see that new super hero film. How about you?"

Beverly looked away, both amused and touched by his change of subjects. If he were going to let her off the hook so nicely, surely she could match his attitude. A date! What did the kids call it, hooking up? No, that was casual sex with no strings. In her case, maybe no sex. "Sure."

She stood up and adjusted her blouse. "I've been meaning to see that new foreign film at the Market Street Theater. Subtitles don't bother you do they?" She had to laugh at the expression on his face. "That's a no, then.""No, now, let a man think a minute. I guess we can do that.""I won't ask you to make the sacrifice. Denise and I have plans to see together anyway."

"That's classy." He slipped on his shoes, smiling to himself. "Not forcing a man to prove himself by doing something he'd rather not do."

She had a feeling he was talking more about how he was treating her but, truly, she hadn't been feeling pressured, exactly. Well, a little. Best thing was to leave it vague so neither of them would have expectations. "So we'll see the super hero film sometime."

"Next Friday. No, wait. I got to work the weekend." He slipped on his jacket. "How about a Thursday? It's just a movie."

She shrugged. "It can't be a late night. I have to work the next day."

"I hear that. I won't keep you from your bed." The way he smiled at her made her wonder if that was a good thing.

No, she'd been down this road before. It took some men about the time required to drive home to realize that they didn't need her kind of grief. She was a stranger. They had enough on their plates. Who needed a frigid woman?

She followed him to the door thinking it was been, for her, mostly a good night. Except for her blouse, his attitude in the beginning, the lightning strike --! Okay it had been a mostly shitty evening. Until he kissed her.

Just when she thought he was going to slip out with the lovely lie about a next time intact, he turned abruptly, took her by the shoulders and pulled her close.

He kissed her so long and thoroughly she thought he had changed his mind about leaving altogether. But then he pulled back, laughing at something only he knew about.

He rested his forehead against hers. "I'll give you this. Each time we meet, you give a man a helluva lot to think on!" And he was gone.

"How was your dinner?"

"Fine."

"It must have been. Look at you, Miss Thang!" Denise made a fluffing gesture with her hand, indicating Beverly hair. "Late nights look good on you. What have you been up to?"

Beverly smiled. "Not much."

She was late to work, a rare thing on a Monday. Saturday had been a downer. Her pity party lasted until she couldn't stop remembering how much she had enjoyed Will's company. Then there was the kissing. She must have it going on to interest a man like him. And he'd seen nothing but her bad sides every time they were together. So who was she feeling sorry for? It was like she wanted to be miserable the rest of her life.

After a soul-searching Sunday, during which she decided she owed herself that chance at a different kind of Beverly Freeman life, she had made an emergency call to her beautician. Promising to double her regular pay if she would come in early and do Beverly's hair had done it trick. It was worth it. Her hair looked good. And she felt her confidence returning. Superficial? Absolutely. But it worked.

Beverly picked up her mail from Wanda's reception area. "There's something special about a bright spring morning. Don't you agree?" Denise looked at her partner over the tops of her reading glasses. "I think it has to do more with what went on in the dark of the night before. You want to comment?"

Wanda, who was playing a video game on her desk computer, looked up. "What I want to know is did the fireman bring the big hose and have to put out any raging fires?"

Beverly leaned over her secretary's desk. "You do remember that we have a checking device on all computers in this office that measures and docks your paycheck for every minute of time spent on unofficial business?"

Stricken, Wanda punched the exit button on her game. "I was just waiting for a fax to come in. You know I do my work, Ms. Freeman."

Laura Castoro

"Just so you know, you're paid to be busy. Have you checked with the insurance agent who wasn't returning my calls on Friday?"

"I'm on it!" Wanda swiveled around the picked up the phone.

We have a checking device? Denise mouthed over Wanda's head.

Beverly gave a slight shake of her head and turned to head for her desk.

"That was just mean!" Denise whispered through giggles when she'd caught up with Beverly. "But I like it!"

"She's a good secretary but she forgets I'm her boss. There are limits."

"I agree. So, let's get a cup of coffee and talk." Denise put an arm around Beverly's shoulders to steer her toward the back room.

When Denise had poured herself a cup and was perched by a hip on the back of a chair she began what Beverly knew would be a thorough interrogation. "What's Mr. Solomon like when he's not rescuing damsels in distress?"

Beverly added one percent milk to her coffee and stirred. "He's nice."

"A gentleman?"

Beverly nodded thoughtfully. "In every way."

She told Denise about the rocky start, the woman at the bar, how he came back, and their dinner.

"Duck grease fries!" Denise snorted her coffee she laughed so hard. "Girlfriend some of them chefs are tripping these days!"

Denise sobered quickly when Beverly described the lightning strike.

"Like you need another stressor on your plate! I prayed for you extra hard at church yesterday. Now I know why the feeling came over me. I thought you weren't in a pew because you were into some deep sinning."

Beverly shook her head. "I was just emotionally rung out and decided to stay in bed all weekend and read and think."

Denise gave her a look. "Does that mean you were alone?"

"Alone."

"Humph! I had hopes for that man. I truly did."

Beverly laughed. "You are going to make me feel sorry for myself."

"And yet you don't." Denise calculating look saw more than Beverly

215

wanted. "He did make a move, didn't he?"

"If I talked about such things, and you know I don't, I would have to say he was everything a woman could want, and still a gentleman."

"But you didn't let him go too far. All right, sista! You know you can't trust a man who insists on sex on the first date. No matter if there's a rubber involved. A man who spreads himself around like that is likely giving away more than Santa Claus. It'll be naughty but it won't be nice. I ask for a medical record these days. I do."

"I thought you wanted me to get laid."

"I do. When the time is right. And the man is right."

Beverly held up her mug in salute. "We're just a couple of old-fashion women."

Denise clicked her mug with Beverly's. "We're a couple of particular women. Rashes and blisters and bad health are not worth the risk for no man's dick!"

"So, are you going to see him again?"

Denise just smiled and sipped her coffee.

"How was your dinner?"

"Fine."

Will inclined his head in greeting as Eddie entered the fire station locker room.

"Come on, help a brother out with some de-tails. I haven't been on a date since Bush took office, the first time. I think I know what it's like but a brother can lose his touch."

Will grunted in good humor. "I had a burger and fries."

"Say what? The sister shorted you on your reward dinner?"

"Not at all. I had sweet potato fries cooked in duck fat, too."

"You lying!"

"And then I almost got struck by lightning."

"Awite! Don't talk about it. But if you got to lie, don't tell no tales about duck fries." Eddie started to leave the dressing room but swung back. "Sherrae called before you came in."

Will swore under his breath. "She wants me to call her back?"

"Is the president a black man?" Eddie grinned. "She said something about you keeping Mykel this weekend."

"I'm on duty."

"She said her job is sending her out of town on Friday for the weekend and her mother's got the flu and her sister is—."

"One tired excuse for a babysitter." Will glanced over at the assignment chart hanging on his locker door. "Got Friday off but from Saturday through Monday I'm on call."

"Me, too. You could bounce him over to Clarice. What's another child at my house? He does know how to dog fight for his share of the food?"

"If Clarice hears you talking about her children like that, you'll be the one in the doghouse."

Eddie snorted. "Dog sleeps on the couch."

Will nodded. "You and Fido, nice couple."

"So what are you gonna do about Mykel?"

"Take him. She'll leave him with her crazy sister if she has no other choice." He reached into his locker for his boots. "I'm petitioning the courts. Got to get a judge to review my case. I need joint custody so I can have some say-so over his life."

Eddie seemed to remember something in his locker and walked over to start working the combination. "You let me know, you change your mind about Clarice keeping him. She likes Mykel."

Will nodded. One problem more or less solved. On to the next.

He glanced over at Eddie. "You ever try to seduce a woman?"

Eddie cracked a smile a mile wide and opened his locker. A series of photos of nearly-naked video vixens lined the door. "Only every day since I was fourteen."

Will balled his t-shirt into a mass and tossed it into his locker. "I'm talking about deliberately setting out to make a woman so hot she can't keep her hands off you."

"Awwgh man! They done asked you again to do that annual Chippendale-style review for charity! Don't do it. A real man don't take his drawers off in public."

Will chuckled. "You're just jealous because they never asked you."

"What you mean?" Eddie rubbed his front. "I got a six-pack."

"Six bags of chips, and a pack of wind is what you've got."

"Who you trying to seduce?" Eddie's face took on a look of horror. "Not the grandma?"

Will clipped the buckles closed on his boots. "Someone I met this weekend. Someone unexpected."

"So the Will Solomon magic is losing its charm. If you got to start working at it, I know I need to stay married. Clarice may have packed on a few but she's reliable."

"One of these days Clarice is going to hear about how you talk about her and that flea-infested couch is gonna look down right comfy compared to where she's going to kick your behind."

"True. True. Still, she knows she's the only woman for me. And as long as I got her thinking the same about me, I plan to keep my home a happy place."

"You said something serious and true." A fellow fireman named Bruce, had walked into the tail of the conversation. The men exchanged greetings, and changed the subject.

As Will finished dressing out, he kept thinking about Beverly and her 'problem.' He'd done some deep thinking on it. She'd felt good in his arms, and tasted even better. No doubt! And she'd been grooving on him until it got to the next level. He hadn't expected to go much farther. He was passed jumping on anything that lay still long enough. Never really had been into that. These days he was after something serious, that much he had figured out before he met Beverly Freeman. But sex couldn't be off the table. If a woman wasn't having as good a time as he was it wasn't going to last. So he'd checked out the internet for advice.

Will wagged his head and chuckled to himself. When he got past all the porno sites posing at medical sexual dysfunction sites he'd learned a few things. Beverly said she could have fun alone. So she probably didn't have a hormone or physical problem. Maybe she'd just been turned off early by a lousy lover, and she'd given up thinking she could have a good time. She liked sex, he guessed. Lawdy, she kissed like she'd invented it. She just thought sex didn't like her.

Will slammed his locker shut and set the lock. It seemed to him the only way to get her past what had become fact in her mind was to arrange it so she wasn't thinking about what was lacking, but what she wanted so badly there was no doubt but that she had to have it.

Will snickered. Not that he was any wonder-boy lover. That was going to take some imagination, some subtlety, and an iron command of his Johnson.

Chapter Eight

"You've always wanted to fly?"

"Yes." Beverly popped into her mouth the last of the chocolate raisins from the box they'd shared at the movie. "When I was a kid I would lie on my back in the grass and watch the clouds sailing by. I'd pretend I was up there flying like a bird. I'd sit on one then glide to another. Sometime I'd fly past just to take a scoop out of one."

"What did they taste like: whip cream, vanilla ice cream, or mashed potatoes?"

"Mashed potatoes, definitely."

Will grinned. "Now see, that's a woman after my own heart. Stick to the basics. I swear I lived for a year when I was ten on my mom's mashed potatoes."

Beverly laughed as they stepped off the sidewalk into the theater parking lot. She'd enjoyed the super-hero movie with its special effects that let the viewer experience what flight must feel like. "I thought at one time I'd take flying lessons."

"Why didn't you?"

"First I didn't have the money. Then I didn't have the time."

"And now?"

"Oh, I'm too—."

"Lazy? Grinchy? I know you weren't about to say old. A friend of my pops just got his license last year, at sixty-one. So don't go using that make-believe crutch."

"You're right. Maybe I'll take flying lessons this year. If I can find time."

They got into Will's truck and headed for her home. He had promised her it wouldn't be a late night. He was happy enough that she was relaxed in his company, wearing a pretty top and jeans with her hair arranged softly around her features. Tonight, even her smile had a softer curve.

He reached out and took her hand in a friendly manner. "Any more flashbacks?"

Beverly shook her head. "I've been going to bed early and getting up late for a change. I think I was so stressed from everything all at once that I was due for a crash."

"Still, you need to check with your doctor." He rubbed her soft knuckles with his thumb. "Just to make sure you're taking care of you."

"I already did. He says I need to take a vacation. I asked him if he could just take off from his business and go away. He laughed and said, try to take a vacation, soon."

"Will you?"

"I would take a few days off if I could find somewhere cheap and simple to go."

Will nodded. "I'll think on that."

When he pulled up to her door a little while later he turned to her, stretching out an arm on the seat to play with her hair. "I had a good time."

"I did, too." She held his gaze. "Would you like to come in? For a drink?"

"No." Will shook his head. "You don't want me in there tonight."

She frowned. "Why not?"

"I'll show you." He slid over and cupped the back of her head with one hand and turned her chin up to meet his kiss with his other. He kissed her softly at first, barely letting his lips slide over hers. When she relaxed a little against him and opened her mouth, he licked the edges of her lips until she sighed. And then he really went to work, using every technique he could think of and invent on the spot that would prolong that kiss. But his hands stayed above her waist. That was his rule. She's been fine until he reached below her waist that first time.

She didn't seem to be thinking about that. As he drew back a little for air, she followed him onto his side of the seat, arms sliding around his neck, body angling toward his touch, soft and warm with all that womanly weight against his more than welcoming body. Here he was trying to give her space. He was going to have to break his rule before he's observed it if she didn't back away soon. Okay, now.

He reached for her, pulled her in next to the steering wheel, and then slid a hand under the edge of her skirt, and up her thigh.

The moment she stopped feeling and started thinking, she stiffened and pulled back. Will murmured his relief. Things had gotten a lot further a lot faster than he intended.

He watched her, torn between desire and uncertainty, slip back onto her side of the truck. He didn't have any divided feelings. He was hard.

She smoothed her hair then looked at him from a tilted angle. "You're sure you don't want to come in?"

Damm! He would never understand women. "You have to work in the morning and what I need --. Let's just say you wouldn't wake up fresh as a daisy for work."

She looked embarrassed. For a second he wondered if he was making a mistake. But then she was leaning in to kiss him and he just took whatever she wanted to offer.

This wasn't about him. It wasn't about him being a hero or a success or winning an award. He just wanted her to have what she deserved, good loving, and to be feel cherished. Special. Damn! He was getting serious!

He made the trip to the door to see her safely inside and back to his auto in record time. Then he gunned his engine, threw his truck into gear, and laid rubber for half a block.

Will chewed his thumb as he stared at his cell phone. This was asking a lot, too much. But he was desperate. He punched the number.

"Hi, Will." Beverly's voice held the welcome he longed to hear.

"Hi, Ms. Freeman. How are you doing?"

"Welcoming Friday with big howdy." He liked her laugh. It was as if she were sliding into a new view of herself overnight. "What can I do for you, Mr. Solomon?"

"I'm glad you asked. This is really short notice, and we don't know each other that well so if you say no it won't affect anything between us because it's a lot to ask."

"What is it, Will?" She sounded amused because he sounded nervous.

"It's about my son, Mykel. My ex is leaving town this weekend and she needs me to keep him. I love keeping him but I'm on duty this weekend. I asked a friend to sit him but now Eddie just called and said his wife and kids have the flu. So I got a problem."

"How long does he need supervision?"

"From about noon on Saturday until Sunday night. His mother will pick him up after her flight arrives."

"I suppose I could look after him."

"Oh, now, no. That is not what I was thinking exactly." But it was. He just didn't now how to ask.

"Okay." The serious Ms. Freeman was again on the job. "I didn't mean to get into your business."

"It's not even about that. I just don't want to drag you into my drama."

"The way I dragged you into mine?" He could feel her thinking through the phone. "How do two people have a relationship if all their relatives and friends are off-limits?"

He could have kissed her. "See, you always have to be right about things. Thank you. I could use some help. If it's not putting you out or anything."

"I'm a grandma. I can handle one five-year-old boy for thirty-six hours. The question is will he want to be with me?"

He hoped she could hear his smile in his voice. "Why don't we find out?"

Will stopped calling every hour on the hour after the first three hours Beverly and Mykel were in his apartment alone. He'd ordered the pizza to be delivered, laid out all the appropriate video games for Mykel, and even rented a couple of his favorite movies for Beverly to watch after Mykel was asleep.

He'd even found a moment to buy new sheets for his bed, in case she would feel strange sliding between his covers without him there. Okay, he was feeling strange about that. His new lady's first sleepover at his place and he wasn't even there. How messed up was that?

Yet, they'd agreed that if Mykel were going to be looked after by a stranger at least the surroundings should be familiar. Mykel had his own bedroom and toys, and even a few clothes, at his dad's apartment. Turns out this was good thing since Mykel's mother got stuck in Chicago overnight when her flight got cancelled. Beverly was gracious enough to stay over until Monday at noon when Will got off his shift.

They sounded like they were fine, every time he called. He was the basket case.

"Man! You're wearing a rut in the floor!" one of his fellow fireman complained of his restless pacing that first evening.

When the fire house alarm sounded for the first time Will was almost cheerful about it. Not that someone was in trouble, but that he had something to take his mind off what was going down at his place.

By the time he returned from the second alarm Mykel was in bed. Though Beverly sounded a little tired, she didn't seem unhappy or anxious. She was making sugar cookie dough, the kind she said she had to put in the refrigerator overnight, so Mykel could make cookies the next day.

"I didn't even know I had ingredients for cookies in my place."

"You don't. We went to the store and bought butter, vanilla, baking powder, flour and sugar. You live lean."

"I can cook. I just don't like to eat alone."

"Uh huh." Her laugh was beginning to be enough to get his attention.

"Seriously. Next time you come by my place, I'm cooking."

"You certainly are."

He eased up on the calls on Sunday. Between sports on TV and the guys, he decided Beverly knew where and how to get him if she needed him. Even so, he was glad when Monday rolled around and he could go home.

"Dad!" Mykel burst out the apartment door, backpack already strapped to his back, when he saw his father coming up the walk.

"My man!" Will picked up his son and swung him around.

Mykel frowned. "I told you about that babyish stuff."

Will popped him lightly on the head. "And I told you 'til you can pick me up, I'm gonna pick you any time I want."

Mykel tilted his head back to look up at his dad. "I am catching up to you."

Will grinned. "You are, for sure. So, tell me. What do we think of Ms. Freeman?"

Mykel shrugged. "She's all right. She plays tough. For real. She won't let me beat her at games like you do."

"That's because I can't beat you all the time. Sounds like we got some competition in the house."

Mykel shrugged as they walked toward the door where Beverly now stood. Her hair was a little wild, as if she'd pushed a hand through it quickly. Her shirt had a streak of flour on it, yet she looked right at home framed in his doorway. A Kodak moment!

Will bent toward his son as they neared. "So you like her?"

"Yeah, she's strict. But she's nice, too. She let me have seconds on the—." Mykel pulled up short when Beverly put a finger to her lips.

Will made a big show of looking from one to the other with suspicion written large on his face. "What have two you been up to?"

"Nothing," Beverly struggled to keep a straight face.

"Nothing!" Mykel's giggles got the better of him.

Will swept his son's head in against him with a hand, then bent and gave his head a kiss. "You got all your things?" Mykel nodded. "Then hop in the truck, I'm coming."

Mykel started down the sidewalk and then stopped and turned. "Thank you, Miss Beverly."

"Thank you, Mykel. See you soon."

Mykel's expression brightened. "For real?"

"I'd like that." Beverly glanced at Will. "If you daddy is okay with it."

Mykel nodded and went on down the walk to climb up into the open truck, as both adults watched.

"Come here." Will grabbed her wrist and pulled her just inside the doorway out of sight.

Once there, he backed her up against the wall and kissed her with his whole body, pressing every part of himself against every part of her he could manage. And then he kissed her lips long and lingeringly.

When he leaned away from her he kept his eyes shut for a moment, a smile on his face. "Sugar cookie! That's what you taste like."

She was breathing a little hard when he did open his eyes, her mouth glistening from his kiss, but there was a smile forming, too. "What was that all about?"

"I just wanted you to know how much you taking care of Mykel meant to me."

She touched his chest. "You got a unique say of saying thank you."

He smiled slowly. "You have no idea how many ways I want to thank you."

The trunk horn sounded. "Got to take Mykel home." He freed her. "You'll still be here when I get back?"

She answered with a shake of her head. "You forget I work for a living."

"I'm off next Saturday. Movie? No dancing. Let's go dancing."

The place Will chose was not one Beverly knew about. They arrived after ten p.m. He had assured her that nothing would be jumping off much earlier than that. Beverly tried to take mental notes. It was the kind of place Wanda would know, or want to know, about.

The family-style restaurant during the week became a bar/dancehall/meet-and-greet spot for the single set on the weekend. The restaurant's tables were stacked against the wall to create a dance floor. Only a few tall bistro-type tables and stools were available. The D. J. was set up in one corner, pumping tunes to match the heated atmosphere. The folks were excited. They were snapping photos in the darkness, smiling, laughing, drinking, and dancing. The small area was packed to capacity. She was glad Will had a tight grip on her hand or she was certain she would have lost him in no time.

"Will! Is that you?" A big man, twice Will's width, had blocked his path. "What are you doing not hollering at a brother when you're in town?"

"How you doing, Dee?" Will and other man gripped hands and bumped shoulders.

"Hanging." The man's gaze swiveled past his friend to Beverly. "Who's this fine woman with you?"

Will put his arm around Beverly's waist to pull her close. "This is Ms. Freeman, Dee."

Dee held out his hand. "Please to meet you Ms. Freeman. You can't be from around here. I know all the foxy ladies up in the Rock."

"Don't embarrass yourself, Dee. I got this covered." Will steered her quickly past his friend and into an alcove nearby.

Beverly looked back with reproach. "That was cold."

Will shook his head. "You don't know him like I do. Brother falls in love every weekend. First he'll ask for a dance, then he'll ask for your digits. Before the evening is out, he'll be naming the children you're going to have together."

Beverly laughed.

Several other male friends of Will's came up, speaking to him but eying her with a kind of interest she hadn't felt in years. Was it being in Will's company or was she pulling male appreciation on her own? Will's hand stayed on her waist with easy familiarity as he introduced her, proprietary and even a little proud. He knew how to make a woman feel special. Only other women kept their distance.

When a break came in the introductions Will said, "What are you drinking tonight, Ms Freeman? Martini?"

Beverly had checked out the bar, which seemed serviceable but limited. "Do they serve those here?"

"I'll check." He kissed her cheek. "Don't get lost."

Will plowed through the crowd that instantly enveloped him.

It wasn't long before Beverly realized that even in the crush people could pick up on who other people were checking out. For instance, the group of women at the far end of the room had drawn a bead on her. The way they all kept glancing at her made it obvious that they were talking about her.

Their clothing showed a lot of young, well-toned body. She never had the nerve to dress like that when she was twenty-five. Now, it was not an option. She'd felt the force of Will's interest when he saw her form-fitting plum sheath with the deep key-hole baring a lot of her back. But she couldn't compete with this group. A little intimidated, she turned away and began concentrating on the D.J.

"You're with Will Solomon?"

Beverly turned in surprise to the young woman addressing her. It was one of the women who'd been discussing her. Two others were with her. "Hi."

The woman stirred the drink she held with a tiny straw. "I'm Jaime. This is Yolanda and Rochelle."

Beverly smiled at the women. "I'm Beverly. Nice to meet you."

"We didn't know Will was seeing anybody." Jaime paused. "Though he hasn't been in circulation lately."

"Are you seeing him?" Yolanda asked. "Regularly?"

"Because we are wondering if you are the reason he turned down our charity benefit," Rochelle completed.

Beverly wasn't sure how to answer so many personal questions with potential traps in them. "I don't know what you're talking about."

The women exchanged glances.

"You've heard about our sorority's Divas-Only Charity Event?" Beverly shook her head in answer to Jaime's question. "We hold a high-ticket dinner and auction where some of the best-looking bachelors in the Rock offer to strip for charity. The higher the ladies bid, the more the men take off. Will promised he'd consider participating this year."

"It's for a good cause. We raise money for special needs kids in the community."

"But no cause gets women up off their wallets like the sight of a fine man's bare-naked ass!"

There were high fives all around but Beverly didn't participate.

Jaime examined her silver glitter nails. "Will's a good man. That's why we asked him. He's nice."

"Got that right!" Yolanda turned and made a circular motion with her fingertips over the dance floor. "Some men up in here won't recognize the woman whose bed they jumped out of this morning."

"You must be new to town." Yolanda smiled at Beverly. "Because you sure don't look like you belong in here."

"Why?" Were they about to comment on her age?

"You look like you'll go to church tomorrow morning and mean it."

Beverly laughed. They joined her.

"So if you could just put a good word in with Will for us…" Rochelle's voice trailed off. "Never mind. I wouldn't let no man of mine to show his goods, either."

"How's Mykel?" Jaime was still staring at her intently.

Beverly hesitated on a second. "Fine. He's a sweet child. But all boy."

The women exchanged knowing glances. "We've never met Mykel. You have a good evening. Okay?"

Will broke through the crowd at that moment. "Hi, Jaime, Rochelle, Yolanda. Everything okay?"

"Fine, Will. We like your lady." They each kissed him on the cheek in turn and then departed.

Will followed them with his gaze for a second then turned to Beverly. "Listen, I don't know what they said about me…"

"They said you were a nice guy."

"Is that all?"

"Is there something else?"

He smiled but dropped his gaze, and shook his head.

Beverly wondered if she should tell him what the women had said about him stripping for charity. As long as Will had refused, did it matter? "What did you bring me?"

He looked down at the drink he held in each hand. "Gin and tonic. The closest I could get to a martini that I was sure would come out right."

"I like gin and tonic."

They sipped their drinks in silence, staring at each other over the rims of their glasses.

Finally Will put his glass down. "Sounds like your boyfriend is getting a spin." The D.J. had put on a John Legend tune. "Let's dance."

By the time they found a space on the dance floor the room was electric with the physical pulse of dance.

"Ready to go right now!" the crowd roared over the recorded vocals. They were eating it up, with frantic dance steps and the energetic jerk and fall of hands and hip gyrations. The lyrics and rhythm were riding the beat, a beat that would not be denied. But Will had other plans.

He pulled Beverly in close and began to move slowly, barely shifting his feet. The way he held her, one hand fanned across her bare back and the other splayed over the curve over her lower back, she felt every shift of muscle in his body. At first Beverly felt awkward, with everyone about them moving at double or triple their tempo. But then she remembered that Will was a musician. His rhythm went under the pulse to catch the lullaby lilt in Legend's lyrics.

They danced several songs like that, a slow slow drag, him playing with her hair, leaning in occasionally to whisper something that made her laugh.

His hands were hot and strong on her and when they drifted lower onto the swell of her hips to bring her even closer she didn't resist. She liked the way he held her, as if she were something he needed to hold onto to be happy. They stayed on the floor until the sweat began to tickle down her back and between her breast and thighs and she found herself rubbing up against him, just to watch the sparks of desire jump in his golden eyes.

Finally he whispered. "Let's get the hell out of here."

"Um hm," she murmured.

She felt drunk, dazed by the desire, pulsing and throbbing, sweet and hot all at once, within her. She giggled as they stumbled out hand in hand into the welcome cool of the night.

"Wait!" She bent over and pulled off her heels. "My feet are killing me."

He laughed. "That's not what's paining me."

When they reached the deep shadows by his truck he pulled her in against him. She lifted her face, expecting his kiss. But he stopped just short of her lips, forcing her to decide to make contact. She did.

She kissed him, writhing and twisting slowly against the harder places of his chest, their pelvises bumping and touching, grinding to the music still playing inside her. After a few seconds he leaned back against his fender, shimmied her dress up her thighs and spread her legs with a knee so that she was astride his thigh as his hands guided her hips back and forth. She felt like a teenager, dry-humping in the dark.

When they heard the sound of footsteps crunching gravel, Will groaned and reluctantly released her. "Damn, woman! Let's get the hell outta here before we get arrested!"

Chapter Nine

"Damn! Damn! Damn!"

Denise looked up from her desk. "What's the matter, Beverly?"

Beverly bent to pick up the pile of papers that only seconds before had been three separated perfectly collated stacks. "I'm butter-fingered and so tense I could pop!"

Denise looked up at the ceiling. "I wonder why that is?"

Beverly cut her eyes at her friend. "Don't even start!"

"All right, Ms Freeman! Scared of you."

Beverly rubbed her brow, as annoyance scrambled like ants over her skin. She was a wreck! A complete basket case! And she knew who to blame.

It had been ten days! Ten incredibly frustrating days since she and Will had gone dancing and then, incredibly, he had left her at her door with a slack jaw and enough sexual desire to light Little Rock for a week.

She was so keyed up that the mere sound of Will's voice on the phone was enough to make her chest tighten up and, contrarily, melt lower down. She had never quite known what sexual frustration meant until she met Will Solomon.

Their last phone call had ended in a huge fight over absolutely nothing! Even now she couldn't believe that her final words to him were to tell him to get lost! Thank goodness he had laughed it off and said he'd be in touch. That was three days ago.

What sort of twisted, evil game was he playing? Okay, she said she didn't have sex on the first date. But they'd had three now, four if Mykel-sitting counted, which she guessed technically it didn't. Still, wasn't a woman allowed to change her mind?

Once she never thought about sex. Now it was only thing on her mind: at work, driving home, at home, in bed, in the shower, every time she let her mind drift it drifted to Will. If it hadn't been so excruciatingly maddening, she would have thought her situation hilarious. Beverly Freeman, the Ice queen who never thought sex was all that, was dying to jump a man. Not any man, William Solomon.

During her marriage she'd felt like a failure as a woman. Her ex's parting shot had been that he wouldn't miss her in bed, where he'd felt alone anyway. Later when she'd let her guard down with the few men she thought worthy, sexual disappointment had inevitably followed. So, alone had become a habit. Ignoring her body's urges as much as possible had become a habit. No more. Will had changed all that. Sexual desire dogged her every step.

If they didn't get together soon, even if she were ultimately disappointed, something inside her was going to snap!

Will listened intently to the courthouse secretary's words. He would have his day in court for his custody petition to be heard. In sixty days he would know if Mykel could again be a permanent part of his life. "Thanks. This is great. You're welcome. And have a good, no, have a great day!"

"What are you so happy about this morning?"

Will looked up at Eddie. "I'm going to get a chance to get co-custody of Mykel. The date is set for next month."

Eddie slapped his friend on the back. "That's just fine. A boy needs his father."

Will nodded and snorted, wiping his hand over his face to keep his emotions from getting the better of him. He was beginning to get his life in order again. And all that was going on in it was good. Mykel and Beverly.

Beverly! He needed to call her with his news, but he knew he was going to have to have a plan before he did that. If things between them didn't come to head, in more ways than one and soon, he was going to walking crooked permanently. There were thing he wanted to say to her that couldn't be handled in a phone call or over dinner. He needed an excuse to be alone with her for more than a couple of hours.

"Eddie, you remember that house up on Beaver Lake you once rented as Clarice's birthday surprise. How much did that cost?"

"Not that much. We rented for a weekend. It's cheaper by the week if there's not something special going on in Eureka Springs, or War Eagle. I got the paperwork in my locker. Let me look."

Beverly waited three rings before she answered Will's call.

First off he told her about the court date. Will was so happy his enthusiasm was infectious right through the phone. Then he moved to the next topic. "Remember how you said you needed time off? I found you a cheap retreat." he quoted the amount. "This Thursday through next. It's not a vacation unless you can take weekdays off."

"I don't know, Will. It's already Tuesday." But she was already calculating in her head how much washing and preparing she needed to do to get ready.

"If you want I can drive you up so you don't have to use the loaner. Then I'll drive back up and get you the following Thursday."

"That's a lot of miles on your truck." And he didn't seem to be inviting himself to join her. Was that good or bad news?

"So, pay the gas tab." He wasn't going to let her say no.

"Yes. Thanks. I accept." She could hear him sigh in relief. "And, Will, I'm praying for you and Mykel."

"Aren't you the woman with the pull? Knowing how things are going to turn out before they do?"

Beverly hesitated. This was serious. "It feels right, Will."

"There you go. Pick you up early. Want you to make the most of the time."

The Ozarks were in full display. Pink and white dogwood blooms and redbud trees laced the new-green under growth of the mountainsides with color while wisteria trellised the canopy overhead with scented lavender stalks. The house Will had rented, unseen, was tucked away off a hard-pack rutted road.

"Are you sure this is right?" Beverly watched the road ahead narrow in with shrubs while tree limbs arched and met overhead.

Before he could decide how to answer, the road rose sharply. At the summit, the land opened up on a view of treetops and a small shingled cottage and the vista of a sparkling lake below.

"Oh Will!"

He grinned. "Well, daaa-yam! I did all right."

They scrambled out of the truck, and while she ran down the path that led to the water's edge, he stayed behind to store the groceries they'd stopped in town to buy so she wouldn't need supplies while he was gone.

She came flying back up the path, looking like a young girl, her face gleaming with joy. She threw her arms about him, crying, "This is perfect, Will. Perfect! You've saved my life again."

He hugged her, hard, and then he backed off. "Ok. You got everything you need. If not, you got the number of the service station back on the main road. He said call if you have any kind of a problem. He's got my number, too."

Beverly noticed him backing up. "You're really going to leave me here alone?"

Will paused, his golden gaze not quite meeting hers. "That's what you said you needed."

She turned her head in puzzlement. "I need peaceful days and some good times. I don't have to be alone for that, do I?"

"I don't know." He looked straight into her eyes. "Do you?"

Beverly held his gaze. "Not anymore."

"We need to talk."

He took her hand and led her to the porch swing of the cottage where they sat.

"You know how it was the night you had that flashback? I've been thinking on that." He dipped his head. "I think I've been taking advantage of you ever since."

Beverly chuckled. "What are you talking about? You've been a complete gentleman about everything."

See, that's just it." He shook his head. "I'm not a gentleman. I've been playing you, Beverly, for my own selfish reasons.

I don't understand."

"Let me break it down for you. I'm not bragging, but I have a job that makes the people I deal, with whose houses and pets and even themselves sometime, beholden to me. You've been into me because you see me as a hero. I did what I did because it's what I do, saving people."

"Oh." Beverly felt the icy tingle of disillusionment run down her spine. "You're saying women come onto you all the time after you've helped them out. You expect that, and exploit that."

"No, I didn't say that. I'm saying if you think I'm a hero then you're wrong. I'm not close to that. I'm a man who lusted after a woman and when I got close, I saw a way to become memorable to her. But it can't be like that between us. Because sooner or later you're going to wake up and notice your hero ain't for shit." He took her hand and rubbed it between his own. "And then I might lose you."

Beverly remained silent, trying to hear all the nuances of what he was saying while trying not to be overwhelmed by her own visceral responses. He said he'd played her? And now he was tired of playing. Was that it? Lose her? What was he saying?

He tried to touch her face but she backed up. "Let me finish, all right?" She gave a tight little nod.

"It wasn't about playing you. Never. You're the kinda woman I like. No, you're the woman I like. I like everything about you. Your bossiness and your strength, and your courage and your reserve. The way you hold yourself and how make even a bad date good. A man knows he's got class just walking down the street beside you. But that's not all.

"I like the way you look, and smell." This time she let him touch her cheek. "I like the way you feel when I run my hands over your body. You're all woman but don't need to advertize that fact every minute of every day. A man has to work to know about that inner fire. That's special. And I like the way you look at me, like you can see something in me I didn't even know was there. But it's got to be real between us, Beverly. No hero bull. No savior complex. You don't need to be

234

grateful to me. I want you to want me, as a man. Flaws and all."

Beverly bit her lip. That was the most eloquent speech any man had ever made to her. There were a lot of promises in his eyes that she didn't know if she was ready to accept. "We haven't known each other long," she began.

"Love never was about time." He smiled at her expression. "I know. It's too soon. But you need to know how I see this. I'm for real. I got a child to think of. If you're not feeling it, like even a future possibility, then I might not want to get hurt like that."

Beverly licked her lips. "What did you mean before, about taking advantage of me?"

"Oh that." He rubbed his chin with a hand. "You presented a challenge, telling me about being with a bunch – a few," he amended when he saw her expression. "A few lousy men. It set me up to want to change your opinion of men."

"You mean sex." She tucked her lips to keep back her smile.

"Yeah. Sex. You're just too much woman not to know the joys of a physical relationship."

She looked away from him. Her heart was hammering and her pulse was leaping. Maybe lust was playing its part, it was impossible to be with Will and not feel it. Yet something else superseded even that. She was looking at a future. Her future. Not as part of someone else's life, but her own.

She turned back to him, letting everything she was thinking show on her face.

"You told me how you feel. I think it's time you know how I feel about you, Will."

She kissed him with everything she had. Everything seemed to be more than enough.

By the time they found the bedroom the lovely melting pleasure invading her body was so welcome to the long frozen places in her soul that she gasped in need for it to continue.

They lost their clothes in scattered piled on the floor and then he was bending over her, kissing her all over, in every place that could be kissed. And she was doing to same, wanting to please with a depot of desire she had never tried to please anyone, even herself before.

When he moved up and over her, her back arched off the bed in welcome. She had felt carnal pleasure before, if only at her own hands. But this was different. This was not within her control. She was giving up and letting go, going places and feeling things that had never been hers to feel before. And it was better, bigger, higher, wilder, freer.

"What just happened?"

He grinned and kissed her sweaty neck. "What do you think?"

Beverly breathed a laugh. "A little miracle!"

He wagged his head. "No, what happened is what's supposed to happen. It's the most natural thing in the world when two people are right together."

She looked at him, at that nice smile that had first greeted her with the promise of rescue, and wanted to thank him. But that would sound ridiculous, as if he had performed a service for her. What he'd done was made a liar of her acceptance that one of the ordinary things in life was never meant to be hers. Thank you wouldn't cover that.

In her expression Will saw all the thoughts flooding through her mind. Some he could guess at. Others he knew would always be a mystery to him. But that was all right. More than all right. It was all good.

He nuzzled her breast. "Just don't go chalking this up to some stupid idea about young stud service. This is about you Beverly and me Will. That's all it is."

"I just want--." He put a finger to her lips.

"We don't need to talk about this ever again. Whatever is is. We go with the flow. Understand?"

"Understand."

He flipped over on his back and pulled her half over him. "There's something else you may as well know about me."

She looked alert. What is it?" Her expression fell. "You're still married."

"No, hell no! I'm just not as young as you think. I'll be thirty-five in August."

She gasped. "You told me you were thirty, or even twenty-nine."

"I never said. You assumed. So, I thought you should know. If I'm not the young stud you want, you got to kick me outta your bed now. Because I intend to stay with the good thing I found."

Beverly tried to hide her smile. "Hm. I was really grooving on the fantasy of seducing a man a decade younger. Six years doesn't quite have the same cache."

"What if I said I'd be thirty-four on my next birthday?"

"Now you're just trying to tempt me into thinking I'm robbing the cradle."

"Yes, ma'am, I am tempting you. Tempted?"

"Show me what you got, and then I'll decide."

Much later she curled a hand around the column of his neck. "Twenty years is a long time to be wrong."

"Yeah, you were due to be wrong about something sometime. I'm just glad it was me who showed you the error of your ways." He framed her face in his hands. "I did pack a bag. I can stay until Saturday. We got a lot to make up for."

"I want to make up for lots of things. For instance, I think I'll try skydiving."

His eyes widened. "Why would you want to jump out of a plane with a perfectly good motor running?"

"You won't go with me?"

"How about a hot air balloon ride? Something gentle."

"Wuzz."

"Wild woman!"

The End

Multi-award winning author Laura Castoro loves to travel. She's been part of ship christening in Norway, scuba dived on the Great Barrier reef, and climbed glaciers on two continents. Her spirit for adventure may have been born when she was. At only six weeks, she made her first trip from Texas where she was born to Arkansas where she grew up. She's lived in Washington D.C., Connecticut, New Jersey, with long stretches in between under the big sky of Texas. An avid traveler, she's logged miles in England, Ireland, Denmark, Norway, Germany, France, Belgium, Italy, and Australia. The Caribbean, Mexico and Canada? Of course! Just now, she's trying to finagle a trip to China.

Married with three children, Laura began her writing career while taking time off from a degree in microbiology to take care her of personal biology experiments at home, two wearing diapers, and one in kindergarten. Two years later, she sold her first book, a historical romance Silks and Sabers. Always adaptable, she decided to see how far this enterprise would take her. Twenty-six years later with more than (36) thirty-six published books in print is such genres as contemporary romance, westerns, sagas, and romantic suspense; Laura is now writing about the modern woman's life as she sees it.

A sought-after speaker and writing workshop leader, Laura puts her passion for the written word to good use. She is the President of the Board of the Communications Arts Institute, which oversees the Writers Colony at Dairy Hollow, a working writers' residence program in Eureka Springs, AR. She is on the board of the Arts and Science Center of Southeast AR. Her most thrilling award was being named recipient of the Arkansas Writers Hall of Fame Award for 2005.